PRAISE FOR RAY HARRISON'S SERGEANT BRAGG-CONSTABLE MORTON MYSTERIES

DEATH
— OF A —
DANCING
LADY

RAY HARRISON

*A Sergeant Bragg-
Constable Morton Mystery*

B
BERKLEY BOOKS, NEW YORK

This Berkley book contains the complete
text of the original hardcover edition.
It has been completely reset in a typeface
designed for easy reading and was printed
from new film.

DEATH OF A DANCING LADY

A Berkley Book/published by arrangement with
Charles Scribner's Sons

PRINTING HISTORY
Scribner's edition published 1985
Berkley edition/September 1988

ISBN: 0-425-11047-8

A BERKLEY BOOK ® TM 757,375
Berkley Books are published by The Berkley Publishing Group
200 Madison Avenue, New York, NY 10016.
The name "Berkley" and the "B" logo
are trademarks belonging to Berkley Publishing Corporation.

PRINTED IN THE UNITED STATES OF AMERICA

10 9 8 7 6 5 4 3 2 1

To Sue and Julian

CHAPTER ─────────
─────── ONE

"It was very accommodating of you to see me at such short notice, Mr. Commissioner." John Goddard drew his chair up to the desk with a smile. "I hope you did not regard as presumptuous, my suggestion that our meeting should be attended by an officer experienced in the investigation of fraud."

Lt. Col. Sir William Sumner CB, Commissioner of the City of London Police, looked at the insurance underwriter with foreboding, then flapped his hand toward the window. "This is Detective Sergeant Bragg," he said.

Goddard raised his eyebrows in surprise. "I am sorry," he remarked, "I was anticipating someone of much greater seniority."

"Rank does not always reflect ability, Mr. Goddard," Sir William said gruffly. "You should know that."

"Indeed!" Goddard replied with a smile. "Well now, I should explain that I am a senior member of the Committee of Lloyd's; though after your last remark, I am not sure that carries any automatic claim on your time. However, as such, I from time to time become involved in matters which bear on the interests of the Lloyd's community as a whole."

To Bragg, Goddard seemed the embodiment of a City committee-man. In his early fifties, he was expensively though soberly dressed, well-groomed, and wearing a heavy gold albert and a pearl tie-pin. Everything about him discreetly proclaimed wealth and social standing. His public-school accent had been carefully retained and lovingly polished, he was bland in manner and address . . . Bragg felt like giving him a shake, to see if he were capable of a reaction that was not carefully weighed and considered in advance.

"I am sure I would be stating the obvious," went on Goddard, "if I were to say that the City is unlike any other society. After all, London is the economic center of the world, and it is in everyone's interest that it should remain so."

The Commissioner shifted restlessly in his chair, and began to fiddle with his paper-knife.

"The reason for our supremacy is our experience and our financial integrity. If the latter could be undermined, then other financial centers would arise in Holland, France, America; and our dominance would be lost. It goes without saying that there is no lack of persons in those countries who would welcome such a development, or even conspire to bring it about . . . One of the gravest threats to our financial stability is fraud," Goddard paused impressively, "international fraud."

"Perhaps I'm not following you, sir," remarked Bragg diffidently, "but I don't understand how the integrity of the City could be undermined if someone defrauds it."

The underwriter's manner lost some of its suavity. "It's a matter of scale, sergeant," he said sharply. "If a business cannot honor its bargains, it is of little concern whether it is sinned against, rather than sinning."

"I see," remarked Bragg. "So it is really a matter of what fraud is costing you."

With a look of distaste, Goddard turned back to the Commissioner. "I can assert with some confidence that the police have little idea of the extent to which the resources of the City have been eroded by fraud. In most cases there is no tangible evidence, often we have little more than a suspicion, and so the police never become involved. Over all the City's activities, however, it could easily amount to a million pounds a year."

Sir William put down his paper-knife, and began to gaze stonily out of the window.

"If I consider my own area," Goddard went on, "I must admit that we have always been prepared to accept a certain level of fraud. Take, for example, a man who fails to find a buyer for his pleasure yacht. He could well be tempted to insure it, then *accidentally* run it onto a rock . . . having made sure, of course, that it was not too far from land!" Goddard smiled expansively. "That kind of thing we can absorb within the normal premium levels, because the amounts are small, and it is unlikely to happen frequently in such an exclusive circle. There has, however, been a steady trickle of claims relating to larger vessels, in recent years, which appear to have sunk in circumstances that are decidedly suspicious. We cannot view such a development with comparable equanimity, the more so since many of the cases have international connections. That is the reason for my coming to see you today."

Sir William swivelled round to face the underwriter. "The establishment of my force, Mr. Goddard, is no greater than is necessary for the normal policing of the Square Mile," he said brusquely. "I cannot spare men to investigate the suspicion of a fraud, where there is no evidence."

"Then we shall have to see to it that your establishment is increased," Goddard replied smoothly. "Just as the City is unique, so the City Police should be acknowledged to be unique. To my mind, there is no duty so important to the economic health of the City as the suppression of fraud. Indeed, if I am elected chairman of Lloyd's when Lord Revelstoke retires at the end of this year—and there is every indication that I shall be so honored—then I intend to press the Common Council to set up a separate division within the City Police, which will deal exclusively with fraud."

"I hope you have more success than I do, when I ask for more men," Sir William retorted grumpily.

"I have no doubt about it." Goddard allowed himself a self-satisfied smile. "But that is for the future. My purpose today is to ask you to institute inquiries into the sinking of a ship, which has all the hallmarks of fraud. It is not a case which is devoid of evidence; indeed there is said to be a witness, now in America, who would no doubt give testimony as to the facts."

"I cannot waste the taxpayers' money, sending officers to America," protested the Commissioner, aghast. "It would be more than my job is worth. Even in eighteen ninety-two, it takes a week to get there."

"I would beg you to remember," Goddard said icily, "that we have only resisted the attempts of the Metropolitan Police to absorb your force, because we believed that you would protect the interests of the business community. I would be sorry to discover that we were wrong."

Sir William's face turned puce with anger, but he did not reply.

"These are the details of the case, so far as I know them," Goddard resumed affably. "Some two weeks ago, an American named Ryan called on the Lloyd's agent in New Orleans and gave an account of the sinking of a British freighter called the *Dancing Lady*. He said he was a marine engineer, and was traveling on the ship from London to New Orleans. According to his allegations, the *Dancing Lady* did not call at New Orleans. Instead, it proceeded down the coast to Galveston, where the cargo was off-loaded on to lighters, at night. Thereafter, the ship sailed down the coast for some distance, and was then scuttled."

"And did Lloyd's insure the *Dancing Lady*?" asked Bragg.

"We were involved on two levels; the ship itself, and the cargo it was carrying, which consisted of a cotton-seed mill. If you want details of the hull and machinery policy, you should talk to John Frankis; the cargo insurance was led by Peter Whitlock's syndicate. If you need any further assistance or advice, do not hesitate to approach me . . . I need hardly say that the committee of Lloyd's sets great store by this investigation. For some time we have been waiting for a case to arise, through which we could demonstrate that fraud cannot be practiced against us with impunity. In this case we have a witness who is an experienced seaman, and who communicated with us voluntarily." Goddard rose to his feet. "We rely on you to ensure that the perpetrators are brought to justice. Good morning, gentlemen."

"Pompous bugger," muttered Bragg as the door closed behind him.

Sir William contemplated his blotter dejectedly. With his round balding head and pointed beard, he looked like a petulant Prince of Wales. For the first time, Bragg felt a twinge of sympathy for him.

"This is a far from easy job," Sir William said with a sigh. "It may seem so to you, Bragg, but at times I wish I were back in the army. At least when you are in command of a regiment, you don't have civilians interfering and telling you what to do. Here, I no sooner make a decision, than someone is pressing me to alter it."

"Surely you can ignore him, sir?"

"Stop being stupid, Bragg. You heard what he said. Unless we comply, we shall be absorbed into the Met. You would not want that anymore than I do."

"That was just bluff, though."

"Not a bit of it. It is at the bidding of such as he that the City authorities and the Tory party have fought to prevent us from being swallowed up. Make no mistake, they pull the strings."

"Then it looks as if you have no option, sir."

"Do you believe in this theory of an international conspiracy to destroy the City?" asked the Commissioner.

"Not the way he put it. But no doubt there are plenty of people who would like a shovel or two of the money that piles up here."

"I suppose he is right, in a way. There is little point in keeping the traffic flowing, and watching out for burglars, if we allow financial crimes to go unchecked. But then, everybody who comes here pleading a special case is right in a way."

"It sounds as if he will fight your battles for you on staff, anyway . . . That is, if he does become chairman."

"I would think it is certain. He will have been tipped the wink already. That's how things are done in the City. Nothing so vulgar as an election."

"Well then, it seems that you can only gain, sir."

"Maybe. But that's in the future, perhaps a couple of years away. In the meantime, we are expected to take on a commitment we are not staffed for. And you know better than I the time that a fraud case can consume. I cannot send an officer gallivanting about America. The first Alderman whose warehouse was broken into would have my head on a platter."

"There is Constable Morton, sir."

"How do you mean, Bragg?"

"You did give him permission to come back from Australia by way of America. He left me the address of his uncle in Boston. So we could easily telegraph him, and tell him to stay and have a look around."

"I don't know, Bragg . . . Is he capable of working alone yet?"

"I think so, if this damned cricket tour hasn't made him forget everything I've taught him."

"That kind of thing is good for the reputation of the force, Bragg," said Sir William with a frown. "We consistently get a better standard of recruit than the Met. In my view the two are not unconnected."

"But, in the meantime, I have to go short-handed."

"From what Inspector Cotton tells me, you are accustomed to surmount any obstacle, by legitimate means or stratagem, and often at the expense of your fellow-officers. You can hardly expect sympathy."

Bragg smoothed his untidy moustache to conceal his smile. "At any rate," he said, "Constable Morton is paying his own expenses, so it would not cost you any more than if he were working in London."

The Commissioner's face brightened. "That's true, certainly. Yes, Bragg. That rather lets us off that particular hook, does it not? Good! Will you telegraph him to go down to Galveston, and see what he can find out?"

"Very good, sir. And I will let the police there know that they can expect him."

"I suppose we will have to pay his railway fares and hotel bills," said the Commissioner, relapsing into gloom. "They are sure to be high. Why does it have to be such a damned enormous country?"

Bragg wandered over to the barrack-like Customs House, down by the Thames. The May day sun was warm, and, surprisingly, he was glad to reach the cool gloom of the entrance. He looked around in vain for a messenger, then climbed the balustraded staircase to the high-vaulted Long Room overlooking the river. Here the counters were thronged with men making declarations of cargoes, and arguing over the duty payable. Bragg pushed his way to the front, and, waving his warrant card, attracted the attention of a clerk.

"Can you tell me where the Ship Registry is?" he asked.

"No, I can't," the young man replied perkily. "This place is such a rabbit-warren that if I tell you, you still would never find it. I will only be a moment." He spoke briefly to the man he was dealing with, then beckoned to Bragg. They went up stairs, down stairs, and along echoing stone-flagged corridors, until they reached what Bragg judged to be a basement, in a distant wing of the building. The clerk knocked on a door and opened it.

"A police officer to see you, Mr. Rappaport." He stood aside to let Bragg pass, and turned on his heel. The room was gloomy, with the musty smell of old books. A black-coated man of sixty rose from a table in front of the barred window, and peered myopically at Bragg's warrant card.

"I would imagine that they don't regard your department as the most important job around here," Bragg observed lightly.

"What? Oh yes, I see," chirped Rappaport. "No, the Customs are only agents of the Board of Trade for registering ships. Not that these are our permanent quarters. We are to be given rooms on the ground floor, off the entrance hall, next year. It is so inconvenient for the public to have to come down here."

Bragg surveyed the deserted room. "Perhaps they never find you."

Rappaport gave a wheezing laugh. "Examining shipping registers is not the most popular of pursuits," he said. "Mostly it is clerks from ship-brokers or solicitors, when a ship is changing hands. There are days when no public foot crosses the threshold."

"I had never thought of my foot as being either public or private; but I would prefer not to pay your shilling," said Bragg with a smile.

"Then I will extend the courtesy of one maligned species for another. How can I help you?"

"I want to find out about a ship called the *Dancing Lady*."

"That should be simple enough," Rappaport said. "There is the minor complication that the current year's register has gone for binding, but we can look it up in last year's."

He crossed to some racking, and standing on tiptoe, eased an enormous leather-bound volume to the edge of a high shelf. Bragg started forward to help.

"No, no, I can manage," cried Rappaport. "It's easy when you are used to it." He gave a final tug, and with the great tome threatening to break out of his puny grasp, he tottered rapidly to the table and dropped it there.

"You see?" he said with satisfaction, wiping the dust from his hands onto the front of his coat. "Now, in that register are the particulars of every ship flying the British flag. Where are we? The *Dancing Lady* . . ." He opened the register and quickly turned the pages, "Here we are. What is it you want to know?"

"At the moment, the only information I have is that it was a freighter, and it is alleged to have been scuttled. Perhaps if you just tell me about it, I shall get a feel for what I'm after."

"Well now, it was built in eighteen seventy-two, which makes it just twenty years old. The builder was James Laing of Sunderland, and the first owners seem to have been H.A.F. Naumann of Hamburg." Rappaport's finger was flitting from one part of the page to another as he looked for the details. "When I say that, I am making an assumption. All the register really shows is that it was sold by Naumann to the Green Funnel line, three years ago. That was the first time it came under the British flag."

"What kind of ship was it?" Bragg asked.

Rappaport's finger leapt to the right-hand page. "She had an iron hull, with a large hold forward and a smaller one aft. She had three masts, and was schooner-rigged, and there was a deckhouse forward of the mizzen mast."

"I really meant, how big was it?"

"Oh, quite small. Her gross tonnage was only a little over one thousand tons."

"What does that mean in size?"

Rappaport's finger found another column. "She was two hundred and thirty-seven feet long, and thirty feet wide."

"Now you're talking my language. So it was really small. Would you expect a ship like that to cross the Atlantic in winter?"

"I cannot say as to that," replied Rappaport. "Our concern is to measure the ship and determine its carrying capacity. We are not qualified to form opinions as to the use to which it should be put."

"You can see what I'm driving at, though. Here is a ship

which has sunk. A man who was on it says it was scuttled, but it could have gone down by natural causes, as you might say, and he could be having us on.''

"One moment, I will consult the file." Rappaport opened a large wooden cupboard in the corner and extracted a thin manila folder, which he placed on the desk before them. "The ship was, of course, surveyed when it first came onto the register in 'eighty-nine. I was wondering if the report gave any indication of the vessel's condition . . . but you can see that it does not. Nor is that surprising, it is not our concern.''

"I thought the Shipping Acts were to do with safety, and the conditions British seamen served under," said Bragg in surprise.

"Well so they are. A ship is not allowed to carry in excess of the ascertained tonnage, and in addition they have to provide enough lifeboats for the crew, and suchlike.''

"But you are not concerned if the hull consists of layers of rust held together with paint?''

"It may seem odd to you, but that is the case. Unless there are structural alterations, a ship is only surveyed by us once. You might get some help in that area from Lloyd's Register. They are an offshoot of the insurance people, and they are concerned with seaworthiness.''

"Thank you, I'll see them . . . Oh, can you tell me the address of the Green Funnel line?''

"They went out of business at the end of eighteen ninety. Their ships were bought by Harvey & Crane Ltd. of Twenty-four, Leadenhall Street." He turned over the letters on the file: "I could give you the name of the managing agents, if you like.''

"Please." Bragg took out his notebook.

"They are Taylor Pendrill & Co., of Fifteen, St. Mary Axe.''

Bragg looked at his watch on regaining the street. With any luck he might catch someone at the owners' office before they went home for the night. He hurried up the steep street from the river. Really, he was getting too old for this kind of exertion. It was either his forty-one years, or the numerous barrels of beer he'd consumed in that time. He could positively feel his paunch quivering as his feet pounded the pavement. He arrived in Leadenhall Street breathless, vowing to give up either exercise or the beer. He was still puffing when he pushed into the offices of Harvey & Crane, and rang the bell on the counter. The young man who answered was already wearing his coat and bowler hat.

"I want to see the boss," Bragg growled, thrusting his warrant card under the man's nose.

"Mr. Cakebread? I think he may have already left. Just a moment . . ." He disappeared through a door in the back of the office.

Bragg studied the pictures of ships around the walls, but although they all had green funnels, none of them bore the name *Dancing Lady*.

"Will you come this way, sir?" The young man conducted him down a corridor and ushered him into a gloomy office at the back of the building.

An oldish man, with faded fair hair and yellowing skin, was sitting behind the desk, engaged in putting his pencils and pens into a drawer. He glanced at Bragg through his pince-nez, without getting up.

"Six o'clock is a most inconvenient time to come calling," he said in a high querulous voice. "Will it not keep till morning?"

"I'm afraid public business is often inconvenient, sir," Bragg said gravely. "I will not detain you long."

Cakebread closed the drawer with a bang, and sat back in his chair. "Very well," he said peevishly. "What have you come to see me about?"

"I am making inquiries concerning a ship called the *Dancing Lady*. I understand that it was owned by your company."

Cakebread suddenly became tense. "That is correct," he said warily.

"From information we have received, it appears that the ship was lost in the Caribbean Sea on or around the fifteenth of February this year."

"Why does this concern you?" asked Cakebread sharply. "We have not asked you to make inquiries."

"That is true, certainly. But Lloyd's think the vessel may have been scuttled as part of a plot to defraud them on the insurance, and have asked us to look into it. I am bound to say that we have little evidence one way or another, at the moment, but I'm sure you will be able to help us."

Cakebread rose jerkily to his feet. "I am not prepared to answer any questions unless the legal advisor of the company is present," he said edgily, and strode out of the room. He had given no indication that the interview was terminated, and his hat and coat still hung in the corner, so Bragg stayed in his chair. After some moments he heard Cakebread's voice speaking loudly in the front office. He could not distinguish what was being said, though he heard the word "police" several times. Then the conversation ceased, and Cakebread reappeared.

"I have just been talking to the solicitor over the telephone," he said in a tight voice. "He is unable to come at such short notice, but agrees that he ought to be present at any interview."

"I was only going to ask about the condition of the ship, and suchlike," protested Bragg. "Nothing to get in a muck-sweat about."

"Nevertheless, I must take his advice. He instructs me to say that you should submit any questions you may have, in writing. They will be considered, and we will give such answers as are proper, at an interview to be arranged two or three days later."

"That is a very peculiar way of proceeding," said Bragg roughly. "It almost suggests you have something to hide."

"Nevertheless, you will have to put up with it," retorted Cakebread defiantly. "Now I suggest you leave the premises, so that honest people may go home."

It was Bragg's usual practice to stay down in the basement kitchen after supper, with Mrs. Jenks, his landlady. In the winter it was warm and companionable, he with his pipe and library book on one side of the range, she on the other with her knitting. Anyway, it was more like the living room of his childhood home in Dorset than the prim parlor he rented on the top floor of the house. But tonight he felt restless. He took a turn around the weedy patch of earth at the back, where Mrs. Jenks tried to grow delphiniums and roses. The untidy dejection of it tugged at his conscience. The very least he could do would be to fork it over, and get the weeds out. It wasn't really a woman's work, though she swore she preferred to do it herself. Women! They were supposed to be sweet and charming and amenable, yet he hadn't met one who wasn't cantankerous and wrong-headed and bossy. And dammit, she should have pruned the roses back harder. They'd end up straggly, with a lot of small flowers, instead of the big blooms that delighted him. But tell her that, and he'd feel the edge of her tongue. To hear her talk, you would think they grew nothing in the country but grass.

"Mr. Bragg," her sharp voice cut into his reverie, "Miss Marsden has called to see you. I've put her in your sitting-room."

He hastened up the back stairs, and found Catherine peering at an indistinct snapshot of his late wife on the mantelpiece.

"It's good to see you, Miss Marsden," he said. "How are you? And how is the foot you dislocated last autumn?"

"It has almost wholly recovered now, thank you."

"Nasty business."

"Yes. I stayed for three weeks with the Mortons, and it really was not improving at all. Then one evening a doctor friend of James—er, Constable Morton—called in. He looks after the Kent cricket team. He made me put my foot on a low stool then pressed down with his thumbs, and the bones went back with the most horrid click."

"But it is all right now?"

"Yes. If I walk on an uneven pavement, I sometimes feel it. But it will soon be completely healed. I can tell you one thing, though; I have given up jumping out of trees!"

"If it's not that, it will be something else. I have known you barely a year, and you have been within a whisker of death twice. You will never make old bones."

"I certainly intend to try."

"You have no brothers or sisters, have you?"

"No."

"Don't your parents get anxious about you?"

"My father indulges me, my mother thinks—or perhaps merely hopes—that I can look after myself."

"And here you are miles from home, at eight o'clock at night."

"Don't you start chiding me, sergeant," Catherine protested with a smile. "You know perfectly well that I have to work late on Fridays, until they have put the Saturday edition to bed."

"So you are still intent on being a journalist, then?"

"Not merely intent on it, I can really say that I am one. My probation at the *City Press* is over, and I have been confirmed as a full-time permanent reporter. And, moreover, I am no longer restricted to social and charitable occasions. Whatever you may say about that last escapade, it got me noticed in my profession."

"And are you still writing the occasional column for the *Star*?"

"Of course! . . . I can regard myself as a success, sergeant."

"Not bad for a woman. How old are you?"

"Don't condescend, sergeant . . . I have just turned twenty-one."

"So now you will take advice from no one. But you know what I think."

"Yes indeed!" she replied, smiling broadly. "Practically your first words to me were that I should be at home dandling a baby on my knee. I cannot recollect whether you advised me to get married first, or not."

"I've seen a good few of you professional women in my time—teachers, hospital matrons, the odd doctor—and never a one but feels she's missed out in life."

"Goodness! You are becoming more maternal than Mamma ever was. No, sergeant, I have a stimulating, responsible job that most men would give their eye-teeth for. I am not about to relinquish that to embrace a domesticity which, so far as I can see, means that I would stay at home with the children, while my husband was enjoying himself with a mistress."

"Not every man is like that, miss."

"In my circle they are."

"Very well, I've had my say. Now I don't suppose you came just to exchange pleasantries with me. What can I do for you?"

Catherine's face colored. "Well, as a matter of fact, I did want to pick your brains."

"You are welcome, such as they are."

"I have a friend who is a compositor on the *Lloyd's List*. He sent me round a note about a paragraph in tomorrow's edition. It will say that the City police are inquiring into the sinking of a ship in the Caribbean last February."

"They wasted no time," grunted Bragg.

"I gather it is based on a statement made by the committee of Lloyd's. Do you know anything about it?"

"I know I am in charge of the investigation. Beyond that I know precious little. Although I worked in a shipping office as a youngster, we were only import and export agents. The business of owning and running ships is a new world to me, and at the moment I am more than a bit lost."

"But if you have been asked to investigate, then there must be a suspicion of a crime."

"Fraud. The Lloyd's people think the ship was scuttled for the insurance money."

"And was it?"

"Hold on, young woman, I was only given the case this morning."

"Well, you will keep me in touch with developments, won't you?"

"On the usual basis, that you do not publish anything till we say you can."

"I suppose so, though it has not served me particularly well in the past."

"Now, there is ingratitude from a newly-appointed, permanent lady reporter."

"Sorry!"

"We shall, in fact, be investigating the allegations from both ends. I shall be making the enquiries here, while those in America will be made by Constable Morton, who conveniently happens to be there at the moment."

"Oh." Catherine's voice sounded flat.

"So he will not be home for quite a time yet."

"I suppose not."

"But when he does come back, he will be able to tell you all about it himself."

Catherine smiled, and Bragg thought he detected a blush on her cheek. "On the usual basis, of course," she said.

"But of course."

CHAPTER ———— ———— TWO

James Morton gave a final tug at his bow tie, and glanced out of the window at the scene below. It was a relief to have his feet on something that was not moving. For over seven months he had been travelling on a ship or a train, with an occasional few days snatched for a cricket match. By the time the tour of Australia was over, it had seemed that the relentless travelling was its object, and the cricket merely a series of pleasant interludes. The voyage to San Francisco had allowed him to relax, to regain his individuality, instead of being merely one of an ill-assorted group whose collective bonhomie was wearing ever thinner. But even so, he felt suspended in a vacuum. The excitement of his selection had receded, and the experience of playing for England, satisfying as it had been, was gradually diminishing in importance. Yet he was still insulated from normal life by the two weeks of travel in front of him. He had thought that on the train to Boston he would be able to marshal his thoughts, achieve a new perspective, if one were needed. But once through the Rockies, the numbing tedium of the journey had stultified any attempt at self-appraisal.

At least his uncle's manservant had brushed and sponged his evening clothes; so he felt less like a piece of baggage with a Union Jack pasted on it. He put on his jacket, and pulled down the sleeves of his shirt; then, with a final look in the mirror, went downstairs. He received a welcoming smile from one of the maids.

"Mr. and Mrs. Harman are in the drawing-room, sir."

"Thank you," Morton replied. "I have an idea that I should recognize you, but it is over three years since I last came. Surely you were a chamber-maid then?"

"That's correct, sir," she said with a smile. "My name is Annie Johnson. I'm a parlor-maid now."

"Well done. It's good to see you again." He pushed open the heavy mahogany door. "Sorry to have been so long," he said, "I'm afraid that I found it impossible to drag myself out of the bath."

"I can well understand that," his aunt Amelia assured him with a smile. "In the days when I used to go to Philadelphia with your uncle, I would come back feeling as grubby as a hog! Well, it's only the four of us this evening, as Joshua and I are going out to a charity concert after dinner. Shall we go in?"

Morton found himself sitting opposite his cousin Violet. She was certainly very handsome. Last time he'd seen her she had been a somewhat gauche seventeen-year-old, with acne. Now she was elegantly dressed, and appeared mature and self-possessed. She did not have the fine contained beauty of a Gainsborough, more the full-blooded promise of a Titian. In middle age, she would be just like her mother, comely and contented.

"And how is everyone in England, James?" asked his uncle.

"I'm sorry, sir. I was day-dreaming." Morton saw an amused glance pass between Amelia and Violet. "I am afraid I have been out of touch for so long that I was hoping you could tell me."

"We had a letter from your mother last week, but there was not too much news in it. Charlotte still regards me as her little brother, and preaches at me all the time. She exercises the prerogative of an expatriate American, and berates me about what we are doing wrong."

"I am sure that everyone must be well, or she would have told you."

"Your father is still Lord-Lieutenant of Kent?"

"Yes. He seems to enjoy it, even though it is mainly an honorific appointment. At least it absorbs his energies. After the army, he would have found it difficult to settle down to the life of a country gentleman."

"And your mother?"

"I think she is very happy. What with the estate and local affairs, and official functions as well, she barely has time to fit everything in."

Joshua dabbed at his mouth with his napkin. "Is the estate doing well?" he asked.

Morton laughed. "Well, if you were asking me whether or not it was a profitable enterprise, I think I would have to say 'No'. Since your people began flooding Britain with cheap grain . . ."

Joshua held up his hand with a smile. "You have no need to tell me. Your mother's letters, for the past year, have said all there is to say."

"I would like to switch from cereals to milk. You remember the land in the valley bottom? In my view that would be perfect for grass. I want to refrigerate the milk, as you do, and send it to London; but my father will not hear of it."

"I suppose you cannot expect him to take on board new ideas at his age. From what your mother tells me, even men who have done nothing all their lives but farm their estates, are sticking stubbornly to the old ways."

"It's not only that. When they brought Edwin home from the Sudan, my father said that he was making over the management of the estate to him. Mother says it is to give him something to do, to give him a sense of achievement. But I think, in addition, they want to let him feel that he is running the family estates, which would have come to him, if he had not been wounded."

"But they still will, won't they?" asked Amelia. "He's still the elder son."

"You are touching on a very sore area, aunt," said Morton gloomily. "I genuinely do not mind that he will inherit the baronetcy. How could I? And, anyway, it must come to my children ultimately. But I do object most strongly that he should inherit The Priory. How can a man who is paralysed from the waist down, and who can only leave his room on a good day, in case he takes a chill; how can he run a large agricultural estate? And yet my parents seem determined on it."

"Perhaps they feel that Edwin has not many years left," remarked Joshua reflectively. "How is he?"

"Not much different from when you saw him last. Only his will-power, and resentment at his fate, keep him going; but they show no sign of abating."

"So who runs the estate in practice?"

"No one." Morton put down his wine-glass. "Edwin makes the decisions of policy, out of the full measure of his inexperience and the bailiff deals with the day-to-day problems."

"It sounds as if the property could be not worth the inheriting, by the time it passes to you."

"I'm sorry to be so sour about all this," Morton said with a grimace. "It's just that The Priory has been in the family for centuries, and I cannot accept that my father has the right to allow it to decline, just to give a spurious sense of purpose to one member of the family, however unfortunate."

"Come now, James," said his uncle jocularly. "If it were not for money from this side of the Atlantic, The Priory would be in irreversible decay by now."

Morton flushed. "That is undoubtedly true, uncle, but since family money is available, I can think of no better way of using it."

"That seems a little sterile, to me, James. Here you are, performing a lowly office in the police force, waiting to obtain an inheritance that can only come to you on the deaths of two people . . ."

"Daddy!" Violet exclaimed. "You are being quite unnecessarily cruel."

"No, cousin," said Morton. "He is only saying what I have thought to myself increasingly, over the last year or so."

"Suppose it does come to you?" Joshua asked. "What will you do then? Spend your life restoring and maintaining a mouldering collection of buildings that represents a bygone age? Surely life is about people, not stones?"

"It is the family tradition to run the estate, and anyway the livelihood of a good number of people depends on it."

"You cannot fight against economic laws, James. That way

of life is passing, and I do not see you should mourn it. As a tradition it has consumed the energies of countless people, and given very little back. America is the land of opportunity, James. You could do worse than join us here. We must see that the future of our business is in good hands, and we could give you a job that would really stretch you . . . Come along Amelia," he said, peering at his watch. "We will leave these two young people to their own devices for a while."

Violet and Morton watched the carriage disappear down the long winding drive, then explored the grounds hand-in-hand, as if they were still children. She showed him the new tennis court; and clambering onto a pile of stones, attempted to explain what the Italian garden would look like, when it was finished. But she was a tomboy no longer, and Morton had to take her by the waist and swing her down, lest her gown should be soiled. Even so, there seemed to be an impish excitement in her, and calling that she would race him back to the house, she gathered up her skirts, and took to her heels. He ran after her without pressing, fearful that in the dusk she might miss her footing, and they arrived at the house together. She flopped against him as she used to in the old days, gasping that she felt like a rag doll, and on a sudden impulse of happiness he planted a kiss on her upturned forehead. She drew away from him, once more the young society lady, and walked quickly through the front door and into the sitting-room. There was no hint of censure in her manner, however, and they chatted easily about her visits to England, and the times they had spent together on the Massachusetts farm.

Then she played the piano to him—a Mendelssohn Song Without Words; soft cascades of arpeggios, with just a touch of sentiment. Morton observed her speculatively, remembering that as children they had always enjoyed each other's company. More than once he had been admonished for being sullen when it was time to go back to England. She had the ability to make him feel relaxed and content, and at the moment it was a quality he greatly prized. Violet rose from the piano, and the style of her dress accentuated her shapely body and wide hips. Good breeding-stock, his father would say.

They stood in the window, looking down at the street lights, and the carriage lamps crawling slowly up Beacon Hill. Violet would certainly be a successful hostess, and was already a

great favorite at The Priory . . . Of course, some people said
that cousins should never marry under any circumstances; but
it was not as if there had been inter-breeding in the past. She
was perhaps a bit superficial, but a happy and amusing
temperament more than compensated for that. On the whole, it
would work very well. He had an easy, enduring affection for
her, which could prove a more stable foundation for marriage
than the wild infatuations he had experienced to date. And
when did members of his class marry for love, anyway? She
moved closer to him, and he felt the stirrings of physical
excitement . . . Then they heard the sound of hooves and
carriage-wheels on the drive. Violet started away from him in
confusion, and hastily drew the curtains. When his uncle and
aunt came into the room, they were sitting decorously on either
side of the fireplace, with all the lights turned up.

"How was the concert, Mamma?" asked Violet.

"Much as these things usually are, dear," her mother
replied. "And what mischief have you two been up to? I
always used to ask you that, James. Remember? And often
with good reason, too!"

"Oh, we had a wonderful evening, Mamma, talking over
old times." Violet's face was suffused with a happy excitement. Morton thought he would be well content, if his own
daughters looked like that. She was really very pretty.

"Well, come along, dear. It's time we got our beauty sleep.
You won't be long, Josh, will you?" she called over her
shoulder, as she and Violet went out.

"Scotch, my boy?" asked Joshua.

"Thank you, uncle."

"No ice, as I recall."

"That's right."

Joshua brought over the drinks, and stood with his back to
the fire. "I suppose they are necessary," he said, "but I find
these charity concerts just one big bore . . ." Then he crossed
over to a bureau. "A telegraph arrived for you a couple of days
ago," he said. "I am sorry to say that it was opened by my
secretary; and since I was fearful that it contained bad news, I
read it, in the hope that I might shorten your journey home."
He handed the buff envelope to Morton. "I kept it back from
you," he went on, "because I wanted you to have at least one
evening of relaxation. I guess it means you need not have
unpacked your bags at all!"

Morton scanned the page. "Where is Galveston?" he asked.

"It must be about as far south from here as you can go—on the Gulf coast, in Texas. I suppose it might take four days to get there."

"Oh well," replied Morton with a grin, "I thought it was too much to expect that the world would stay still for a while."

Joshua placed his glass on the mantelpiece. "I have a meeting with your uncle Thomas in Newark tomorrow afternoon, so I shall be making an early start."

"Do you mind if I come with you as far as New York?" asked Morton, rising to his feet.

"I should like that," replied Joshua warmly. "I will see that you are called. The carriage will be at the door at seven. Goodnight, James."

Morton slept soundly, and was awakened by a discreet tapping on his door. It was already broad daylight, and the strengthening sun was coaxing the mist from the hollows. While he shaved, his uncle's valet packed his bags. Then with a regretful glance around the room, he went down to breakfast. His uncle and aunt were already there, Amelia dressed in a brightly colored peignoir.

"I am so sorry that you have to leave us, James," she said.

"The law has a long arm, nowadays," replied Morton with a smile, "even for its own."

"You must have a big breakfast," his aunt enjoined. "Heaven knows when you will get some decent food again."

He was just finishing his coffee when the door was pushed open, and Violet entered. She was wearing a blue morning-dress, and her hair had been carefully dressed. "Oh, James," she said reproachfully. "Why did you not tell me last night? I did so want you to stay for a time."

"The reason is simple," said Joshua. "I only gave James the telegraph after you had gone to bed."

"You will come back for a few more days, before you sail home?" she pleaded.

"You may be sure that I shall try," Morton replied. "If not, I shall see you when you come to England next spring. I promise that I shall squire you all over London!"

"Come along, my boy," said Joshua, "the carriage will be waiting."

Violet insisted on accompanying them to the station. She

hugged Morton warmly before he boarded the train, and looking back down the track he could see her fluttering handkerchief till the train swung round a curve, and hid her from sight. He sighed, and took his seat by the window. Opposite him, Joshua was buried in his newspaper—no doubt absorbing the commercial news . . . So his uncle would like him to join the family business in America; take a job that would really stretch him. At the moment, the idea of traveling two hundred miles for a meeting, year in year out, had little appeal. But in time he might think differently. He decided not to raise the matter himself, but to wait till it was broached more formally. In the meantime he could be thinking about it—and about Violet.

It was when the train was running down from Montgomery to Mobile, that Morton noticed a marked change in the climate. From New York they had been ambling along the flank of the Appalachian Mountains. Across the wide plains of Maryland and Virginia, it had seemed like a lush English summer; and when they came to the Carolinas, the train had taken to the hills—orange-brown slashes of rock in the green mantle of trees. So he was unprepared for the steamy heat of the southern plain. He followed the example of his fellow passengers, and took off his jacket. Even so, he was being slowly broiled by the mid-morning sun, and the only breeze seemed to be that created by the passage of the train itself. Reaching the coast provided no relief. If anything the air was more humid than ever. By New Orleans, Morton had suffered enough, and abandoning the train, he took a room for the night at Ziegler's. He caught the first train for Houston next morning, and by four o'clock he was sluicing himself down in a hotel in Galveston.

He put on his lightest clothes, and taking instructions from the porter, strolled off in the direction of the police station. In contrast to New Orleans, the buildings were insubstantial; mostly constructed of wood, and erected on piles sunk into the ground. There were none of the great granite slabs that paved the streets of New Orleans. Here the roads were of beaten earth, and the lightest buggy trailed a plume of dust. But at least there was more air, because, he had been proudly informed by the porter, Galveston was built on an island. He tried to purchase a street plan, or a map of the immediate vicinity, but none was available. The locals evidently had no need of them, and regarded his inquiries as evidence of mild eccentricity.

The police station proved to be a single-storeyed wooden building, with a shingle roof. Only its length, and the inscription painted over the door, distinguished it from the other buildings in the street. It was to be hoped that the jail was more strongly built, thought Morton. You could break out of this with one hefty kick. A man in shirtsleeves was occupying the outer office. His heels were on the desk, and the chair was tipped back so that his head rested on the wall. Apart from the badge pinned to his shirt, he might have been a civilian snoozing in his summerhouse.

"Good afternoon," Morton said pleasantly.

The man opened an eye experimentally.

"Yeah?" he asked.

"I would like to see the officer in charge of the police force."

"Oh, yeah?" The information did not appear to stimulate any spirit of inquiry in the man.

"You should have received a cable to say I was coming."

"I guess Lieutenant Gregory is a mite busy just now."

"Look," said Morton irritably, "I have come down from Boston to see him. At least tell him I have arrived."

The man reluctantly slid his heels off the desk, and sauntered over to a door on the right. He stuck his head through it, and called, "Greg, there's a guy from Boston to see you." There was a muffled shout from beyond.

"What d'you say your name was?"

"Morton. Constable Morton from the London police."

The man's eyes registered puzzlement and suspicion. "I thought you just said you was from Boston," he said.

"No. I am an officer in the City of London Police, but I have just traveled down from Boston."

"Are you English, then?"

"Yes."

"My folks came from Lincoln, England, way back. Boston's near Lincoln, ain't it?"

"Ah, did they? Good. However, I have come down from Boston, Massachusetts," Morton said patiently. "I have an uncle there."

"But you're from London, England?"

"That's right."

"Hold on, will you?" He pushed through the door, which flapped closed behind him. After a few minutes he reappeared. "Last door on the left," he remarked laconically, and sitting in his chair, resumed his former posture.

Morton walked down the short corridor, and rapped on the door indicated.

"Come on in."

A powerfully-built man rose from behind the door and held out a huge hand.

"Mighty good to see you, son. My name's Matt Gregory; mostly they call me Greg. Take a seat, will you?"

He had a large fleshy face, with heavy sideburns, but otherwise was clean-shaven. A few strands of hair were carefully combed across his balding head. There were deep creases at the corners of his eyes and mouth, as if he smiled habitually.

"Are you fixed up with some place to stay?" he asked genially.

"Yes, thank you. I have a room at the hotel by the station."

"Good. You won't do better in this town. This your first visit over here?"

"My first to the South. I have an uncle, Joshua Harman, in Boston. We have exchanged visits fairly regularly."

"Joshua Harman, eh?" Greg murmured reflectively. "Should I know that name?"

"My mother's family have coal mines and iron works in Philadelphia, and various other parts of America."

"Ah." Greg filed the information in his memory, then smiled again. "I got a cable from your folks in England, sayin' I was to expect you. But it said nothin' about the reason."

"This will tell you as much as I know," said Morton, passing over his telegraph message.

Greg read it slowly, his lips silently forming the words as he did so. Then he placed it on the desk, a frown puckering the smooth skin of his brow.

"Your people in England are investigatin' what they call the 'diversion' of a cargo from New Orleans to Galveston. What d'you reckon they mean by that word?"

"'Diversion'? Why, I assume that the goods were being

dispatched to New Orleans, but they did not arrive there. Instead, they were off-loaded in Galveston harbor, at night, presumably for the benefit of someone in this area."

"Are you just lookin' for the cotton-seed mill, or what?"

"Not only that," replied Morton. "The clear implication of the cable is that this was a criminal act. I would therefore assume we would be interested in all the individuals involved in it."

Greg looked up cautiously. "And where would you say this 'diversion' took place?"

Morton frowned in thought. "I suppose it must have happened at the point where the master of the *Dancing Lady* altered course to go to Galveston instead of New Orleans."

"That must have been off the Mississippi coast, or maybe even the open sea," said Greg with a smile. "This state ain't got a law against piracy, leastwise none I've ever come across!"

"But surely there are federal laws?" Morton protested.

"What's that?—I suddenly gone deaf." Greg gave a high-pitched titter.

"At the very least, it is possible that someone in this vicinity is in possession of stolen property," said Morton.

"Now we do have a law about that. Right, what d'you want me to do?"

"Trace the shipment, so that we can question the person who has received it."

"Now ain't you a little in front of yourself? First we've got to be sure the man that gave this information to your folks was speakin' the truth."

"That is tantamount to saying that you cannot help," said Morton.

"No, it ain't. You just got to tread lightly in this town. Texas has not been in the Union very long, and there's plenty folk around still think we should never have given up our independence. I can't see people gettin' steamed up about somethin' that should have gone to New Orleans, and arrived here instead!" Greg giggled once more . . . "Then again, if it was landed in Galveston, I'd want to know who's got it now—or maybe better, who ain't got it."

"So what do we do?" asked Morton.

Greg looked at the watch propped up by his ink-stand.

"Why, we go for a drink at the Cotton Club." He reached for his jacket. "What did you say your first name was?"

"James."

"Right." He led the way to the street. "Tell me somethin' about yourself, and take care not to let them know you're a policeman."

After a few hundred yards, Greg led the way into a colonial-style building, with a pillared portico. "Hello, Tom," he greeted the white-gloved, liveried servant. "Let's have a couple of bourbons, will you?"

"Yes, Massa Greg. Right away." His teeth flashed white in his ebony face.

"Where is everybody?"

"Massa Langbe and Massa Coyle are on the veranda." He handed them each a tinkling glass wrapped in a white napkin.

Morton followed Greg into a large high-ceilinged room, and through a mesh door to the veranda. They approached a table placed under a lazily-revolving fan.

"Gentlemen," said Greg, "I would like you to meet a young friend of mine, James Morton, from England."

Each man rose courteously to his feet as he was introduced, and shook hands.

"James is a nephew of Joshua Harman—you know, the Philadelphia coal and iron people."

"Is he now?" Langbe seemed impressed.

"Old John Harman's daughter got herself married to a lord. Ain't that right, James?"

"A baronet, actually," murmured Morton.

"You didn't know I moved in them circles, did you?" Greg tittered.

"Welcome to the South, Mr. Morton," Coyle said in a soft voice. "May I ask the purpose of your visit?"

"Largely holiday. I have never been to this part of America before."

"First time I ever heard of anybody coming to Galveston on vacation," remarked Langbe with a smile.

"If you ask me, he's goin' to buy you all up," said Greg.

"I wish he would," retorted Langbe. "I could take my wife back to Savannah then."

"Cotton is comparatively new around here," Greg drawled. "And Sam, here, was sent by his old Dad down to Savannah to learn the trade. Now Sam was a good looking, devil-may-care youngster in those days . . . You'd never believe it now, would you?" he chaffed. "Anyways he brought back the most beautiful belle the South has ever seen. Only trouble is, she can't wait to get back to Georgia."

Coyle and Greg laughed heartily, but Langbe's smile was threadbare.

"I did not realise that the cotton industry was so recently established in Texas," Morton said.

Greg gave his broad smile. "They're still only beginners, James," he said in a bantering tone. "D'you know, there ain't a single mill to crush the cotton-seed, in this whole area. They ship it out in sacks to New Orleans for crushin'; they're happy with ten cents instead of a dollar, around here. That's not my notion of carryin' on."

"Old Jefferson Harris used to talk of buying a mill," Coyle mused. "Nobody took up the idea, once he died."

"He never had the capital, anyway," replied Langbe. "And if he'd borrowed, his profit would have all been swallowed up in interest."

"Maybe we ought to get up a syndicate to run one," said Coyle. "Or maybe the Harmans will build one, if they are buying into cotton here."

"I'm afraid that Greg is pulling your leg, gentlemen," Morton replied with a smile.

"Wouldn't be the first time," said Langbe sourly.

"Come along, James," tittered Greg. "You've a deal of cotton fields to see before sundown."

Morton took his farewell of Coyle and Langbe, and followed Greg into the street.

"Does that mean that there is no truth in the allegations?" he asked.

"No, you can't say that," replied Greg. "Sam Langbe is a big planter from the north of this county, and Jimmy Coyle is the most important cotton-broker in Galveston. I'd bet ten dollars to a pole-cat's tail they ain't heard a whisper about any cotton-seed mill comin' in. And since they are well in with the folk that control this town, it means none of their cronies have either. So, we can push our enquiries a mite further . . . Don't look so pained, son. I'm here to keep some kind of order in this town, not stir it up for the sake of folks in England. I'll walk with you to the hotel, to see they don't fleece you."

CHAPTER ———— ———— THREE

The chief surveyor of the Lloyd's Register was a surprisingly young man, with a lean face, and hair cut modishly close to the head. Bragg shook the proffered hand, and eased himself into a rather flimsy chair.

"I want to find out about the seaworthiness of a British freighter called the *Dancing Lady*," he said. "It is alleged to have been scuttled, but for all we know it could have foundered. It was twenty years old."

"I shall have to get the register." He rang a small bell, a pimply youth answered, and was dispatched for the book.

"What is your interest?" asked the surveyor.

"Lloyd's insurance people think it was an attempt to defraud them. I want to get an idea of the odds."

"We may not have up-to-date information on the vessel. We do not insist on an annual survey in every case; and where we do, we have to fit it in with its voyages. So the hull might be surveyed in Liverpool and the engine and boilers in Cape Town, months later. Often by the time the information gets here, it is time to begin again."

"What is the value of the register, then?"

"It began as an aid to Lloyd's underwriters, in fixing the insurance premiums on a vessel and its cargo. But the information was of value to people like shippers and ship-brokers, so we became independent of Lloyd's."

"I wish you had changed your name as well. It would have been less confusing. But you still do surveys for insurance?"

"Not as such. We classify the ships we survey, and the underwriter can take our classification into account—or not, as he desires. I would say that shippers make more use of us nowadays. With the value of cargoes constantly rising, it is important to consign your goods on a ship which you can be confident will reach its destination. A vessel with a *100A1* classification will be able to earn higher freight rates than one with a lower classification . . . Ah, here we are." The pimply youth reappeared with a comparatively modest volume under his arm. The surveyor riffled through the pages.

"We have details of virtually every ship afloat in this register," he remarked. "Here we are, the *Dancing Lady*. Well, I can give you a very short answer to your question, but it will not be very helpful—the ship has not been submitted for classification."

"What does that mean?" asked Bragg.

"One cannot draw any inferences as to its seaworthiness, if that is what you think. Some shipping lines decline to have their vessels classified as a matter of policy. And if they are well known in the trade, the fact will not necessarily count against them."

"It's a funny world, this," grumbled Bragg. "The Board of Trade, who are responsible for safety at sea, don't concern themselves with the seaworthiness of vessels; you produce seaworthiness classifications that people can ignore; and neither of you seem to have up-to-date information."

The surveyor shrugged and smiled. "A good number of us get a living in the process."

"I begin to think this is all a put-on," said Bragg. "What was a ship's engineer doing on a sailing ship, anyway?"

"Oh, she had an engine." The surveyor turned to the register. "It was a one-hundred-and-twenty horsepower, compound engine . . . the steam pressure was fairly low of course, only seventy-five pounds to the square inch."

"What does that mean?"

"Well, it was more than a mere auxiliary engine. Despite her three masts, I suspect she was used as a steamer most of the time."

"What I want to know," said Bragg, "is whether it could be expected to survive an Atlantic crossing in winter. Having said that, we have information to the effect that it did, in fact, go down in the Caribbean . . . I suppose what I really would like is someone to look at all the details and say 'It could not have sunk, it must have been scuttled.'"

"You would never achieve that," the surveyor replied with a smile. "But we could indulge in some speculation, if you like."

"It would be helpful—as long as it doesn't send me off on a wrong track."

"You will be the judge of what action to take." He scrutinised the register sheet. "For our purposes, we can ignore the fact that she carried sails, and regard her as an iron-hulled steamer. I can fairly confidently assert that she was not designed for trans-Atlantic voyages—more for short sea-crossings. I am therefore mildly surprised to find her in the Caribbean."

"The first owners seem to have been German—Naumanns of Hamburg," said Bragg.

"That's more her ticket—feeder services into a large port. It by no means follows, however, that she would be incapable of crossing the Atlantic. The Royal Mail line has modern ships of just such a size, serving the Caribbean ports. It is something to bear in mind, though. Another factor is that she was twenty years old. That is no great age for a vessel constructed of iron, providing she has been properly maintained. She is owned by Harvey and Crane, which means she must have been one of the Green Funnel line ships. Since we have never surveyed her, I can only guess as to her condition, and I would not want you to put undue weight on my speculations."

"Even if they are guesses, they will be vastly more informed than mine."

"Very well. The Green Funnel line was one of the pioneers of steamships, and made the switch from paddle propulsion to screw, early. This gave them a big commercial advantage, and they expanded quickly. They concentrated on cargo ships, carrying the occasional passenger, and they were very successful. Their ships were well built and immaculately maintained, so they had no difficulty in obtaining cargoes. Had it not been for the engine developments in recent years, they would have been sitting on top of the world."

"What developments are these?"

"Well, the first marine steam-engines were unbelievably inefficient. They had only one cylinder, and their boilers could not produce above five pounds per square inch pressure. They burnt so much coal that a great deal of the hull was taken up by bunkers. Outside short sea-crossings like the English Channel, they were hopelessly uneconomic. Then, in the early sixties, the compound engine was developed."

"What was different about that?"

"Essentially, the steam was made to work twice over. It was forced into the high-pressure cylinder, and, as the piston was pushed down, it was exhausted into a low-pressure cylinder, where it drove a second piston before its energy was spent. Effectively, this meant you only needed half the coal to carry the same cargo on a voyage. Coaling stations were set up all over the world, and suddenly sailing ships were obsolete. By the early seventies, freighters like the *Dancing Lady* were to be found in every ocean of the world. It was during this era that the Green Funnel line expanded—with hindsight, one would say, 'over-expanded'."

"Why?"

"Well, there was constant improvement in boilers, and steam pressures rose as a result. We know that the boiler installed in the *Dancing Lady* could produce seventy-five pounds per square inch. By the end of the seventies, that figure had doubled, and now the ordinary working steam pressure of boilers is around two hundred pounds per square inch."

"Does that mean they can drive the engines faster?" asked Bragg.

"Not exactly. Rather, they made possible a new kind of engine. The higher boiler pressures meant that the energy of the steam was by no means exhausted, when it has passed through the second cylinder of the compound engine. So they added another, and the triple-expansion engine was born."

"So the steam was made to work three times instead of twice."

"That's right. The commercial effects were dramatic. A modern engine can drive a cargo ship at nine knots, using only half an ounce of coal per ton for each mile steamed."

Bragg smiled. "I'm afraid that doesn't convey anything to me. I am totally ignorant where engineering is concerned."

The surveyor opened a drawer and took out a sheet of vellum writing paper. "You see that?" he asked crumpling it in his fist and dropping it in front of Bragg. "A modern ship can carry a ton of cargo for a mile on the heat you would generate by burning that."

Bragg looked up incredulously. "I always had a picture in my mind of armies of sweating stokers shovelling coal."

"They are still there, have no fear. But the economics of running a ship have been transformed. You carry less coal for a given voyage, so you can carry far more cargo. The compound-engined ship has become obsolete. No-one wants them."

"That sounds like a damned good reason for a scuttle, to me," Bragg said.

"Perhaps, but I would prefer to regard the effects as somewhat more insidious. Once the new generation of ships became established, the shippers preferred to use them. To compete, the lines like Green Funnel, with a large fleet of old vessels, had to drop their freight rates. In turn that meant less money for maintenance and replacements, and as their vessels deteriorated, they commanded ever lower freight rates."

"Are you saying that the *Dancing Lady* could have been in such a bad state that she might have sunk, rather than been scuttled?"

"It is certainly possible."

"Who would know?"

"The owners, though whether they would tell you the truth is another matter. The ship's husband would be a better bet."

"The what?"

"Sorry! It does sound a rather sterile relationship, doesn't it! That is the term we use for the person who manages a ship."

"Ah. I was given a name by the Ship Registry . . . Taylor Pendrill & Co."

"They are a reputable concern. I would imagine you could trust their judgment."

Bernard Ingham, principal of Taylor Pendrill & Co., turned out to be a breezy, outgoing fifty-year-old. He received Bragg affably, assuring him of his readiness to help the police on any matter within his competence.

"It is about the *Dancing Lady*," Bragg said. "You will have seen in the *Lloyd's List* that we have been asked to look into the circumstances surrounding her loss."

"It would be more accurate to say 'presumed loss', sergeant. So far as I have heard, no one has yet found the wreck."

"Have it your own way, sir. I wanted to find out about the ship, and I am told you can help."

"Where did you get our name from, sergeant?"

"The Customs people."

"Ah, yes. Well, we have certainly looked after her for some years. What is it you want to know?"

"For a start, what exactly does a ship's husband do?"

"Basically, we take over the chore of running the ship. It varies from one owner to the next; we do what they cannot be bothered to do." Ingham smiled expansively.

"And in this case?"

"That depends on whether you are referring to the old Green Funnel days, or the period since Harvey & Crane took over."

"Both."

"In the old days, we did the bare minimum; but as we were husband to their whole fleet, it was a very satisfactory connection."

"I've heard all the jokes about ships and their husbands," growled Bragg. "Just tell it to me straight."

Ingham was not abashed. "Our function was to see that the ship was victualled, properly crewed, and in all respects ready to go to sea."

"Were you responsible for seeing that necessary repairs were carried out?"

"No. The Green Funnel line surveyors examined each ship every time it came into its home port, and arranged for repairs to be done where and when convenient."

"I gather that in the later years, it was not often convenient to have repairs done to vessels like the *Dancing Lady*."

Ingham pursed his lips, then shrugged. "Certainly their standards dropped as they got into financial difficulty."

"What about the Harvey & Crane period?" Bragg asked.

"We have a much wider remit from that company. In addition to our normal function, we are expected to draw attention to specific deficiencies, and advise on general matters."

"It has been suggested that Harvey & Crane have little or no background in shipping."

"That is true enough." Ingham smiled broadly. "Though with us looking after their ships, the public have no cause for anxiety."

"Who is behind the company?" asked Bragg.

"I have often wondered, myself. My contact has been exclusively with the manager of the Leadenhall Street office."

"Mr. Cakebread?"

"Yes. I would not have thought that his knowledge of shipping was very extensive, either."

"The *Dancing Lady* was a small ship. Some people are surprised to hear that she was on a voyage to the Caribbean."

"Are you asking me, or telling me?" remarked Ingham.

"I am inviting you to comment," replied Bragg, irritably.

"I don't know that I am able to. She was a substantial vessel, built for such voyages."

"What kind of condition was it in?"

"Well, she complied with the regulations applying to British ships. We could not have let her go to sea, otherwise."

"I've been reading them, and they don't impress me. You could go to sea in a bath-tub, if it had the regulation number of life-belts, and nobody had weighted the boiler safety-valve to get more power."

"It would have to be at least a fifteen-ton bath-tub," replied Ingham with a laugh.

"What I keep asking, and what no one will tell me, is 'Was the ship seaworthy?'. You must know there are allegations that it was scuttled. I want to be satisfied in my mind that the condition of the vessel was such as to make that a probable explanation of its loss. Lloyd's Register cannot help me because the ship was never surveyed by them."

"Have you asked the owners?"

"I've not obtained an answer."

"Then I suggest that you should," said Ingham firmly. "It is their responsibility. We are only their agents, and if we had any views on the seaworthiness of the vessel, it would be quite improper for us to communicate them to a third party—even the police."

"You might find yourself in the witness-box, being compelled to answer," said Bragg angrily.

"I doubt it, sergeant. Our views would carry little weight in a court of law. No one would regard us as experts in the maintenance of ships . . . You could, of course, apply a little robust common-sense. You know the particulars of the ship from the register, and therefore are aware that she was somewhat old-fashioned. Some people are apparently prepared to take the view that she might not survive a tropical storm."

"Are you saying that it could have sunk through bad weather?"

"Any ship can sink, if the weather is bad enough, sergeant. I am saying nothing."

As Bragg approached the Royal Exchange, he was more than ever struck by its massive proportions. Across the road, the Bank of England, windowless and dumb, was reticent in comparison. This building squatted arrogantly on the east of the crossing, like a guard-dog baring its teeth against the indigent. Why was it, Bragg wondered, that financial institutions needed to barricade themselves behind vast piles of masonry to overawe the populace? He noted with quiet satisfaction that, although it was barely fifty years old, its towering Ionic columns were stained with soot, and birddroppings encrusted the elaborate pediment. He passed through the immense wrought-iron gates, and found a red-coated Lloyd's waiter.

"I want to see Mr. John Frankis," he said.

"I think you will find he is away for a few days, sir," said the man. "Another gentleman was asking for him a short while ago, and that was what I was told."

"Mr. Peter Whitlock, then."

They went along an aisle, between rows of cubicles

consisting of pew-like benches facing each other, with a desk in between. Bragg supposed that they must have derived from the tables in Lloyd's coffee-house where the market originated. The waiter turned along a side aisle, and pointed to a cubicle by the wall.

"That is Mr. Whitlock's box, sir."

In one pew, a couple of young men were writing diligently in ledgers—obviously clerks. The other was occupied by a big man with a fleshy face, and unkempt iron-grey hair. His coat was rumpled, and his neck-tie like a twisted bit of rag. He was listening intently to the words of a younger man standing respectfully in the aisle. There was a snatch of conversation, then Whitlock nodded, wrote briefly on the wide piece of paper in front of him, impressed a rubber stamp on it, and handed it to the man. He hurried away, with a mixture of satisfaction and relief on his face.

Bragg approached the box, and showed his warrant-card. "Mr. Whitlock?" he asked.

"That's me."

"I would be glad if I could talk to you for a few minutes."

"What about?"

"Insurance generally, and one of your cases in particular."

"Right. Then let us get out of this mad-house, and have a cup of coffee. John," he called to the older of the clerks sitting opposite, "mind the shop, will you?"

He shambled out of the exchange, to a coffee-shop in an alley.

"What is it you want to know?" he asked, when the steaming cups had been placed before them.

"To begin with, I would like to understand how the Lloyd's market works."

"Right. Well, we will ignore its origins. There is a damned sight too much history and precedent about the place, as it is."

"Fine. I need to know how it operates now."

"Firstly, the capital of the market is provided by wealthy individuals, who quite probably have no knowledge whatever of insurance. They are, nevertheless, trading as independent insurers in their own right, without the protection of limited liability. So they are putting their personal fortune at the disposal of the insurance market, down to their last shirt-button. That places a great responsibility on the next tier in the structure, the professional underwriter."

"Which is you?" Bragg asked.

"Yes. I write the insurance risks for a syndicate of those individuals. We call them 'names,' because originally the names of all the participating merchants appeared on the policy. That does not happen any more, but no one has been able to think up a better term for them. I have eighty-odd names on my syndicate, which makes it one of the largest. Every box in Lloyd's writes for at least one syndicate, so you can appreciate that there are scores of syndicates active in the market."

"That means that there are a great many wealthy individuals behind them."

"Yes, though not so many as you would think. Any individual will normally become a name on a number of syndicates—up to five or six. By doing that, he reduces the risk of being bankrupted. If, in any year, one syndicate does badly, it is probable that another will do well. In that way the name spreads his risk—it's a basic insurance principle that you will meet over and over again."

"Where do the insurances that you write come from?"

"Brokers. Lloyd's has accredited an alarmingly large number of brokers, and if you want to insure at Lloyd's you have to go through one of them."

"That sounds very cosy," remarked Bragg.

"For them, it is. Some underwriters feel that the brokers have too much power, in that they really control the business rather than the insurer. But that is how the market has grown up, and it is too late to change it."

"Suppose I had a ship I wanted to insure, how would I set about it?"

"You would go to a Lloyd's broker, and explain to him what risks you wanted to cover, the values, the period of time involved, the details of the voyage. He would reduce all that to a proposal for insurance on what we call a slip."

"That sounds like a lengthy job."

"Again, a practice has evolved which allows the system to function. Some underwriters, because of their experience and success in various classes of business, are regarded as leaders, and the broker will approach one of them first. Once he has put down a line—for, say, five per cent—other underwriters will follow without making an independent scrutiny of the risk."

"So who are the leaders?" asked Bragg.

"People like Charles Harris, Ben Archibald, John Frankis, in the hull market, with John Goddard and myself in the cargo market."

"Good. Now the particular case I wanted to ask you about is a freighter called the *Dancing Lady*."

"Goddard told me to expect some queries from the police, so I have looked up my records."

"What was your involvement?"

"I led the cargo risk. It was a cotton-seed mill being sent by Thurgood & Jackson, the engineers, to an agent in New Orleans. We got a slip from Frewer Biddle & Co., the brokers, and I took a ten-per-cent line."

"Wasn't that rather high?"

Whitlock laughed. "In retrospect, it was; but it seemed a reasonable enough risk at the time. I knew Frankis was leading the hull insurance, so it seemed safe."

"Who was the person insured? The manufacturer?"

"No, the policy was taken out in the name of the American import agent, but no doubt he would assign it to his client."

"Would you be happy about that?"

"It makes no difference to us, so long as any claim is valid. We have to work that way, because ships are often sold in mid-voyage—even cargoes. The insurance policy has to be transferable also."

"So if the ship were lost, you would get a claim from the true owner of the cargo."

"You can put it in the present tense, if you like. It seems that the ship has been lost, and we have received a claim in respect of the cargo."

"And is the claim valid?"

"Insofar as we accept that the claimant has the insurable interest in the cotton-seed mill, yes."

"So will you be paying the loss?"

"By no means! We don't pay out on a scuttle, just like that."

"I suppose that since the ship was deliberately sunk, it will be outside the terms of the policy," remarked Bragg.

"Oh, it is covered all right. 'Barratry of the master and mariners' is how it is described in the policy."

"Barratry? That's a new one for me."

"It covers any fraudulent or criminal conduct against the owners of the ship or goods."

"I don't understand," said Bragg. "You seem to accept that the claim lies within the terms of the policy, and yet you are refusing to pay it. How do you justify that?"

"I am carrying on a business, sergeant. The insured value of that cargo was thirty thousand pounds. I don't pay out that kind of money till I have to."

"But you said you only wrote ten per cent."

"That is so, but the whole is my responsibility. If I pay out on the claim, everyone else will follow my lead. Where there is a possibility of fraud, I like to see which way things develop."

"I confess I was surprised to hear that one could insure against fraud," remarked Bragg. "But since you have committed yourself to such a policy, surely you are bound by its terms?"

"Oh, I shall abide by the policy. It covered a voyage from London to New Orleans. From what I hear, the *Dancing Lady* did not call at New Orleans, but went beyond, to Galveston. It was not entitled to do so, and I have voided the policy for deviation."

"So what happens now?"

"Why, we just wait and see."

"This is Mr. Pocklington, the company's solicitor," said Cakebread. His face was haggard, and his skin even more sallow than at their previous meeting.

Bragg shook the solicitor's hand perfunctorily. He was a cheerful, brisk man. The bald top of his head gleamed in the light, his smooth cheeks shone, and a smile hovered around his lips.

"I am sorry to have taken so long to consider your questions, sergeant," he said. "However, we should be able to deal with them satisfactorily this evening." He looked down at the sheet of paper in front of him. "I can confirm that the *Dancing Lady* was one of the vessels purchased by Harvey & Crane Ltd. from the Green Funnel line. She was one of their freighters, and was some twenty years old. As to the Lloyd's survey, it was not the policy of the previous owners to submit their vessels for classification, and this policy was continued by the company. I should emphasize that nothing should be read into this circumstance."

"You are just telling me things I know already," Bragg grumbled.

"I am passing on such information as the company is prepared to give, sergeant. You must be patient . . . The name of the master is, or was, Ben Gadd. He was appointed for this voyage in place of the previous master. As to your last question, I am not convinced that knowing the names of the shareholders in Harvey & Crane Ltd. is relevant to your inquiries, or will advance them in any way. I have therefore advised the company that it should make no answer."

"It is important to know who are the real principals in the affair," retorted Bragg.

"In law, the company is the principal, as I am sure you know, sergeant . . . Now then, in order to demonstrate that the company is co-operating in all relevant matters, I will give you some information which does not flow from the questions you have asked." Pocklington smiled self-righteously. "The *Dancing Lady* was demise chartered from the first of January this year, until the thirty-first of March. Half of the consideration for the charter-party was received in advance."

"What is a demise charter?" asked Bragg.

"Sometimes it is referred to more graphically as a bare-boat charter. Under such an agreement, the shipowner hires out the vessel only. The charterer effectively becomes the owner for the period of the charter. He appoints the master and provides the crew, he arranges for the stores and victualling."

"But the ship still belonged to Harvey & Crane."

"That is true, but beyond the obvious precaution of insuring the vessel, this company had no responsibility for it whatever."

"Who appointed the new master?" Bragg asked.

"The charterers. And this point I cannot stress too strongly; in everything he did, he was acting as their agent."

"Who are these charterers?"

A momentary frown puckered the solicitor's brow, then he

turned to Cakebread. "I think we can make that information available to the police."

Cakebread crossed to a cupboard, and took down a scuffed leather-bound ledger. He turned towards the middle of the book. "It was a French company," he said in his squeaky voice. "Michel Tissier et Cie, of Rue de la Garonne, in Paris."

"And how did this charter come about?"

"It was arranged through the Baltic Exchange, in the usual way."

"What will happen to the balance of the charter money, now the ship has been lost?" asked Bragg.

Cakebread looked doubtfully towards the solicitor.

"I am certainly of the view," said Pocklington, "that none of the advance is repayable. As to whether we could sue the French company for any or all of the remaining balance, that would depend on the date of loss, which appears to be by no means certain."

Bragg looked at Cakebread. "Was this ship fit to go on a voyage to the Caribbean, in winter?" he asked.

"That is enough supplementary questions," Pocklington interrupted. "We are not in the House of Commons, sergeant."

On leaving the shipowners office, Bragg hurried down Cornhill, and managed to find Whitlock still working at his box.

"I have discovered," he announced, "that the *Dancing Lady* was demise chartered to a French company for the voyage to New Orleans. Were you aware of that?"

"No."

"Does it alter the insurance position?"

"Not so far as the cargo is concerned. The contract of affreightment would be with the character, so my assured position would be unaffected. That might not apply to the hull insurance. You had better talk to John Frankis about that."

"If I ever catch up with him, I will," replied Bragg.

"There is one point that has come up since we spoke, and may be of interest to you. The master of the *Dancing Lady* was a man called Gadd."

"Ben Gadd, yes, I know."

"I have been reminded that he was master of another vessel in eighteen eighty-eight. That ship," went on Whitlock significantly, "was lost off British Honduras, in circumstances not unlike those of the *Dancing Lady*. There was an inquiry, and Gadd stated that they were struck by a tornado, and had to abandon ship. It is possible; these whirlwinds can be very local. But it is odd that no other vessel in the area reported having encountered it. And there was another surprising aspect to it. Despite being forced to abandon his ship by the violence of the storm, he managed to get his crew ashore in the lifeboats without losing a man."

"You think it was scuttled?"

"Interestingly enough, the water is very deep, close to the shore. We shall never know."

"Our friend Gadd becomes more fascinating by the minute," murmured Bragg. "I think I will get a warrant for his arrest. It can do no harm."

CHAPTER ——————
—————— # FOUR

Morton had barely seated himself in Greg's office when there
was an insistent jangling from the corner. Greg turned round
expectantly, and reached for the telephone instrument.

"Hello," he shouted, pulling an apologetic face at Morton.
"Speak louder, will you? . . . Oh, it's you, Mary Ellen . . .
No, Joe's not here right now . . . No, he's out with the
paddy-waggon . . . Mary Ellen, if everybody knew just
where every officer was at a particular time, you might just as
well not have a police force . . . Yes, I'll give him a
message." Greg picked up a pencil. "Yes? . . . not to forget
the crawfish . . . make sure they are peeled, yes . . . can of
condensed milk . . . one pack of the new gelatin des-
sert . . . Sounds a mighty interestin' dish, Mary Ellen. I
might just invite myself over . . . No, I won't forget."

Greg replaced the ear-piece sheepishly. "Mary Ellen works
at the drapery store on Houston Street," he commented.
"We've been connected to the telephone exchange maybe a
month, and not one real call have I had in all that time. The

darned thing has turned me into an errand-boy for the likes of Mary Ellen,'' he giggled.

"Perhaps you should have it transferred to the outer office,'' Morton remarked with a smile.

"Maybe you're right. Randy might think it was his alarm-clock, and wake up from time to time! Well now, I arranged to see Bill Capo this morning, so let's take a walk down to the port.''

They strolled in the humid sunshine, towards the center of the town.

"Why do you build houses on stilts?'' Morton asked.

" 'Cause of the blamed termites. They eat the wood, d'you see.''

"But the piles are of wood.''

"Yeah, that is so. But every year you get a boy to crawl under the house, and paint them with creosote . . . You forget one year, and most like you'll wake up one mornin' in a small heap of dust!'' Greg tittered.

"Why not use iron piles?''

"You're a true Harman, I'll say that for you. Do you know the cost of iron piles delivered down here?''

"I cannot even guess,'' Morton replied with a laugh.

"It's a whole heap of money, that's for sure.''

Greg led the way down a narrow alley, which became more dejected as it twisted and turned, then suddenly debouched onto the quay.

"That's Bill Capo's place.'' He pointed to a tall green-painted warehouse. "Bill is the biggest lighterman hereabouts. We'll see what he has to say.''

Greg seemed to be well known, and chatted easily to the counter-clerk for a few minutes. Then he asked if Bill Capo were available. In reply the clerk went over to the corner, and taking a plug out of a copper tube, uttered a piercing whistle. He then set his ear to the end. There was a faint murmur, and the clerk spoke in reply.

"Never seen one of them before?'' asked Greg, noting Morton's amazement.

"No, never.''

"It's a naval speakin' tube. Gives Bill time to escape round the back, while I'm climbin' the front stairs.''

"It is somehow more appropriate for a lighterman, than a telephone," remarked Morton.

"He's waiting for you," said the clerk, "you know the way, don't you?"

They labored up six flights of stairs, and entered a small office with a magnificent view over the harbor. One wall was taken up with shelving, which was crammed with dusty bundles of papers. A man in his early forties was sitting in his shirtsleeves behind a desk. His hair was pitch black, and his mustache curled at the ends in Mexican style. His smile revealed teeth yellowed from chewing tobacco.

"Well, lieutenant, have my boys been misbehaving?" he asked.

"Not more than usual, I guess," replied Greg taking a chair. "It depends on what you can tell me."

"You know I only employ men of integrity, Greg. I am not aware of anything to their discredit." Capo's jaws were chewing slowly, his eyes watchful.

"At this moment, Bill, I'm not handin' out credit or discredit. I just want information."

"About what?"

"Now, we both know that not a matchbox floats by in this harbor, without you know about it." Bill's only answer to that assertion was to send a jet of brown juice towards a spittoon on the floor by his desk.

"So it's only a question of whether you want to tell me, or you don't," Greg went on. "I heard a rumor of a freighter comin' into the harbor at night, and off-loadin' into boats."

"I don't know anything about that," Capo said quickly.

"And this ship sailed out again, the same night, without checkin' in at the port," continued Greg, ignoring Capo's denial. "It was the tenth of February, Bill. The cargo was in wooden crates, some of them large. They would have been hoisted over the side by the ship's own derricks, but it would need skilled lightermen to handle it. I'm sure you would know about it."

Capo shook his head emphatically.

Greg smiled broadly. "You know, Bill," he said, "I'm gettin' a new recruit, tomorrow. Bright kid he is; can count beyond his fingers and thumbs. Now you're supposed to have fifteen lighters workin' in the port, but I'd be surprised if my new countin' cop didn't make it more—say twenty-four."

Capo stared at Greg for a moment, then transferred his gaze to the harbor outside. "You are wrong, lieutenant, when you say I know everything that happens," he said slowly. "I wouldn't know, for instance, if my boys used one of my lighters to take some furniture along the coast for a friend. If it happened, it wouldn't be a commercial load, and all it cost me would be the fuel for the tug. Of course, if I became aware of such a happening, I would have to take action; and all my boys might walk out on me. I'm just fortunate that it doesn't occur."

"And it would be just as impossible, for your men to take a couple of tugs and several lighters, to help a friend who had a ship full of big heavy furniture?"

"I cannot imagine it happening, lieutenant," said Capo, poker-faced.

"I thought not . . . Tell me, Bill, as a quite separate matter: if you wanted to off-load some bulky goods here, without sendin' them through the port, what would you do?"

"I find such an idea shocking, Greg. Still . . . I think I would avoid Galveston Bay. I would get the ship to drop anchor in the channel towards the other end of the island. Then I'd take the cargo in lighters to the mainland."

"Where would you land it?"

"That I don't know. You would need lifting gear, but there are one or two small piers along there that could handle it."

"Interestin'," Greg remarked. "Pity it never happened." He rose to go, then turned at the door. "On second thoughts, I'll put my new lad to countin' the girls on the street corners. He'll go a damned sight higher than twenty-four."

When Bragg once more sought John Frankis in the Royal Exchange, he was not there. The assistant underwriter suggested that he might catch him at the management office in Birchin Lane. Although it was a mere step, Bragg felt somewhat aggrieved. This was one of the most irritating cases he had ever investigated. Whatever skulduggery had gone on, it would not easily be brought within the framework of English law. On top of that, the facts were obscure, and the people who could clarify them were either not available, or obstructive. He looked for something to kick, but there was not even a pebble in sight. His grumpy mood was somewhat mollified at the sight of a pretty young woman at the reception desk. She smiled sweetly at him, disappeared briefly, then ushered him along a thickly-carpeted corridor to a large office with a panoramic view over the roof-tops. A man rose from a desk littered with papers. He was of medium build, with dark hair, and gray eyes behind tortoise-shell spectacles. His demeanor was scholarly, rather than brash, but like everyone else in this case, he exuded the confidence of wealth and position.

"I apologize, if I have been a little elusive," he said with a faint smile. "I had to spend some days in Glasgow, to settle a claim."

"I imagine Mr. Goddard will have told you to expect me."

"This is about the *Dancing Lady*?"

"Yes. I am told that you led the insurance of the vessel itself."

"That is correct. The hull and machinery were insured for twelve thousand pounds."

"Was that all placed at Lloyd's?" asked Bragg.

"Yes. The brokers only go to the insurance companies as a last resort, I am glad to say."

"And what line did you write?"

"I can see that I am dealing with an expert," Frankis remarked with amusement.

"I am getting the hang of the jargon," replied Bragg, "but there is no real knowledge behind it."

"I wrote a ten-per-cent line."

"You decided to give this one a bit of a push, did you?" Bragg said quizzically.

"I do not understand, sergeant."

"From what I can make out, sir, a line of five per cent would be the most even a leader would write."

Frankis pushed his spectacles up his nose with a forefinger. "There is nothing sacrosanct about five per cent," he said. "I may have felt that it was a good risk, I really cannot remember. Anyway, one reinsures."

"Now you have lost me," Bragg admitted.

"It is simple enough, sergeant. One accepts a proportion of the primary risk, and then one reinsures it with other syndicates. It is rather like a bookmaker laying-off the bets he has taken, although we like to think that we are more scientific about it. If I write a five-per-cent line I might cede four per cent to other syndicates by way of reinsurance, so that my own syndicate is only liable for one per cent of any loss."

"Spreading the risk," murmured Bragg. "And did you in fact reinsure this particular risk?"

Frankis smiled deprecatingly. "I am sorry to say that we had not got around to doing so before the ship was posted as a loss. Even the best-run syndicate falls down sometimes."

"The risk was placed with you by a broker?"

"Yes. Frewer Biddle & Co."

"Did they give you full details of the risk involved?"

"I would be very surprised if they had not."

"Then why did you agree to insure a ship with a master who had already been involved in a suspected scuttle?"

"Who is that?"

"Ben Gadd."

"I know the name well enough, of course. Was he the master of the *Dancing Lady*?"

"He was."

"Perhaps Ingham did not mention him, after all."

"Ingham?"

"Bernard Ingham. He is the principal of Frewer Biddle."

"I thought he was a shipping agent."

"Ship broking and insurance broking go together. Most people are involved in both areas."

"I see. And have you received any claim under the policy?"

"Not yet."

"If you get one, will you pay it?"

"In principle, yes. Barratry is covered by the policy, and barratry includes scuttling the ship."

"Why do you take a different view from Mr. Whitlock? He is refusing to pay the cargo claim on the grounds that the *Dancing Lady* deviated from her route."

Frankis gave an embarrassed smirk. "Peter Whitlock holds rather robust views, which fortunately do not reflect the attitude of the Lloyd's community as a whole. Not many people would regard putting in to Galveston instead of New Orleans as a significant enough deviation to render the policy voidable."

"I see. Well, that is all for the moment, sir. I would be glad if you could give me your address in case I need to contact you urgently."

"Yes, of course. My London address is Three, Grosvenor Mansions, Park Street. It is in a modern block of apartments near Marble Arch."

"Oh, by the way," remarked Bragg as he rose to go. "Did you know about the demise charter to the French company?"

"Why, yes. I knew about that."

On the stroke of nine o'clock, Bragg was at the shipping office of Taylor Pendrill & Co.

"Is Mr. Ingham in?" he asked the clerk.

"I'm sorry, sir, he has not yet arrived. He usually calls at Clements Lane first, and comes on here between half past nine and ten o'clock."

"Clements Lane?" asked Bragg.

"The insurance broking office."

"I see. Very well, I will come back."

Bragg had an impulse to watch Ingham as he walked up the street, to see him when he was off guard, pondering his problems. He concealed himself in the shadow of a doorway and waited. Some youngsters were coming along the pavement. They weren't toffs' kids, by the look of their clothes—probably from the East End. They ought to be at school, instead of larking about in the City. Now they were following an elderly gentleman, pressing round him cheekily. He raised his stick to them, and they scampered off up an alley. At least, they had inherited the lively disrespect common to their kind.

Across the road, old Tom stood on his pitch, his eyes turned sightlessly heavenward. On the tray suspended from his shoulders were a few boxes of matches. Round his neck was a square of cardboard, on which had been printed

BLIND
WIFE AND
SIX CHILDREN
TO SUPPORT

To Braggs recollection he had been supporting those six children for fifteen years . . . A well-dressed young man approached, and taking a box of matches, dropped a penny on the tray.

"God bless you, sir," piped up Tom in a quavering voice.

The old fraud. Still he was providing a service, and no doubt the young man felt a wholly spurious glow of virture.

Out of the corner of his eye, Bragg saw that the children were back on the street. They crossed over, and gathered in a squirming huddle, about ten yards from Tom. Then one of their number crept along the pavement, and gently took a box of matches from Tom's tray as he passed. Tom appeared to be totally unaware of the theft, and Bragg wondered if he ought to interfere. The miscreant had halted a little distance away, and was mouthing and beckoning to his companions. Bragg sighed, he had better things to do than run in a few kids for pilfering. Now another lad was creeping along, grinning all over his face. He stopped by the tray, and with an elaborate flourish, made to take a matchbox. At that moment, Tom pivoted slightly and stuck out with his open hand. It caught the boy below the ear, and knocked him into the gutter. It was all over in a blink. Tom was back by the wall, his eyes probing the skies. It was as if God himself had intervened. The child sat up, bewildered, and burst into tears. Then they all scurried off up the street towards Whitechapel, and Bragg caught the ghost of a smile on Tom's lips.

After a few minutes, Bragg saw Ingham striding purposefully towards his office. He stopped to buy a box of matches, and went up the steps with old Tom's benison fluting in his ears. No sign of stress there. If anything he seemed cockier than ever. Bragg waited five minutes, then followed.

Ingham received him with unruffled composure.

"Good morning, sergeant. Have you made any arrests yet?"

Bragg ignored the sally. "Why did you not tell me you had brokered the insurance of the *Dancing Lady*?" he demanded.

"Because you did not ask me," Ingham replied simply.

"You must have known that it is relevant to my enquiries."

"I am happy to say, sergeant, that I have never come into conflict with the authorities, and therefore I have no idea of what you would regard as important. I will answer your questions as best I can, but you must not expect me to anticipate them."

Bragg glared at him. "How come you are acting as ship manager and insurance broker at the same time?"

"My dear sergeant," replied Ingham indulgently, "there is

no possible conflict of interest between the two roles. Indeed, one is able to act more effectively as an insurance broker, because of the intimate knowledge of a vessel one acquires as manager."

"How long have you been doing both for this ship?"

"Since it was bought by the Green Funnel line in eighteen eighty-nine. But I have carried out both functions in respect of some of their vessels, for around twelve years . . . And in case you accuse me again of withholding relevant information, let me add that in another manifestation—that of a ship broker at the Baltic Exchange—I secured the charter for the *Dancing Lady*, which was in operation when she was lost."

"How did that come about?" Bradd demanded.

"I received a letter from Paris, asking me to fix a demise charter for three months, and giving broad details of the type of vessel required. The *Dancing Lady* exactly fitted the bill."

"Have you ever dealt with the French company before?"

"No."

"How did they get to know about you?"

"One does not inquire, sergeant. One does not positively seek an obligation to pay an introductory commission."

"So you were managers to the ship, you acquired a charter for it, and you arranged the insurance," said Bragg sarcastically. "You have it all nicely sewn up, haven't you? Whoever loses, it isn't going to be you."

"My brokerage is a fixed percentage in each case," cried Ingham angrily. "I take great exception to your remarks."

"I have no doubt you do . . . Why did you not tell me about the charter?"

"As I recall our conversation, your concern was firstly to learn something about the function of a ship's husband, and secondly to discover if the vessel was seaworthy or not when it set sail."

"Do you accept that the *Dancing Lady* has been lost?" asked Bragg.

"As it has been entered in the loss book at Lloyd's, I have no alternative."

"Has any claim been made by Harvey & Crane?"

"Yes."

"When was that?"

Ingham pulled a thin folder from a drawer in his desk, and extracted a letter. "The thirtieth of April," he said.

"Why does Frankis, the underwriter, not know about it?"

"I felt at the time, that the claim was somewhat premature. It was a matter of rumor only, and I hoped that the vessel would turn up somewhere."

"Did you place the cargo insurance?"

"Yes."

"Who asked you to?"

"I advertised for cargo in the usual way, and the engineering company in Manchester booked space for their piece of plant. They asked me to arrange the insurance on behalf of their customer."

"You are not very consistent," Bragg sneered. "How does it happen that a claim goes forward on the cargo insurance policy, but you withhold the claim on the ship policy?"

"Harvey & Crane left it to my judgement, the consignee of the plant did not," replied Ingham evenly.

"Did you find the crew for this voyage?"

"Only the master. He found the rest."

"Ben Gadd, eh? Why did you not tell Frankis about him?"

"I am sure that I did tell him."

"Frankis denies it. Did you tell him that Gadd has been involved in a scuttling before?"

"No. I had no idea that was so. What ship was involved?"

"I'll find out for you . . . Now here's your chance to put yourself in Frankis's good books. Tell him you have withheld a material fact. He would be able to void the policy. That would please him. But perhaps you would lose your commission then . . ."

Whitlock was standing beside his box, when Bragg arrived, and his senior acolyte had taken his place.

"You only just caught me," he cried, "I have a horse running in the Derby, hence the go-to-meeting suit!"

"Blasphemy will get you nowhere. Can you spare me a moment?"

Whitlock consulted his watch. "My wife will be pawing the ground," he remarked. "But, on the other hand, my horse is not performing for another four hours."

"I promise not to keep you. Can you tell me the name of the ship that Gadd may have scuttled in eighteen eighty-eight?"

Whitlock addressed his assitant. "You looked it up, John. Do you remember?"

"The *Pearl*, sir."

"There you are, sergeant. Now, there has been a development on the cargo claim that you ought to know about. We have had a writ issued against us for payment of the loss, on behalf of the New Orleans shipping agent. That complicates things from our point of view, since we have no evidence acceptable to a court of law which would justify our refusal. What we need is someone to go into the witness box."

"I don't know if it will help you, but one of my constables is down in Galveston at the moment. I got a cable from him this morning. It seems that he has found enough circumstantial evidence there to make him believe that Ryan was telling the truth about the diversion of the cargo."

"Has he, by God?" Whitlock pounded his palm with his fist. "Is there any chance of your man bringing Ryan back with him? I would gladly defray all the expenses."

"There could not be any question of compulsion," said Bragg. "If he is willing to come, I would have no objection to my constable's acting as escort. I wouldn't mind having a chat with Ryan myself."

"If your man is going to be in New Orleans, he might do us both a bit of good. All our dealings are with De Wolf & Fletcher, through Ingham. I would love to know who the ultimate assured is."

"That is the person who was actually going to receive the cottonseed mill?"

"Yes. And another thing, he might have a word with Luigi Rossi, the Lloyd's agent there. You never know, he might pick up something interesting."

"How are your investigations progressing, sergeant?" Goddard asked amiably.

"We have an officer in Galveston at the moment, sir, and he will go on to New Orleans in the next day or two."

"Excellent!" Goddard smiled in gratification. "And are you getting all the co-operation from our people that you need?"

"I think so, sir. It is not a very clear-cut case, and your underwriters don't seem to be in one mind about it."

"Why is that?"

"John Frankis is inclined to pay any claim he gets on the ship itself, while Peter Whitlock has refused to pay the cargo claim—on what he admits are the thinnest of grounds."

"It is not often that Whitlock and I are shooting from the same butt," remarked Goddard with a smile.

"I must say, that so far I have not got a smell of a crime we could arraign under English law."

"I am sure it is not for want of trying. Keep on with your inquiries, sergeant, and perhaps equally importantly, be seen to do so."

"There is something you could help me with, sir. Mr. Whitlock has discovered that Ben Gadd, the master of the *Dancing Lady*, was also master of a ship called the *Pearl*, which sank in suspicious circumstances in eighteen eighty-eight. Can you tell me who led the hull insurance?"

"I might have done so myself. I know my syndicate had a line on it. Just a moment, I will find out from my box." He picked up a telephone instrument, and spoke for a few minutes.

"No," he said, replacing the ear-piece, "I was wrong. We had only a two-per-cent line on that one. The insurance was led by John Frankis."

CHAPTER _____
_____ FIVE

When Morton received Bragg's cable, he arranged with Greg that he should telegraph London with any information emerging from his investigations. He then took a train to New Orleans, and found himself a room at Ziegler's. By then it was late in the afternoon, and he decided to postpone his inquiries till next day. Instead, he wandered around the streets of the French Quarter, intrigued by half-glimpsed courtyards, and the exuberance of the wrought-iron balconies, which made the houses look like riverboats moored alongside the streets. Eventually, irritated by the repeated importunings of street-girls, he went back to his hotel.

After dinner, the porter suggested that he might like a ticket for the theater, and whispered that if he would like a pretty girl to accompany him, it could be arranged. Then he lowered his voice still further, and said that if the gentleman was partial to a spot of poker-playing, he knew of a place . . . Morton eschewed these delights, and instead took a trip out to Spanish Fort. The pleasure-gardens were festooned with electric lamps, and in the garish light, laughing groups of people strolled to and fro, grateful for the cool lakeside air. The general impression, thought Morton, was of a relaxed and confident affluence. The ladies were gay, the men attentive, and if the elegance and style of Paris was lacking, what did it matter? In some ways he felt more at ease here than in the prim northern towns created by English puritanism.

Nevertheless, he was up early next morning, exhilarated at the prospect of pushing the investigation a stage further. He decided that the best way of tracing Ryan was through the police. They would know the part of the city where a seaman would lodge, and could tell him which employers to approach. So, taking directions from the porter, he strode briskly to Carondelet Street. On hearing that he was seeking a ship's engineer, the clerk in the police headquarters advised him to go to the sixth precinct station in Rousseau Street. As he approached it, Morton was struck with astonishment. If the headquarters building had been nondescript and unimaginative, this was assertive to the point of eccentricity. It looked like a cross between a temple of Osiris and an Egyptian burial chamber. The policeman on duty at the door seemed slight and insubstantial, with that pretentious mass of stone looming over him.

Morton explained what he wanted, and was escorted to the offices of Captain Desmier, who was in charge of the precinct. Desmier received him coolly.

"Is this Ryan a criminal?" he asked.

"Not that I am aware of," Morton replied.

"Then why should an English policeman come to New Orleans in search of him?"

"It is not a police matter, really. I happened to be on holiday in Boston, and was asked to trace him. I shall try to persuade him to come back to England, as a witness in a civil case."

Desmier looked at him in disbelief. "What kind of a civil case?" he asked.

"It concerns an insurance claim over the loss of a ship and its cargo. You can imagine there is a great deal of money at stake."

Desmier appeared to lose interest. "Very well, constable. Go and see Lieutenant Kinsella—the door at the end of the passage." He turned back to his papers dismissively.

Morton was piqued at the condescension in his tone. In a

way it was his own fault, for being content with so lowly a
position. Yet Matt Gregory had not reacted in that way. He had
been friendly and considerate, and had appeared to dismiss the
difference in rank between them. Morton smiled. Sergeant
Bragg would explain it as the inevitable result of working in an
Egyptian temple—perhaps there was something in the theory
after all. He tapped on the lieutenant's door.

"Enter!"

The voice was nasal, the man anything but prepossessing.
Of slim build, he had straggly greying hair, and a sharp nose
jutting over a weak chin.

"Yeah?"

"Lieutenant Kinsella?"

"The same."

"Captain Desmier referred me to you, as someone who can
help me to trace a ship's engineer based in New Orleans."

"It sounds a tall order, mister."

"Morton, Constable James Morton of the City of London
Police."

"Official, is it?"

"Yes. He is wanted as a witness in a court case."

"Name of?"

"Patrick Ryan. Age about thirty-five, of Irish extraction."

"Sure. I know where he is."

"You do?" exclaimed Morton in surprise.

"He's in the charity Hospital, if he's not in the morgue
already."

"Morgue?"

"Yeah. He was done over by some guys in Jackson Square,
about three weeks ago. He was in bad shape then, but I haven't
actually heard he's died. Shall we go and find out?—be a good
excuse to get out of this dump." He ushered Morton out of his
room, and banged the door behind him.

"From your accent, I imagine you would be more at home in
the north," ventured Morton, as they walked down the street.

"New York. That's where I was born. I came down here to
seek my fortune, like any wooden-headed forty-niner."

"Gold?" asked Morton, surprised.

"Ambition. I was in the force in New York. Then in the
years after the civil war, the northerners wanted to keep control
of the South. Reconstruction, they called it," Kinsella gave a

bitter laugh. "They persuaded me to come down to New Orleans as a lieutenant, and as good as promised I would be in charge of the force within seven years. But these bastards down here are still fighting the war. Desmier has no more idea of police work than a piccaninny, but he's a southern gentleman," Kinsella's lip curled in a sneer.

"Why not go back to New York?" suggested Morton.

"I married a southern girl. One year I took her and the children to my sister's for Thanksgiving, and she swore she'd never go near the north again. Anyway, the time is past for that . . . Look, this is Jackson Square; I'll show you where they found him."

Kinsella led Morton through a gate in the iron railings, and he found himself in an elaborate garden, laid out with flower-beds and shrubberies. Paths converging on the center drew the eye to a jaunty equestrian statue of General Jackson. On either side of the square were massive arcaded buildings, not above forty years old; but the cathedral and its attendant buildings on the north side spoke of an older culture, different values.

"They found him here," said Kinsella, pushing away the shrubs, and indicating a patch of ground at the foot of a myrtle tree. "He'd been badly beaten up, and I guess they left him for dead."

"When was he found?" asked Morton.

"At seven o'clock in the morning, by the daytime guard."

Morton looked around him. "Is there a night-time guard, then?" he asked.

"Yeah."

"Why did he not discover him? The shrubs would not have concealed him."

"The guard said he was taken with the runs, and spent all night in the bog-house."

"Was it true?"

"Now how do you prove a thing like that?—No, I reckon he was warned off."

"By whom?"

"Our Sicilian friends, I guess."

"I had no idea the Mafia had spread down here," said Morton.

"We had a police superintendant—a guy called Hennessy. He swore he would throw them out, but they got him first. Shot him dead in the street—not a year and a half ago."

"Did they catch the assassins?"

"Sure they did. Nineteen of them were tried—and acquitted. The folks round here didn't like that. They broke into the prison that same night, and lynched most of 'em. They've been a bit quieter since then, but they are still around."

"It sounds a fairly rough area," said Morton.

"Maybe. But there are times," Kinsella replied darkly, "when the citizens have to take the law in their own hands, if it is to be enforced at all."

"So you are satisfied that the attack on Ryan was not just a random footpadding?"

"That is so. The streets are too well lit, to make that likely. And this Ryan is one hell of a big guy. It would take a good number of men to beat him up like that."

"Do you think the attack might be connected with the fact that he gave information about the scuttling of a ship to the Lloyd's agent here?"

"Could be," said Kinsella pensively, as he led the way out of the square. "Is that what happened?"

"Yes. I'm here to escort him back to England, to give evidence in a court case on the insurance claim."

"It sounds a bit out of the usual run of Mafia concerns," Kinsella said. "But where there's money, you'll find them too. One thing there is no doubt about at all, somebody had it in for him . . . There's the hospital," he added, pointing to a large Grecian building, surmounted by an incongruous cupola bearing a weather-cock. They waited for some time in the stone-flagged entrance hall, and were then taken to the office of a Dr. Caspard. His manner was cautious and non-committal.

"Yes, Mr. Ryan is still alive, lieutenant."

"Is he fit to be questioned?" asked Kinsella.

"I think so, provided he is handled gently, and it does not go on for too long."

"Will there be any permanent effects from the injuries?" Morton asked.

"It is a little early to say yet. There were no bones broken, and he has recovered from the loss of blood. He was badly concussed, of course, and he may have recurrent headaches, but nothing disabling."

"His memory was not affected, then?"

"No, his rational faculties appear to be wholly unimpaired."

"Would he be able to travel?"

"Where to?"

"To London, England."

Caspard considered for a moment. "I would prefer to wait a day or two before giving a definite answer, but as he is progressing at the moment, I see no reason why he should not, providing that he does not exert himself."

"He would have first-class treatment all the way."

"He still has dressings on his head, you would have to arrange for them to be changed."

"That should not be a problem. It could be done when we reach New York, at the latest; and there will certainly be a doctor on the ship."

"Very well. Come back in three days, and we will see."

"Can we talk to him now?" asked Kinsella.

"Of course, but for ten minutes only." He took them to a large ward, and indicated a bed some way along one side. It was impossible to make out much of the man who was propped up in it. His body was clothed in a nightshirt buttoned up to the neck, and his head was encased in bandages like a mob-cap. In between was a heavy-boned face covered with a fuzz of ginger whiskers, and pierced by cornflower-blue eyes.

"Kinsella, lieutenant of police." He flashed his warrant-card under Ryan's nose.

"Where the hell have you been?" growled Ryan.

"I don't follow you."

"Some bastards beat me up three weeks ago, and this is the first time a cop has showed up."

"We thought you were a goner. They refused to let us see you."

"Crap. I've been out of bed every afternoon for a week."

"So tell us now. Did you pick yourself a fight with a railroad engine?"

"The bastards set on me when I was crossing the square—eight or nine of them, with bludgeons. I kept them off at first, but they were too many for me."

"Who were they?"

"I dunno."

"Would you recognize any of them?"

"Not for certain."

"What time did the attack happen?" asked Kinsella.

"Half after twelve."

"No witnesses, I suppose?"

"How the hell do I know? That's what you are for."

"Well, none have come forward. Is there anybody in this town bears you a grudge?"

"Jesus! Not enough to kill me."

"Can you think of any reason why you might have been attacked?"

"No."

"Could it have had any connection with the information you gave to the Lloyd's agent about the *Dancing Lady*?" asked Morton.

"How do you know about that?"

"I've been sent from London to make inquiries. They would like you to come back with me, so that you can give your story in person."

"Back to London? That's a laugh!" snorted Ryan. "I just been through hell, gettin' back from there."

"It might be safer for you than New Orleans, for a time."

"Yeah, that's true . . . Especially with our police force being so concerned." He shot a challenging look at Kinsella. "Yeah, sure I'll come, so long as you get me back here afterwards."

They left Ryan, and sought out the nurse on duty. She proved to be a brisk, cheerful young woman with a self-assured air.

"Did you nurse Patrick Ryan, miss?" asked Kinsella.

"Why, yes. Poor man, he was terribly ill when he first came in. He's doing well now, isn't he?" Her tone held a mixture of pride and satisfaction.

"Where does he live?"

She turned to her desk and picked out a folder from a pile. "He lodges with a Mrs. Moffatt at Seventy-six, Gravier Street."

"Any known relatives?"

"Not that we are aware of. Mrs. Moffatt is the only person who has visited him."

"He is something of a puzzle to us, nurse," said Morton pleasantly. "Has he said anything about himself to you?"

"He has not been exactly chatty," she replied, "and who can blame him? But the night after he was brought in, I was sitting by his bedside; and when the fever was at its height, he kept shouting strange things—I jotted them down somewhere." She turned back in the folder, and extracted a scrap of paper torn from a notebook. "Here we are," she said. "The most frequent thing he shouted was 'Don't shoot!', and interspersed with that was 'I'm an American,' and 'Open the gates.'"

"One gets the impression," said Morton as they left the hospital, "that Ryan is not telling us the whole story."

"I guess he's a hoodlum, like his pals who did him up."

"Do you know where Luigi Rossi's office is? He is the Lloyd's agent, and perhaps he learned more from Ryan than he passed on to London."

"Sure."

They set off at a more leisurely pace, now that the sun was high, and were fortunate enough to catch Rossi at his desk. He answered Kinsella's greeting cordially enough, but Morton felt he was on his guard.

"I have been given a summary of your cable to Lloyd's, of course," Morton said. "But I wondered if Ryan told you anything that you did not include there."

"Young man," said Rossi starchily, "it is my function to pass all information on shipping matters to Lloyd's, whether I regard it as important or not."

"So Ryan did not tell you where the *Dancing Lady* was alleged to have been scuttled?"

Rossi gave a long-suffering sigh. "That would have been the single most important piece of information I could furnish to London."

"Did you believe what he told you, Mr. Rossi?"

"Yes, I think so. He was obviously an experienced seaman, familiar with these waters. I felt at the time that he had decided how much he was going to tell me, and would not go further than that. Obviously, I believed him enough to feel the information was worth passing on."

"When did Ryan come to see you?" asked Kinsella.

"Now let me see." Rossi picked up his desk diary, and began to flick backwards through the pages. "Yes," he said. "I have a note that I sent the cable to Lloyd's on the fourteenth of April. I am certain that he came to see me on the morning of the same day."

"So by the evening of the fourteenth, it was common knowledge that Ryan had sung out about the scuttle."

"I would not go so far as that, lieutenant; we try to keep our shipping intelligence confidential."

"But you dictated the cable to your stenographer, and she took it to the telegraph office, where the operator read it, at the very least."

"To that extent, it must have been known, I agree."

"You would not know anything about Ryan's being attacked in Jackson Square, on the tenth of May, I suppose?"

"Good heavens! How terrible. No lieutenant, I had no idea."

"I thought not. Good day, Mr. Rossi."

"You know," said Kinsella, when they were once more in the street, "I think the sooner you get Ryan out of New Orleans, the better. I'm aware that not all Italians are involved with the Mafia, but I would be surprised if they didn't know by nightfall that we had been sniffing around." He pulled out his watch. "A quarter after eleven. Now is there anything else I can do for you?"

"The only other people I have been asked to see are De Wolf & Fletcher, the import agents. I think it would be helpful if you were there, to give it an official air."

"Great, they are just around the corner, I know Henry De Wolf of old. A very upright-seeming gentleman is Henry."

Kinsella's description seemed amply justified, for De Wolf was soberly dressed in a well-cut morning coat, and he wore a gold tiepin in his cravat. His face was smooth and chubby, his whiskers touched with gray. He exuded artless benevolence and candor.

"I am real pleased to meet you, Mr. Morton," he said, with a firm handshake.

"I understand that you were involved in procuring a cotton-seed mill from Thurgood & Jackson Ltd. in England."

"That is correct, young man. My principal has been chasing me like I was a turkey at Thanksgiving, but there was nothing I could do about it."

"I take it you are referring to the fact that it has not been delivered."

"Correct. It should have been here by the end of February."

"What action did you take when it did not arrive?"

"Why nothing, at first. You can never tell within a month when a cargo is going to arrive. The ship might be calling at ports on the eastern seaboard, on the way here. Sometimes a ship is stuck in the river for weeks, waiting its turn to be unloaded. I was not unduly concerned, as I say, but when my principal started getting hot under the collar, I made enquiries. I had arranged with an export agent in Manchester to place the order with a manufacturer, so I sent a cablegram to him. I got a reply back from the shipping agents in London; let me see if I can find it. Excuse me a moment." He disappeared through a door in a glass partition, and Morton could see several clerks working in the room beyond.

"Here it is," said De Wolf, reappearing with a telegraph form in his hand. "It was sent by a firm called Taylor Pendrill & Co., and it confirmed that the machinery had been despatched via the *ss Dancing Lady* on the twelfth of January."

"What was the date of that cable?" asked Kinsella.

"The seventh of April. About the same time I became aware that rumors were circulating about the loss of that ship. I consulted with my principal, and on the eighteenth of April, I cabled Taylor Pendrill & Co., who had arranged the insurance, and instructed them to lodge a claim with the insurers."

"And did they pay out?"

"Oh, no," replied De Wolf with a look of injured innocence, "Lloyd's refused to pay. They said they were not satisfied that the circumstances of the loss were covered by the policy . . . We are taking them to court, of course."

"Who is your principal?" asked Morton.

"Well, I am not sure that I should tell you," De Wolf demurred.

"It will save me the trouble of sending a cable to Lloyd's."

"You would be wasting your time," De Wolf said with a guileless smile. "The insurance policy was taken out in the name of my firm, as agent for my principal."

"What was the reason for that?" asked Morton.

"He wanted to conceal his identity till the transaction was completed—which is why I am reluctant to disclose it now."

"His name, Henry," Kinsella demanded peremptorily. "There could be attempted murder charges pending; you wouldn't want to get mixed up with something like that."

"Goodness me! I had no idea," said De Wolf earnestly. "You may be sure I will do anything I can to help the police, lieutenant. Yes, well, my principal is a gentleman called Jethro Dillard, who owns the Chantilly Plantation, near Shreveport, in the north of the state."

Morton bade a warm farewell to Kinsella, and ate a leisurely lunch at a restaurant providing French cuisine. Pondering on what he had learned during the morning, he realized that there was one aspect still to be covered in New Orleans. Accordingly, he paid his bill, and set off for Gravier Street.

Mrs. Moffatt proved to be a petite, fading woman of forty, with genteel manners, and work-roughened hands. She showed Morton into a parlor that was dingy, yet scrupulously clean.

"Poor Mr. Ryan, I was so sorry for him. He was so kind." She turned away, and blew her nose delicately into a lace-trimmed handkerchief. "They are animals on the street here, just animals," she declared with unexpected vehemence.

"He is recovering very quickly now," Morton assured her.

"Yes, that is something. He will soon be home now. Then I'll see he gets really well . . . Are you a relation of his?"

"No." Morton hesitated. "Just a friend."

"I thought not. Patrick . . . er, Mr. Ryan never mentioned having relatives. Fancy you coming all the way from Boston to see him."

"He is a fine man. How long has he been lodging with you, Mrs. Moffatt?"

"He knocked on my door in the evening of March twenty-six, Mr. Morton. He looked dead beat then, poor thing. He was all dirty and ragged, and he looked as if he had not had a square meal for a week. I nearly turned him away, but he gave me such a pleading look . . . He had no money, either, not till he got a job at the port. But I trusted him, and he never let me down. He will get an appointment to a ship all right, when the cotton is ready," she added wistfully.

"Did you know him before he came to live here?"

"No, though I believe he spent some years in New Orleans when he was young."

"So you do not know him well at all?"

Mrs. Moffatt appeared flustered, and put up a hand to smooth her hair. "There are some men you just know you can trust," she replied.

"Has he ever spoken to you about any enemies he might have? Anyone who might bear him a grudge?"

"No, never."

"What did he do when he wasn't working?"

"He stayed at home, mostly. He was not too strong at first . . . and he sometimes drank more than I would have liked. But he was never ugly with it," she said with a reflective smile. "It just used to make him silly . . ."

• • •

Faced with three days of kicking his heels, Morton decided to see if he could contrive an interview with Jethro Dillard. Next morning he caught an early train to Shreveport. At first the train seemed to pick its way hesitantly between bayous, where trees veiled in spanish moss dabbled their feet in the water. Once he saw an alligator hauling itself out of the brown water, oblivious of the clanking engine close by. Then, reaching higher ground, the train seemed to gain confidence, and picked up speed.

They arrived at Shreveport on the stroke of noon. Morton took a hasty lunch, and hired a driver to take him to the Chantilly Plantation. It was no great distance, but in the humidity the pony could barely raise a trot. Morton folded his jacket across his knees in the hope of a cooling breeze, but there was none. The sun was now obscured by a blue-gray haze, and he felt as if he were in a steam-bath. The driver seemed to be nodding himself asleep beside him, and Morton had the feeling that they all might slowly run down like a clockwork toy, and stop. Finally, the driver roused himself, and swung the buggy down a long drive bordered by mature oak trees. They drew up before a handsome clapboarded house, shaded by trees. A young black boy ran out, and held the pony's head. Morton got down and rang the doorbell.

"Is Mr. Dillard at home please?" he asked the maid.

"No. Massa Dillard, he gone out." She was smiling as broadly as if she had conferred a bounty on him.

"Do you know when he is expected back?"

"No."

"Who is it, Fanny?" a woman's voice called from within the house.

"Gentleman. He want to know when Massa be back," shouted Fanny, her smiling face still turned towards Morton.

There came the sound of quick footsteps, and a middle-aged woman appeared. "That will do, Fanny."

This was obviously the mistress of the house. She was tastefully dressed in a silk afternoon gown. Morton removed his hat and inclined his head.

"You wish to see my husband?" she inquired with a gratified smile.

"Yes indeed, if it is possible. My name is James Morton. I have to admit that I came up from New Orleans without having asked for an appointment, so I cannot complain if I find him away from home.''

"I expect him back early this evening. Why not send your driver back, and wait till he arrives? One of our men will take you into town afterwards.''

"That is most kind of you. It will save another journey.''

Morton retrieved his bag from the back of the buggy, and paid off the driver.

"Can I get you any refreshment?" asked his hostess.

"Some iced water would be very welcome.''

Mrs. Dillard nodded to Fanny, and led the way into a large airy room which was filled with expensive draperies and fine furniture.

"This is my daughter Rosalie, and this my son Thomas.''

Rosalie was about nineteen, full-bosomed and pale as a lily. Morton bowed gravely over her outstretched hand. "Enchanted," he murmured. The twelve-year old boy scrambled off the settee, and shook Morton's hand.

"D'you live in New Orleans?" he asked.

"No. I have just come from there, but my home is in England.''

"Jeeze," exclaimed the boy incredulously.

"Thomas! You know very well that you are not to use that expression," his mother admonished him.

He disregarded her. "Have you come all the way from England to see my father?''

"This is a little complicated," replied Morton, taking the swathed glass of water from Fanny's tray. "I live in England, but in fact I have just come from Australia.''

"Where is that? Is it a long way?''

"A very long way.''

"Wow . . . Don't go, will you?" He raced off.

"Did you bring your wife with you, Mr. Morton?" asked Rosalie.

Morton smiled. "I am afraid that I am not fortunate enough to be married," he replied.

Thomas rushed in clutching a large schoolroom globe. "Show me where Australia is, sir.''

Morton placed the globe on the table, and knelt by the boy. "This tiny island is England, where I live; this is where we are now;" he turned the globe, "and this is Australia.''

"Jeeze, it's on the other side of the world . . . How did you get here?''

"I sailed in a steamship from Sydney, which is here, up to Fiji," Morton traced the route with his finger, "then to Hawaii, and on to San Francisco. Then I got a train to Boston, and another one down to New Orleans."

"Why did you go to Boston? The railroad goes from Chicago to Philadelphia, you could have changed trains there," the boy asked knowledgeably.

"You are perfectly right," replied Morton with a laugh. "But I have an uncle who lives in Boston, and I went to visit him."

"What were you doing in Australia, sir?"

"Now, really, Thomas, that is enough," said Mrs. Dillard censoriously. "You must forgive him, Mr. Morton, he's just at the age when they want to know everything."

"I assure you, I do not mind in the slightest," Morton replied. "In fact, I was in Australia playing cricket for England."

"What is cricket?" asked the boy.

"It's a game—a bit like baseball."

"Hey!" shouted Thomas in excitement, "will you pitch for me?"

"Why, yes, if you like, though I have never done it before."

"It's easy," the boy grabbed Morton's hand. "Come on."

"Mr. Morton, there really is no need to indulge him," said Mrs. Dillard, "he is becoming thoroughly spoiled."

"I am sure I shall enjoy it, and a little exercise will do me good."

"Well don't go far, Thomas, it looks as if it will rain soon."

Morton allowed himself to be dragged to the back of the house and into the yard. Thomas plunged into a shed, and emerged with a baseball bat, and ball.

"You stand there," he pointed to an area of scuffed grass, "and pitch to me." He took up his stance in front of one of the outbuildings. "Ready?"

Morton lobbed a ball at him, and the boy cracked it past his outstretched hand. Morton toiled after it.

"I won't run," shouted Thomas, "seeing as how there's only us playing."

Morton regained his spot, and sent the next one spinning at waist height. The boy stepped to one side, but was unable to create enough room for a stroke.

"You would have been out then, Tom." Rosalie was watching them from under her parasol.

"No, I wouldn't," retorted her brother, "it was not a proper pitch."

"How should it be done?" asked Morton.

"It should be there," said Thomas, extending his bat sideways.

"And very much faster," added Rosalie.

"Faster?"

"Well, a bit faster," conceded Thomas.

Morton pitched the ball a comfortable distance from Thomas's body, and he sent it curving up into the air. Morton ran to catch it, but it hit the roof of the house, and lodged in the gutter.

"We could get it down," said Thomas hopefully.

"Oh no," countered Rosalie. "Jonas can get it with the ladder tomorrow."

"Perhaps you might show me the garden, instead," Morton suggested.

"That would be delightful." Rosalie took his arm, and they strolled along the path, conversing animatedly, with Thomas trailing behind them.

"I had not expected to find such beautiful shrubs," remarked Morton, stopping to survey the garden, "I have never seen such a profusion of magnolias in my life."

"It is the Louisiana State flower," replied Rosalie. "But you ought to be here when the azaleas are out. They are so beautiful . . . Oh dear, Mamma was right, it is beginning to rain."

"Should we go back to the house?" Morton asked.

"You don't know our rain! We would be drowned before we got there. Thomas, run for the tool shed." They scampered towards a small wooden hut, and perched on boxes, watching the rain lancing down.

Morton glanced at Rosalie, there was a flush of color in her cheeks, and her bosom was rising and falling agreeably. He smiled at her, and she dropped her eyes.

"I am interested to see that the grass in your lawn is much coarser than ours at home," he remarked. "It has much wider leaves."

"It is the only kind that can survive the summer."

"Do you mean that it gets hotter than this?"

"Oh, much hotter . . . So hot, you just long to die."

"What is it like to live in England, sir?" asked Thomas.

"Well, I was brought up in a great stone house, surrounded by a wall, like a castle. Parts of it are over eight hundred years old. It has its own chapel, and a great hall, where the knights used to dine on a long walnut table that they say was brought back from the crusades."

"Are you a knight, sir?" asked Thomas.

"No, but my father is, and I may be someday. My father is a general, and has fought all over the world—in Russia, New Zealand, and Africa."

"Is your castle in London, sir?"

"No!" laughed Morton, "it's in the country, surrounded by farms and woods, like your house. But I can get to London by train in not much more than an hour."

"I would love to see London," Rosalie murmured. "Oh, look! Trust Daddy to get back just as the rain is stopping."

Looking down the drive, Morton could see an elegant phaeton approaching.

"He will be soaking wet," she went on, "so I don't suppose he will see you till he has changed." She put up her parasol. "I will tell him you are here." She smiled excitedly at Morton, and darted through the doorway.

"Can we get the ball down now?" asked Thomas.

"We can try. Do you know where the ladder is?"

"Of course," replied Thomas scornfully.

Nevertheless, it took them some time before they had located it, and carried it to the house. Thomas was eager to clamber up, but the ladder was too short to rest on the gutter. Morton himself ascended, and balancing on the second rung, reached outwards and dislodged the ball. Climbing down after it, he became aware of a slim handsome man standing at Thomas's side.

"My son uses everybody to satisfy his impatience, Mr. Morton." The man held out his hand. "I am Jethro Dillard, I'm glad to meet you."

"How do you do, sir?" replied Morton. "I was hoping that you could spare me a few minutes."

"Certainly, Mr. Morton. However, I make it a rule never to discuss business in the evenings. If I did not, I would never have time for my family."

"I quite understand," Morton replied. "Perhaps you could

set a time for a meeting tomorrow, and get one of your men to drive me to a hotel.''

"I would not dream of it. If you are prepared to indulge my whim, then the least I can do is to see that you are comfortable. I saw your bag in the closet, so I infer that you have not yet checked in anywhere."

"That is certainly true."

"Then I insist that you stay with us overnight, and we can talk in the morning.''

"That is very kind of you, sir.''

"Not a bit of it. Now you will no doubt want to freshen up before dinner. I imagine my wife will already have decided which room will be yours.''

Morton dressed carefully, wiping the dust from his shoes with his discarded socks. He decided that the guest-room was little short of sumptuous, with heavy brocade curtains, and a silk bed cover. It was astonishing that the famed southern hospitality should extend to taking a total stranger as an overnight guest, in such a casual way. It certainly made one feel important. He was impressed, too, with the dining-room. The furniture was elegant, the table gleamed with cut glass and silver, and two young black maids served the meal expertly. At first the conversation was of family matters, then Dillard turned to Morton.

"My wife tells me that you are from England.''

"That is so.''

"And that you have family in Boston. I imagine that they emigrated to America?''

Morton smiled. "That is certainly true in the distant past, but more recently the migration has been the other way. My grandfather was John Harman of Philadelphia. He built up a large coal and iron business there, and for his pains was appointed American ambassador to England by President Buchanan. He took his family with him, of course; and my mother, who was his eldest child, fell in love with a major in the cavalry, and married him.''

"How romantic," said Rosalie, her cheeks flushed.

"We mere civilians can never hope to compete with a uniform, Mr. Morton,'' said her father. "But where does Boston come in?''

"Since my grandfather's death, the business has been run by his two sons. Uncle Thomas stayed in Philadelphia to look after the coal and steel plants. The other interests were the concern of my Uncle Joshua. Since they were so scattered, there was no geographic center to them, so he decided to move to Boston. The family had always owned land there, so it was a logical decision."

"And of course, it is the hub of the universe," remarked Dillard with a smile.

"To Bostonians at least."

"Rosalie tells me that you live in London, Mr. Morton," broke in his wife.

"That is right, Mrs. Dillard."

"Tell me, what are the ladies wearing in London right now?"

"Since I left in October last year, I imagine that my notions of the fashions are liable to be out of date," said Morton with a smile.

"They can't be as out of date as the fashions around here," Rosalie pouted.

"Most people send to Paris," her mother went on, "but we hear that the English fashions are more advanced nowadays."

"What are they like?" asked Rosalie eagerly.

"Well, the bustle has disappeared, thank God . . ."

"That's gone even in the backwoods!"

"The skirts are plain, but still full at the back . . . I think most women wear blouses, and they seem to be very frilly— oh, and the sleeves are puffed up at the shoulder . . . I'm sorry, I never analyze the effect a lady produces, I merely gaze in wonder and gratitude."

"Pretty speeches will not help you," declared Rosalie. "What about evening wear?"

"This is most unfair, ladies," Dillard intervened with a smile. "If you wish to know what is being worn in London, you should go there."

"Oh, might we, Daddy?" asked Rosalie excitedly.

"Of course you may, child."

"What is the best time to visit London, Mr. Morton?" asked Mrs. Dillard.

"I would say June, unquestionably."

"Would you be able to come then, Jethro?"

"June is one of my busiest months, but I am sure Mr. Morton would see you came to no harm."

"It would be a privilege to be allowed to repay your most generous hospitality," replied Morton.

"There then, that's settled." Mrs. Dillard rose from the table. "Shall we take coffee on the veranda?"

After breakfast next morning, Dillard took Morton into an office overlooking the yard. He selected a cigar, and settled back in his chair expectantly.

"How can I help you, Mr. Morton?" he asked.

"First of all," said Morton, "I must tell you that I am a policeman."

"You are what?" exclaimed Dillard, his face darkening.

"I am a police officer."

"You mean you are not a coal and steel tycoon?" demanded Dillard angrily.

"No. I am a constable in the police force of the City of London."

"How dare you, sir?" Dillard spluttered. "How dare you worm your way into this house, and into my daughter's affections, with stories of castles and relatives in Boston." He sprang to his feet. "If I had my way, I'd have you horse-whipped!"

"I've told you nothing but the truth," said Morton in consternation. "See, here is a cable, sent to my uncle's address in Boston." He thrust the envelope into Dillard's hands.

"Ah." Dillard subsided into his chair. "I . . . I must apologize . . ." he muttered.

"I have been sent to make inquiries concerning a cotton-seed mill, which was exported from London to New Orleans in January, but which failed to arrive there. I understand that the plant was to have been delivered to you."

"That is so," acknowledged Dillard shamefacedly. "It should have been here months ago. I have a bill of lading somewhere . . ." He unlocked a drawer in his desk, and withdrew a file. "Here it is." He passed the paper over to Morton. "It was sent to me by Taylor Pendrill & Co. of London, who are the shipping agents. You will see that it is dated the eighth of January this year."

"'Upon the good ship *Dancing Lady*,'" Morton quoted. "I gather that she left London on the twelfth . . . Why is the bill made out to 'Order' instead of to you personally?"

"I wanted it to be at least delivered here, before the other planters found out. I ordered it through De Wolf & Fletcher of New Orleans, back in August of 'ninety-one. De Wolf advised me to have it shipped out to 'Order'. See, the bill has been endorsed by the manufacturer and signed by the master of the ship. I only had to produce it to the master, to claim the cargo.''

"Why did you order the mill, in the first place?'' asked Morton.

"Well, the usual thing is to ship the cotton-seed down the Red River to the Mississippi, and on to New Orleans. That is not very satisfactory; freight is high, and the Red River is often silted up, or jammed with logs. Then we have to use the railroad, but the cost is prohibitive. My plan is to set the mill up in town, by the river, and near the railroad. That way most of the big planters in the area will be able to get their seed to the mill . . . It is much easier to send a few hundred barrels of oil to New Orleans than thousands of sacks of seed.''

"There is reason to believe that the ship was scuttled, and that the cargo may have been diverted elsewhere,'' said Morton.

"Yes, I heard that rumor from De Wolf,'' replied Dillard sharply, "but it is no concern of mine. I paid for the plant to be delivered here, and that should have been done in March. Even if it came today, I would never be able to get it working in time for this year's crop.''

"Would you mind telling me how much you paid for it?''

"Not at all. It cost me nearly one hundred and fifty thousand dollars. There's the manufacturer's receipt.''

Morton whistled. "It sounds a fortune.''

"It is, young man, as the bankers were at pains to point out when they lent me the money. But, up here, it would be like a license to print dollar bills.''

"De Wolf told me that you had made a claim on the insurance policy, and that it had been refused.''

"He told you rightly. Our lawyers have started proceedings in the English courts.''

"I only hope you succeed,'' said Morton.

"You have seen the papers,'' replied Dillard firmly. "I have paid for something that I have not received. I do not see how I can possibly lose.''

CHAPTER ——————

—————— SIX

"Have you anything for me on the insurance fraud case?" Catherine asked. She was perched uncomfortably on Bragg's horsehair sofa, while he sprawled in an armchair by the fireplace.

"The trouble with you newspaper folk," replied Bragg, feeling for his pipe, "is that you are not satisfied with a few facts; you start inventing things to make a good story."

"You have no grounds for accusing me of such practices," said Catherine severely. "Even when I have discovered facts relating to your cases myself, I have refrained from publishing them unless you agreed."

"That is true enough," said Bragg reflectively, knocking out his pipe on the grate. "Well now, you could write that we are continuing our investigations in Britain and America . . ."

"Can I say 'intensifying their investigations'?" Catherine asked, jotting rapidly in her notebook. "It sounds more dynamic."

"If you like," Bragg laughed. "But it will look silly, if nothing comes of it in the end."

"Our readers have short memories."

"You can say that the ship lost was the *Dancing Lady*, and that we are anxious to interview the master, Ben Gadd."

"Anything else?"

"Nothing for publication."

Catherine put her notebook in her bag, and looked at Bragg expectantly.

"It's a great mess is this case," Bragg started to cut thin slices of twist with his pocket-knife. "I begin to feel that the Lloyd's people are using the police. As long as we hang about, and make noise enough to deter other would-be fraudsters, they won't mind if we don't catch this lot. Sometimes I think that the longer our investigations go on, the better they will like it."

"I am sure that you would only be content with a speedy solution, and an arrest," said Catherine emphatically.

Bragg began to rub the tobacco gently between his palms. "At all events," he remarked slyly, "we have finished our investigations in America. Constable Morton leaves New Orleans today."

"Really?" Catherine tossed her head disinterestedly.

"So he should be back in London within ten days."

"And will I be told the results of his investigations?"

"Perhaps. That is assuming there are any."

"You seem surprisingly pessimistic about the case, sergeant."

"Maybe I am. I must confess I get worried when other countries are involved. It's not just the problem of getting there; we can't go blundering about in a foreign jurisdiction without upsetting the local police. So we end up with having to be satisfied with what they can, or will, discover. And this case becomes more international by the minute. I suppose I shouldn't be surprised; both shipping and insurance are international industries. It is just that I get very suspicious when there is an allegation of crime, and all the people connected with it are foreigners or have gone overseas."

"So far as I have heard, the only foreign element is that the cargo was diverted from one American port to another," said Catherine.

Bragg fed the tobacco into his pipe, and pressed it down with his forefinger. "Not a bit of it," he said. "And this is definitely not for publication . . . The *Dancing Lady* was chartered for that voyage by a French company, Michel Tissier et Cie. I telegraphed the Sûreté in Paris, and asked who owned that company. They cabled back to say that it was owned by yet another French company, Lebrun Barré et Cie.''

"Is that so surprising?'' asked Catherine.

"Maybe not. But what better set-up could you have, if you wanted to defraud Lloyd's?'' He laid a match across the bowl of his pipe, and sucked at the flame.

"I knew, of course,'' said Catherine, "that it was the *Dancing Lady* you were interested in, Lloyd's seems to be rife with rumor at the moment.''

"It is the way these markets operate,'' replied Bragg. "A hint or a whisper, and it's as good as gospel.''

"I discovered that the ship was owned by Harvey & Crane Ltd. Are you aware of the action against them?''

"What action?''

"It is all exceedingly obscure. Something involving bottomry. It sounds as if it is to do with the nursery!''

Bragg laughed. "I had not heard about that.''

"The legal correspondent of the *Star* was not very clear on the subject, but it appears that the company borrowed money from a bank in Bermuda to make some repairs, and is refusing to repay it. The Bermuda bank has issued a writ against Harvey & Crane, alleging fradulent intent.''

"Is that so?'' Bragg murmured. "You know, that's another company I am unhappy about. It appears to be one of the injured parties in this scuttling, and yet when I ask about it—things like who the shareholders are—they haul in a solicitor, who reads prepared replies that tell me nothing.''

"I could try to find out the owners if you like,'' said Catherine. "I am going to a ball at Lady Brooke's, this evening. There will probably be some financiers or stockbrokers there . . . Don't worry, I will be discreet!''

"I'm pleased to hear that you keep your social calendar going,'' remarked Bragg with a smile.

"The dancing is fun, but I hate being pestered by vain young City men, and empty-headed subalterns. Still, I cannot opt out of the Season completely. If I did, people would think I was even odder than they do now.'' She rose to her feet. "At least I am going down to the Mortons for the weekend, so that will be pleasant.''

"Are you now?"

"Yes. Emily and I became firm friends last autumn. She wants to do something interesting with her life. James, being a typical arrogant male, forbade me to encourage her . . . but we shall see."

Next morning Bragg went straight to the offices of Harvey & Crane. He was piqued to find that Cakebread refused even to receive him, unless Pocklington was present, and he was kept cooling his heels in the outer office for half an hour until the solicitor arrived. But at least on this occasion the other side had not had the opportunity to determine in advance what they would say, so he might have the edge on them.

"I hear that the company is being sued in connection with the *Dancing Lady*," he began.

"I take it you are referring to the action over the bottomry bond," said Pocklington.

Bragg tugged at one end of his mustache. "You know," he said earnestly, "it would be much better for you, if you told me everything you know."

"You must let us be the judge of that, sergeant," said Pocklington sharply.

"When were you challenged by the Bermuda bank over the bond, Mr. Cakebread?" asked Bragg.

Cakebread cleared his throat. "It would be towards the end of April," he said.

"I understand that the bank is alleging fraud, so you can imagine that I am interested. Are you going to tell me about it, or do I have to go to the bank's solicitors?"

"Since the arguments of both parties have been set out in pleadings to the court," Pocklington said with an impish smile, "I have no objection to telling you. The Bank of Bermuda claims to hold a bottomry bond, in the sum of seventeen thousand pounds, signed by Benjamin Gadd, the master of the *Dancing Lady*, on the twenty-ninth of January this year. I do not know if you are familiar with the function of a bottomry bond?"

"No."

"Well, it is an instrument which allows the master of a ship to obtain funds for essential repairs to complete a voyage. It is in a form approved by Lloyd's, and is only used when it is impossible to obtain credit by other means."

"Is it an insurance?" asked Bragg.

"No. It is a loan which is secured on the hull and machinery of the vessel."

"Then why are Lloyd's interested?'

Pocklington smiled. "Lloyd's arrogate to themselves all kinds of rights in the marine sphere, and one has perforce to accept it. Having said that, there is perhaps some justification in this case, because one feature of the bottomry bond is that the amount advanced is only repayable if the ship completes its journey."

"On the face of it, then, the Bank of Bermuda has no claim," Bragg remarked.

"I should discourage you from coming to conclusions with such alacrity, sergeant," Pocklington quipped. "I would not have it put about that my profession is dispensable. I have to accept, however, that if the bank can demonstrate a fraudulent intent, they could present a colorable argument that the money should be repaid. On our side, we argue that since the ship was demise chartered, the charterer stands in the place of the owner for all matters—including the bottomry bond."

"And will you succeed?" asked Bragg.

"I would be a poor lawyer if I gave a straight answer to that question! It is, however, settled mercantile law, that where there is a bare-boat charter, and the master has been engaged by the charterer, then he is the agent of the charterer, not of the shipowner."

"Suppose that Lloyd's successfully resisted a claim under the insurance policy, would that make any difference to your position?"

"It would depend on the grounds of the decision. However, it could hardly improve our situation."

Ryan was surprisingly weak for so big a man, and Morton had to support him from the hospital door to the carriage. Luckily, it was a cabriolet, and he managed to stumble up the low steps, but the effort exhausted him. By the time they reached the station his newly-shaven face was gray and drawn, and Morton began to wonder about the wisdom of taking him on such an arduous journey. He revived somewhat, after Morton had administered coffee laced with brandy, and managed to stagger to the train. With the attendant pulling, and Morton pushing from behind, they managed to get him safely up the steps, and once in their compartment he fell into an uneasy sleep.

He spent that day, and the next, in a semi-comatose state, eating little, and saying nothing at all. Morton began to wonder if there was some infection under the cap of bandages that was slowly killing him. He decided it was imperative to get him off the train, and to a doctor, as soon as he could. So at Greensboro they alighted and Morton summoned a doctor to the hotel. He gently unwound the dressings, and after a deal of tut-tutting, pronounced that the wounds were almost healed. He replaced the elaborate swathe of bandages with a simple band around the head at the temples. This had the immediate effect of making Ryan look better. Nevertheless, the doctor forbade any more traveling until he had rested for two nights. He left a prescription for a sleeping-draught, which Morton got dispensed at a drug-store near the hotel. It must have been very strong, because hardly had Ryan swallowed a dose than he fell into a deep sleep.

Morton decided to sit up with him. There would now be no chance of a quick trip to Boston, while Ryan was safely tucked up in a New York hospital; so pulling an armchair to the side of the bed, he wrote a letter of apology to his cousin Violet. Most of the night Ryan slept quietly, but from time to time his breathing became agitated, and he would move restlessly, muttering indistinguishable words. Occasionally, he would draw in a long slow breath, the air vibrating his vocal chords like a groan, and hold it—hold it for an impossible length of time, until Morton sprang to his feet, sure that he had breathed his last. Then would come a shuddering agony of exhalation. Sometimes he would keep this up for five minutes at a time, then drift into more peaceful sleep. The pattern was much the same on the second night. Whatever thoughts were chasing each other through this drugged brain, they were not agreeable ones. Morton recalled the words overhead by the nurse, "Don't shoot," "Open the gates," "I'm an American." Something was haunting him—perhaps something relating to the *Dancing Lady*. Morton resolved to gain his confidence in the days to come, and attempt to find out what it was.

Next morning Ryan looked much better. The dreadful pallor was gone, and he ate a reasonable breakfast. Morton cajoled the hotel barber into coming up to Ryan's room and shaving him. Then he managed to dress himself. Morton felt like a hen that sees her chick struggle out of the egg-shell and begin to cheep—except that this chicken was maintaining a morose silence. He packed their bags, and having paid the bill, he helped Ryan down to the lobby of the hotel. The break in the journey had done him good; he climbed into the carriage unaided, and was able to walk to the train without stopping to rest. Once in his seat, however, he fell into a doze, while Morton gazed out of the window at the farmsteads scuttering past. After a time he glanced back to find Ryan's blue eyes fixed on him.

"Ah, you are awake."

Ryan made his usual monosyllabic reply, then seemed to rouse himself, as if to try his new-found strength.

"First time I've been on a train with a cop." He gave a tentative smile.

"As I have told you, I am not with you as a policeman, just as a companion."

"You mean I could get off right now, and go back?"

"Well . . . yes," replied Morton, disconcerted.

"Don't worry." Ryan raised a grin. "I know when I'm well off." He relapsed into silence for a space, then, "Is there such a thing as a drink?" he asked.

"The hospital did not recommend alcohol," replied Morton.

"That damned miserable doctor . . . Do you drink, James?"

"In moderation . . . wine mostly."

"That's my trouble."

"What is?"

"The moderation bit . . . Drink and women, women and drink. It's them have brought me to this . . . Are you married, James?"

"Not yet," replied Morton with a grin.

"You should find yourself a nice girl, and stick to her, James."

"It is not as easy as you seem to think."

"Women are queer about sailors," Ryan said reflectively. "Perhaps it's because their own lives are so dull; maybe a seaman is romantic to them. But put the best of them—hard-working, god-fearing, happily married—in the same room as a sailor, and she'll get an itch between her legs."

"Someone like Mrs. Moffat?" asked Morton slyly.

"Oh, you've met her have you? She's a good woman . . . It's good women that's been my downfall," he said in perplexity.

"I could never get excited over a woman who chased after me," remarked Morton.

"That's a damned prissy thing to say."

"Is it? It was not meant to be. It's just that it takes away some of the spice, some of the satisfaction."

"You'd get a damned sight more satisfaction my way, and for free . . . Women and drink . . . And where they are, there's always fighting. Those three have made me what I am—a freeborn American drifter." He relapsed into gloomy silence.

"How did you come to be on the *Dancing Lady*?" asked Morton in an attempt to keep him talking.

"Now there's an example for you. I was without a ship in the fall, so I made up my mind to go back to the old country . . . My folks left Skibereen, in Ireland, before I was born, and I had a fancy to see the place. I could have saved myself the effort. No wonder they left it. Damp and cold, peat fires that gave out more smoke than heat—even the women smelled like smoked fish. And nothing to do. I hung on, because I did not believe a place could stay so dead. There was some hare-coursing on a Saturday, and a bit of cock-fighting; with Christmas around the corner. Then there was always the drink—and the women. The wife at the pub where I stayed took a shine to me. She would come up to my room when her husband was out. He knew I was humping her, all right, but he just looked sour and took my money, instead of throwing me out like a real man. Until Christmas night, that is. Then he gathered enough courage, and some of his pals, and took me on . . . So there I was, drifting back to the land of the free. I meant to do it in style, to New York by the White Star line. I reckoned I would still have enough cash to get me down to New Orleans—till that Limey bitch in Liverpool took all my money. She left me with two lousy sovereigns in my body belt; and if I hadn't been paralytic drunk, she'd have had them too."

"So what did you do?" Morton prompted him.

"London is the English port for the Gulf trade, so I took a train to there, hoping to sign on a ship. There was only one in the docks, and I was told it had a full crew."

"The *Dancing Lady*?"

"Right—the goddamn rust-bucket."

"And did they give you a job?"

"I didn't give them a chance. I stowed away in a life boat."

CHAPTER ———————
——————— SEVEN

"How did you get on in the Derby, then?" Bragg asked, perching himself on the desk at Whitlock's elbow.

"Don't ask me," replied Whitlock sourly.

"What was your horse's name?"

"Waltzing Matilda."

"You are having trouble with your terpsichorean nymphs, at the moment," Bragg said with a grin.

"That's not bad for the end of a week."

"Pure music-hall, I assure you."

"Oh, the damned thing came in last. It was dead-beat by the time it got to Tattenham Corner. It looked more like a seaside donkey than a racehorse. Everybody else had gone in for the champagne, and I was still standing there, watching it stroll up to the finish. I don't understand why the blasted trainer entered it for the Derby in the first place."

"Think of all the pleasure you have had in the last few weeks," Bragg chaffed him. "You must have gone up in your friends' esteem."

"And down again. Between us, we lost a fortune on that nag. I've a mind to send him to the knacker's yard."

"You should have entered half a dozen, and spread your risks."

Whitlock laughed. "All right, what is it you want?—apart from twisting my tail."

"Did you know that Harvey & Crane were being sued by the Bank of Bermuda in connection with a bottomry bond?"

"No. Did you, John?" he asked his deputy.

"Yes, sir. It was mentioned in yesterday's *Lloyd's List*."

"Do you know who the bank's solicitors are?" asked Bragg.

"I think they were mentioned. Just a moment." John stooped down under the table, and emerged with a newspaper. He spread it out in front of him. "Here it is . . . Yes, they are Carrington Umpleby & Co. of Gray's Inn."

"Was the bond to do with the *Dancing Lady*?" asked Whitlock.

"Yes." Bragg replied. "It was apparently taken out by the master, when he was in Bermuda."

"How much is involved?"

"Seventeen thousand pounds."

Whitlock whistled. "That is a hell of a lot. What was the vessel insured for? Do you know?"

"Twelve thousand pounds."

"There is something very odd here," Whitlock declared. "For a start the seventeen thousand pounds is very high in absolute terms; the ship would have had to be falling apart to justify that. And it is also high relative to the values involved. I expect you will find the cargo was pledged as well, so the insured values would total forty-two thousand . . ." He made a rapid calculation on his pad. "Why, the loan on the bond is over forty percent of the value of the ship and the cargo together! I have never heard of an advance exceeding twenty percent, on a bottomry bond. Generally, they are much, much less."

"But if the ship was in danger of sinking . . . ." began Bragg.

"Then the bank would not have lent the money. The quirky bit about these bonds is that if the ship goes down, there is no repayment."

"Yes, I know."

"Well, put yourself in the banker's position. Is he going to pour money into a ship that looks like sinking on him?"

"I suppose not."

"Of course," said Whitlock thoughtfully, "the whole position would be altered if there was other cargo—valuable cargo—on board."

Bragg spent the weekend pondering on what he had learned. So far as the cotton-seed mill was concerned, the gainer seemed to be the person in Galveston who had ultimately received it. The loser was initially the person in New Orleans who had ordered it, but if he succeeded with his insurance claim, then Lloyd's would be the loser. But how could someone in Texas manipulate events to his advantage in this way? There had to be someone involved who was connected with the ship. On the face of it, Harvey & Crane were losers, because they no longer had their ship, but they would succeed in their insurance claim, so again Lloyd's would be the losers . . . No wonder they were shouting "fraud." And now there was the Bermudian bank. The bottomry business was odd, but, although Bragg did not really understand it, it was clear that the master had been given seventeen thousand pounds. Was that all used on repairing the ship? If not, who was holding out their hand for the rest? The owners of the ship, or the charterers? Pocklington had said that, with this kind of charter, the master was acting for the charterer. That didn't mean he couldn't covertly act for the owner at the same time. But, still, Gadd had been engaged by the charterers—or, more correctly, by Ingham's firm on behalf of the charterers. Bragg made a mental note to ask Ingham if Gadd had ever sailed with the Green Funnel line before . . . . At all events there was seventeen thousand quid rattling around in the puzzle somewhere. It didn't seem to be connected with the insurance, or the diversion of the cargo. It could as easily have ended up with the French charterer as anywhere else—a company owned by another company; as anonymous as the rich men who provided the capital for Lloyd's. He realized that he should have asked the Sûreté more about Michel Tissier et Cie. Since he had been told by the owners of the *Dancing Lady* that the French company had chartered it, he had assumed it was a shipping company. But why should a French shipping company charter a

British ship, if it did not have cargo of its own to transport; if it had to set about advertising for cargo for a voyage to New Orleans?

On Monday morning Bragg telegraphed the Sûreté for information about the French chartering company, and also its parent, Lebrun Barré et Cie. Then he took a cab to Limehouse, and paid it off beneath the thirty-foot walls of the West India dock. His warrant card gained him ingress to this fortress, and he strolled towards the southern dock, which, according to the signs, was concerned with exports. All around were enormous brick warehouses, five stories high. Their lower windows were heavily barred, and hoists like gibbets thrust outward. It must be like working in a vast prison. Yet in one respect, no prison in the world was like this, for the whole of it was permeated by the thick, cloying smell of raw sugar and rum. When he reached the export dock, he popped his head into the little round guard-house, and was directed to the dock manager's office. This proved to be a large well-lit room on the second floor of one of the warehouses. The walls had been white-washed, and the rough floorboards covered with linoleum. Two rows of desks stretched the full length of the room, with a clerk perched on a high stool at each.

A stocky red-faced man approached, and Bragg waved his warrant-card at him.

"Sergeant Bragg, City police," he said. "Are you the manager?"

"I am."

"I want to find out about the cargo of a ship called the *Dancing Lady*. Can you help me?"

"If she loaded from this dock, I can. When did she sail?"

"At noon on the twelfth of January."

"This year?"

"Yes."

The manager took down an index book from a shelf. "*Dancing Lady*," he murmured, flicking over the pages. "Yes, here she is. She entered the dock for loading on the ninth of January. Just a minute." He went to one of the desks, and came back with a heavy ledger. "Page one two seven," he said. "Here we are. We accepted thirty-two wooden crates into the warehouse on the seventh, they were consigned by Thurgood & Jackson of Manchester, via the *ss Dancing Lady* to De

Wolf & Fletcher in New Orleans. You can see that the dimensions of each crate, and its identifying markings, are put down on the left hand page. On the opposite page we have a record of what happened to each one—the warehouse and bay number where it was kept, the date of receipt, the date it was released for loading, and that sort of thing."

Bragg examined the book. "Some of these crates were quite a size," he remarked. "Can you prove that they were loaded, and aren't still in your warehouse?"

"Steady on! We've given a dock receipt for every item, when we received it. If I didn't get a proper release for every one, I'd be out of a job."

"I don't doubt it," said Bragg, with a smile. "I just want to know what the mechanics are."

"The details in the ledger here are copied on to tally cards, and as each crate is loaded, it is ticked off by the tally clerk. That's supposed to be good enough, but I'm a bit particular. The tally cards go to the shipping agent to prepare the bills of lading. And tally cards can get lost. So I make the tally-master initial my book, so there is no argument."

"Are these his initials in the right hand column?" asked Bragg.

"That's it."

"So you can prove that all this cargo was loaded?"

"I can," the dock manager grinned widely.

"There is no record of any other cargo being loaded on the vessel?"

"Not on that voyage, no."

"Does that mean there was no other cargo?"

"No. It just means that this was the only cargo that went through the warehouses."

"There could have been more?"

"Oh yes. Often enough cargo is brought into the docks when the ship is already lying here. They wouldn't go to the bother of putting that through the warehouse, they would load it straight on. You can also get cargo brought into the dock on lighters, and loaded over the ship's side, without ever touching the quay. I don't trouble my head about them. It's only stuff in the sheds that I'm concerned with."

"Do you know if any such cargo was loaded on the *Dancing Lady* in January?"

"Let me think." The manager's brow puckered in a frown of concentration. "No, not that I can recall—and she was berthed right in front of this office. Mind you, I'm only here during the day. I can't vouch for what goes on at night."

The more Bragg brooded on what he knew, the more Ingham seemed to be at the center of the problem. He had been the ship's husband to Harvey & Crane's fleet; he had received the commission to charter a vessel, and had arranged the charter of the *Dancing Lady*; he had appointed Gadd as master; and he had arranged the insurance of both the ship and its cargo. He was like a spider at the center of a web, with a leg touching every radial. It was inconceivable that he could not have received a vibration from whatever knavery had gone on. Why had he said nothing? Would he lose too much financially, if it came out? Or was he implicated? Bragg went through the facts again, but could find no possible ground which would justify applying for an arrest warrant. But that was not to say that Ingham couldn't be leaned on a little.

At nine o'clock next morning, he was hammering on the door of Taylor Pendrill's office. He heard the lock turn, and a man peered out white-faced and trembling.

"Thank God you've come," he gasped, "I thought you'd be an age, I've only just sent word to the beadle."

"What are you talking about?" said Bragg roughly. "Pull yourself together."

"It's Mr. Ingham . . . He's dead."

"Dead? Where is he?"

"In his room. I found him when I unlocked the office at twenty to nine."

"You are quite sure the street door was locked?"

"Yes."

Bragg peered at the door. It was oak, and stoutly made, but the spring-lock that secured it could be opened by a child of nine.

"And what is your name?" he asked.

"Arthur Jones, sergeant."

"Are you the office manager?"

"Yes."

"Did you keep anything valuable on the premises?"

"A little cash, for disbursements. All our receipts are by check."

"Still, a thief would not know that. Is there any sign of a break-in? Has the safe been tampered with? Have the desk drawers been turned out?"

"No, nothing like that."

"Well, don't touch anything. Send your staff home, and tell them to come back at two o'clock . . . I'll be in Mr. Ingham's room for a while."

At first sight, it was normal. The swivel chair was at an odd angle against the wall, but from the doorway the room was as Bragg remembered it. He crossed to the middle of the carpet. A head was projecting from behind the desk. It had been battered until it was hardly recognizable. The face was crusted with dried blood, and one eye was a pulpy red cavity. There appeared to be very little blood on the carpet, despite the ferocity of the attack. Bragg examined the room to see if he could find the murder weapon. There were no fire-irons. Presumably they had been put in store for the summer. A poker would have made a much quicker job of it . . . At all events, it was a spur-of-the-moment murder, or the perpetrator would have equipped himself with a more substantial weapon. That could fit in with the idea of an intruder, finding unexpectedly that the premises were not empty. But a burglar would try to get away, not attack. Bragg rolled the body on to its right side. On the carpet beneath it was a small marble statuette. He remembered seeing it on the desk, being used as a paper-weight. The base was stained with blood, and a fragment of skin and hair adhered to one corner.

There was a sudden commotion in the corridor, and Bragg could hear a loud assertive voice. Then the door was flung open, and Sir Rufus Stone, the coroner for the City of London, entered.

"What the devil are you doing here, Bragg?" he growled. "It is my province to initiate the investigation of violent death. I will not tolerate the police's ignoring established procedures, and worming their way in first."

"It is entirely by accident that I am here, sir," said Bragg deferentially. "I came to question the deceased concerning another matter."

"What was that?" asked Sir Rufus brusquely.

"An alleged marine insurance fraud, on Lloyd's."

"Was this man implicated? . . . Damn it, Bragg, I don't even know his name."

"Bernard Ingham. He was a ship broker, ship manager, insurance broker . . ."

"I know the type, Bragg. Full of bonhomie and bland integrity, yet all of them have their hands in each other's pockets . . . Well, was he?"

"Was he what, sir?"

"Was he involved in the frauds?"

"If I was satisfied there had been a fraud, I would be more able to answer you, sir."

"Come now, Bragg, you sound like an expert witness covering up his ignorance."

"I am out of my depth," Bragg replied with a smile. "I will admit that to anybody. I decided last night that this man must have been at the center of the conspiracy—if there was one. And now I find him murdered."

"It seems to me," asserted Sir Rufus, "that the twin aims of justice and efficiency would best be served, if I requested that you be appointed coroner's officer for this case." He glared at Bragg. "Would that suit you?"

"It would of course have nothing whatever to do with . . ."

"Yes, or no, man?" Sir Rufus interrupted.

"Why, yes."

"Good, good. Now let me view the body."

Sir Rufus stepped round the desk. "Hmn. His last visitor wasn't exactly friendly," he remarked. He stooped down, and rolled the body onto its back again. "I never had much more than a rudimentary knowledge of pathology, even when I was a medical student; and that has been overlaid by thirty years of practicing law. However, from the general stiffness of the corpse, I would say he had been dead for several hours, wouldn't you?"

"No doubt of it, sir. Such blood as there is has completely dried."

"Murdered last night, then," Sir Rufus mused. "Anyway, that is for you. Clearly, there must be an inquest, and equally clearly I shall need medical evidence." He cocked an eye at Bragg. "In view of your other inquiries, would you be content with the divisional police surgeon, or would you want Professor Burney?"

"I would prefer to err on the side of caution."

"Right then, Burney it shall be. When you have finished poking about, Bragg, be good enough to have the body conveyed to the mortuary." With a curt nod, Sir Rufus strode out of the room.

Bragg sketched the position of the body on his pad, and made notes about the various objects in the room. Then he shouted for the manager. Jones came, bewildered and tense. Bragg perched himself on the corner of the desk nearest the battered head, in the hope that he would be drawn towards the corpse. But he stayed resolutely by the door, his eyes fixed on the window.

"What kind of a man was Mr. Ingham?" Bragg asked.

"He was all right. Better than some I've worked for."

"How long have you been here?"

"Ten years."

"So you dealt with the Green Funnel ships all that time?"

"Yes—here, you don't think it's anything to do with that, do you?"

"What do you mean?"

"I . . . well, I don't mean anything, really."

"Did Mr. Ingham have any enemies you know of?" asked Bragg casually.

"Not as you'd call enemies. Brokers are always trying to pinch each others' clients."

"Has he acquired any big clients recently, that other brokers dealt with previously?"

"No."

"Has he lost any big clients, then?"

"Not big ones. A couple of medium-sized ones, and some smaller ones. But none recently."

"The business was running down a bit then?"

"It is not an easy time at the moment. Trade is slackening, and British yards are building more and more ships for foreign owners, nowadays."

"The insurance broking would be all right, though, wouldn't it? Lloyd's is still the only marine market to speak of."

"I suppose so, though most of the business came from the

ships we managed. And, anyway, he has two partners in that business."

"So he was under financial pressure, was he?"

"I should say that he was. He wouldn't even let us hold a stock of envelopes. I had to send an office-boy out for them, a hundred at a time."

"And in the fashion of his kind," remarked Bragg sympathetically, "I expect he took it out on you."

"If you haven't got a dog, you kick the cat," replied Jones with the ghost of a smile.

"Did you quarrel with your employer last evening?" asked Bragg harshly.

"Oh my God!" The man's face went ashen, and his horrified eyes seemed to protude from his head. "No, I never . . . I couldn't have a row with him, I'd have got the sack."

"But it all boiled up inside you, didn't it? All the slights and the snide remarks, the mistakes he made and blamed you for. Then yesterday, your self-restraint snapped, and you hit back at him. And since you would get the push, your only hope was to finish him off properly. That's what happened, isn't it? . . . isn't it?"

"No . . . no." His voice was barely audible, and Bragg thought he was going to faint. "I shall lose my job anyway. There's no one here to carry on. The other firms will carve up the business."

"Then tell me what happened," Bragg demanded.

"Nothing, really. It was much like any other day."

"Was he in the office when you went home?"

"Yes. I went in as usual, last thing."

"Did he have anything to say to you?"

"Nothing special. He told me to leave the street door unlocked, as he was expecting someone."

"Who was it?"

"I do not know."

"Did he ask for any files or papers, for the meeting?"

"No."

"Where is his diary?"

Jones began to walk around the desk, then halted abruptly.

"For Christ's sake," said Bragg harshly, "he's only dead. You won't catch anything. If you're that squeamish, get something to cover him up with . . . And while you are at it, get me the files on the *Dancing Lady*."

Jones disappeared, and Bragg began to go through the drawers of the desk. He soon found the diary, but there was no entry after lunch-time on the sixth of June. He turned back over the previous couple of months. There seemed to be no pattern in the entries, no indication of an important series of meetings that might have gone wrong.

Jones returned with a slim folder, and placed it on the desk. Then with a kind of awkward reverence, he drew a table-cloth over the upper part of Ingham's body.

"There's a drawer that is locked here," remarked Bragg. "The bottom right-hand one. See if you can find a key for it, will you?"

Jones went out, and Bragg settled down to examine the *Dancing Lady* papers. They began with the letter from Michel Tissier et Cie asking Ingham to arrange a charter. Bragg was surprised at this, since he had understood that the ship-broking business was independent. Perhaps Ingham was saving the cost of a separate office. Anyway, it was useful to have it. Next was a draft of the demise charter of the ship, and a cutting from some newspaper of an advertisement for cargo for a voyage to New Orleans. Above that was a letter from Thurgood & Jackson, inquiring about space for a cotton-seed mill; then a draft letter of instructions to them, concerning the dispatch of the cargo, and the freight terms. Next there was a bundle of tally cards held together by an elastic band, and on top was the copy of the bill of lading for the cotton-seed mill, dated the eighth of January. It was made out to "Order," and had been endorsed on behalf of Thurgood & Jackson, and signed by B. Gadd. It all seemed innocent, and in apple-pie order. But there should be more. Morton's cable had said that De Wolf had telegraphed some export agents in Manchester about the non-arrival of the cargo, and had received a reply from Taylor Pendrill & Co. Where was that correspondence?

"I'm sorry, sergeant," Jones poked his head around the door. "We don't have any spare keys to Mr. Ingham's desk. The only ones are on his key ring."

"They'll probably be on the body, then. Come in, Mr. Jones . . . Are these the only papers concerning that last voyage of the *Dancing Lady*?"

"So far as I am aware, they are." Jones advanced hesitantly into the room.

"You remember the cable from America asking why the oods were late? It was sent down from Manchester."

"Yes. Is that not in the pile?"

"No. Nor is your reply."

"That's funny."

"You are sure there are no other papers in the general ffice?"

"I'm certain, sergeant."

"Right." Bragg pulled aside the tablecloth and systematical-y emptied Ingham's pockets. They contained little of interest, personal letter, some small change, a wallet containing six ve-pound notes, and a bunch of keys. At the third attempt he ound a key that fitted the locked drawer, and opened it. Inside vas a manila folder.

"What have we here?" Bragg murmured. "It looks like the apers we were looking for."

"That's right," said Jones, peering over Bragg's shoulder. I would swear I tagged them on the file. I wonder why he put nem in there?"

"Now here's a joker," said Bragg triumphantly. Beneath the apers was a bundle of bills of lading. "What do you know bout these?" he asked.

"I have never seen them before," Jones said with a frown.

"Whose is the writing?"

"Why, that's Mr. Ingham's."

"The first one is for twelve crates of china, being consigned y the Spode works, via the *ss Dancing Lady*, to New Orleans or some merchants in Memphis, Tennessee. What do you now about that?"

"Nothing."

"But you must do. It's been signed by the ship's master, so ne cargo must have been loaded."

"There are no tally cards, are there?"

"Ah, but if it had been loaded alongside, or from a lighter, ou wouldn't have tally cards, would you?"

"I suppose not," Jones's worried frown deepened. "Though nere should be a mate's receipt."

"Let's look at the next one, shall we?" said Bragg auntingly. "It's . . . Good God!, it's just like the first one."

He spread the bills of lading out on the desk, there were five in all, and the details were identical on each.

"How many do you make out in a set?" demanded Bragg.

"Six, usually."

"So if this was a complete set, who would have the missing one?"

Jones looked at the documents in perplexity. "The master has to have a copy, as part of the ship's manifest. It is of no value, because it isn't signed, so no one can collect cargo with it."

"What's to stop him signing it, once he's safely out of British waters? He could sell it to anybody, and deliver the cargo by virtue of it . . . Ben Gadd, eh? Well, well."

CHAPTER

EIGHT

"If the cargo of the *Dancing Lady* was diverted from New Orleans to Galveston, the master must have been a party to it," remarked Morton.

"I suppose so," said Ryan, non-committally.

They were sitting in chairs on the top deck of the ship, soaking up the sun. For the first three days out of New York, there had been a high sea running, and this had seemed to affect Ryan's condition. Morton had thought that it was the rolling motion of the vessel, reviving the residual concussion he had suffered. Whatever the reason, he had been violently sea-sick, and confined to his cabin. On the fourth day the wind had subsided, and the sea had become calm. Now, tucked up in a blanket, he seemed to Morton no better than he had been when they left New Orleans. But at least he was lucid, and willing to converse.

"What was the master's name?" asked Morton.

"Ben Gadd."

"What kind of a man was he?"

"A madman. He was not fit to be in command of a ship."

"Why do you say he was mad?"

"He got violent when he was crossed. Everybody was afraid of him, even his officers. I've seen him threaten to strike the engineer, because the boiler was too leaky to give him an extra knot of speed. Everything he did was kind of crazy."

"When did this manifest itself?"

"You could say right from the start of the voyage. We sailed on the twelfth of January, and all I'd got to eat was a couple of sausages. I made them last till I thought we were well into the Atlantic, and then I went foraging. The lascars caught me, of course, and the mate locked me up in a cabin. That was during the night of the fourteenth. But I had misjudged the speed the ship was capable of, and when I looked out of the port-hole next morning, I could see land. It just had to be Ireland. I waited for the ship to alter course into Bantry Bay, and put me ashore practically where I'd started from. But it just kept going."

"That is interesting," said Morton. "It was almost as if he was reluctant to put into a British port once he had left London."

"We were almost out of sight of land, before the mate came for me. I said something about their having taken their time. He laughed, and said the coastguards would have put away their telescopes."

"So he suspected that something underhand was going on?"

"He must have been in on it. They all must have. Any vessel going to the Caribbean takes the old sailing-ship route and goes south to catch the trade winds from Africa. Yet we were making for New York, in the teeth of a westerly gale. It didn't make sense."

"And what did the master say to you?"

"At first he was all right; a bit abrupt, but civil. I told him I was a ship's engineer, that I had stowed away because I had no money, and was desperate to get back to New Orleans; then I offered to work my passage. At that he went crazy. He pulled a revolver out of his reefer pocket, and made them put me in chains and lock me in the cabin again."

"You had not expected such treatment?"

"You're kidding me! It was as if I were a convict."

"I suppose you had broken the law, by stowing away," remarked Morton.

"Hell, yes. But I wasn't a bum, I was a seaman. And they could have used me, that's for sure. Five days out, the wind worsened and we began shipping water. In the end they had to release me to help with the pumps."

"So you were free after that?"

"No, sir. When I woke up next morning, the cabin door was locked again. But at least I was rid of the chains, they were feeding me, and we were going to New Orleans, so why should I worry? The other officers were a bit more reasonable with me, too. Doig, the engineer, would come to play chess with me, when he felt he could leave the engine-room for an hour."

"Did he not have an assistant?"

"No. He would have had me for his second, if he'd had his way, but Gadd wouldn't hear of it. If you ask me, the whole ship was under-manned. There wasn't even a second-mate; and they'd cut down on the lascars too, or they wouldn't have needed me on the pumps."

"Are you suggesting that it was deliberate?"

"Sure. I don't know about British ships, but no American vessel could put to sea so short of men, and I guess your laws are no different than ours."

"This would be the regulations relating to safety at sea?"

"Right. It was obvious when we got to Bermuda. There wasn't enough crew to have handled the sails, if the engine had broken down. Not that they had to for long . . ." he snorted derisively.

"What is amusing you?"

"Oh, another of the crazy things Gadd got up to. Doig suddenly appeared in my cabin one morning, and said he needed me to help strip down the engine. I asked him what for, because I could hear the thing clunking on as usual. He said the master had told him he had four hours to dismantle it, and he wasn't for asking why."

"So what happened?"

"We doused the boiler fire, and when it had cooled down enough, we began to take the engine apart. In the meantime we could hear the crew manning the sails. By the end of the four hours we had bits strewn all over the engine room, and Doig was satisfied. So we went up for some air, and there we were, clawing our way into Hamilton harbor."

"Whatever was it all about?" asked Morton.

"I don't know. In the afternoon, a well-dressed landsman came aboard. He seemed more concerned not to get grease on his trousers than anything else. Doig spun him a yarn about vibration, and worn bearings, and the crankshaft being out of true; and the guy could see for himself the state of the boiler. Gadd said he would have to sail to Charleston, Carolina, to get them repaired. The swank seemed to be demurring about something, and Gadd took him back on deck. That was the last I saw of him."

"So what happened?"

"About six that evening, Gadd came back in a tearing hurry. He ordered Doig to put it all back together again, and we started tacking out of the harbor. So long as we were in sight of Bermuda, we made for Charleston; but as soon as the engine was reassembled, we got up steam, and he changed course for the Bahamas."

"I wonder what on earth could have been behind that," Morton mused.

"I never found out. I don't think Doig himself knew. So far as I was concerned, it did me some good—perhaps because I didn't try to jump ship. Anyway, after that they didn't lock me up, and I used to help the cook in the galley."

"Were there any other bizarre incidents?" asked Morton.

"Not on that leg, except that I once made to look in the aft hold, and the mate nearly went beserk. If Gadd had been on watch, I reckon I'd have been shark's meat . . . Another time, after we had passed the Bahamas, I went into the chart room, looking for empty mugs. There was no one there, and I had a good look on the table. There was a chart of the Gulf of Mexico, and two crosses on it. One was on the coast, and the other was a short distance out to sea. I was just checking on the scale of the chart when I heard a step, and Gadd came in. By then I was well away from it, but all the same he went crazy. Lucky for me I had a couple of dirty plates in my hands . . . After that I kept out of his way."

"What did you do when the ship did not call at New Orleans?" asked Morton.

"Nothing. I was aware of it, of course. I have sailed along that coast for ten years, and I reckon I know every creek and inlet there is. But I had not told them that. I was leaning over the starboard rail, when I saw the mouth of the Mississippi and realized we were sailing past. The mate was on watch, and I turned to shout that we should alter course . . . Then I saw the look on his face, strained, almost desperate, and kind of hunted."

"Then what happened?"

"Something totally unexpected. That night, Doig and the mate invited me to a celebration."

"What of?"

"They didn't say. But they broke open a case of whisky, and we went at it with mugs. I hadn't even smelled a drink for six weeks, and I wasn't for passing up this chance. Not that they stinted me. If ever they saw my mug was half-empty, they would top it up, and it wasn't long before I was rolling drunk. I remember them helping me down to my bunk, then I must have passed out. When I came to, it was still dark, and the ship was riding at anchor with the engine stopped. I could hear voices—American voices—calling from below, and the screech of the ship's derricks. I looked out of the port-hole, and saw that they were unloading big wooden crates over the side, onto lighters. I could not think where we were. There were a few scattered lights in the distance, so we were just offshore, but I didn't recognize it. I climbed off my bunk to go on deck, but my door was locked, so I went back to sleep. I was awakened by the noise of the engine, and peered out. The sky was beginning to lighten, and I realized that the ship had turned around and was steaming eastward; and on the starboard bow was the port of Galveston."

"Were you absolutely sure?" asked Morton.

"See here, James, I've sailed into that harbor twenty times a year for ten years. There was no way I could have been wrong. What they had done was to sail down the channel between Galveston Island and the mainland, and way past the port. All I saw, when I looked out during the night, were the few homesteads along the shore. But when we sailed back, I couldn't mistake it. Anyway, I watched as we went round the headland, and out of Galveston Bay."

"So what happened next morning?"

"When I finally woke up, the door was unlocked. I went on deck as if nothing had happened. The officers looked at me speculatively, as if to invite questions, but I said nothing. I did not need confirmation. The *Dancing Lady* was riding high and frisky; it was obvious that a great deal of cargo had been off-loaded, without being replaced by ballast.''

"You did not trust any of them by this time?"

"Dead right! And they didn't trust me, not even Doig. I reckon they had already decided that I must never get back to America. It would have suited their book if I could have fallen overboard, but I wasn't obliging them. I kept away from the ship's rail, and from then on spent most of the time in the galley or my cabin.''

"Surely that would confirm their suspicions that you knew something odd was going on?"

"Maybe, but by then it didn't matter. In a way, everyone accepted that I had to be got rid of, it was just a matter of when they would try it. We sailed along the coast for three days, keeping out of sight of land once we were off Mexico. Then on the evening of the third day we hove to, and the mate proposed another drinking session. I went along with it, because I reckoned they didn't trust the lascars enough to murder me in front of them. This time the master joined in too, and they questioned me about where I had sailed in those waters. I made out that it was mostly to the eastern seaboard of the States, and across to Brazil and Venezuela. I don't know whether they believed me or not, but they stopped questioning me after a time. I drank as little as I could get away with, and pretended to be drunker than I was. About midnight they helped me down to my cabin, and I heard them lock the door.''

"The same procedure as before," remarked Morton.

"Almost exactly so. There was little or no cloud that night, and as we crept in to the shore, I could make out an estuary. We dropped anchor, and I heard the hatch covers coming off the aft hold. Then some lights showed ashore, and soon several small boats emerged from the mouth of the river. As they approached, I could see that each was being rowed by four men, and from their lingo, I guessed that they were Mexican Indians. I counted a dozen wooden boxes being lowered into the boats, most of them rectangular. Then they pulled away, and we raised anchor. We steamed out to sea, and as I didn't expect anything else to happen, I went to sleep.

"When I awoke next morning," Ryan went on, "everything seemed unusually quiet. The engine was stopped, and nothing seemed to be happening on deck. I listened for a while, but I couldn't even hear the lascars chattering to each other. Then I realized there was something different about the motion of the ship, she was heavy and sluggish, and the noise of the waves seemed to be close to my ear. I swung off my bunk, and dropped into a foot of water. The damned ship was sinking! I wrenched at the door, but it was locked. It was made of solid mahogany, and as it opened inward, there was no chance of breaking the lock. I even opened the port-hole, but I knew I could never get my shoulders through. And all the time the water was inching upward. My only chance was to break through the upper panel of the door. There was no implement I could use, and I hammered at it with my fists till they were bleeding, but it wasn't even dented. What I needed was to get my boots at it. I tried leaping up and kicking it, but there wasn't enough room to bring any force to bear. I had given up, and was trying to remember a few prayers, when I noticed that the bunk was only secured by a few small screws. I wrenched it away from the bulkhead, and wedged it across the cabin. Now I could lie on top, and pound the panel with my heels. I battered it for an age, then it began to splinter. By now the water was up to the lock. It took me a frenzied five minutes, before the hole was big enough for me to wriggle through. I waded along the passage and climbed on deck. Three of the four lifeboats were gone; I thought I could see them away on the horizon. I dashed to the last one, hoping I could launch it on my own, but I might as well have saved my energy. The bastards had staved it in. So they intended that I should drown.

"I guess I went a little crazy myself. Instead of getting out of it, I lowered myself into the aft hold, and ducking down under the water I eventually found a sea-cock. It was wide open, and the wheel had been removed. It was a deliberate scuttle, and I was meant to go down with it. By the time I got on deck again, the ship was beginning to settle. It was my good fortune that they had not bothered to replace the hatch covers. I managed to maneuver one over the rail and jumped after it. I paddled like hell with a piece of broken plank, and just got far enough away to avoid being sucked under as she went down."

"And were you picked up?"

"No such luck. There I was without food or water, without even a pole to tie my shirt to. And there are some damned

hungry fish in those waters. I reckoned I was a goner . . .
The breeze and the current must have brought me ashore. I
knew very little about it. I remember the fierce heat of the sun,
and my lips cracking with thirst. The next I knew I was being
cradled by a native woman, feeding me coconut milk. They
looked after me for over a week, till I recovered my strength,
and my burns healed somewhat. Once, they took me to the
beach and showed me my raft. It had come ashore not a
hundred yards from the estuary I had seen from the *Dancing
Lady*."

"Had they encountered the other members of her crew?"
asked Morton.

"They said they had seen them rowing up the river, but I
can't say what truth there was in it. I never saw any of them
again."

"And how did you get back to America?"

"I just walked out of the village one morning, and foot-
slogged it back. Was I glad to see the Rio Grande!"

"And where do you think the scuttle took place?"

"It's not a question of thinking. You remember the chart
with the two crosses? One was on the coast at the estuary, the
other was some miles out to sea. It was all planned down to the
minute."

"But where was it?"

"Off Poza Rica, south of Tampico."

CHAPTER ──────────
────────── NINE

Mr. Kenyon of Carrington Umpleby & Co. was a short man, with a shock of white hair, and an urbane manner.

"The bottomry bond?" he repeated in a desiccated voice. "Ah yes, an interesting case."

"I understand," said Bragg, "that if the ship does not complete its voyage, the money lent is not repayable. Can I ask why the Bank of Bermuda is suing for repayment?"

"As to that," Kenyon replied, "I suspect that the officials of the bank are under some pressure from the shareholders, and want to be seen to be striving to retrieve the position. My instructions contained detailed reports from the officials to the directors of the bank, which are obviously exercises in self-justification. It is my view, from such evidence as is available to me, that the manager who granted the bonds had initial doubts, but suppressed them because the master of the ship agreed to a higher than normal rate of interest. It is the usual story of greed clouding judgment, though it does not often occur with subordinate employees."

"You said 'bonds,'" remarked Bragg. "Was there more than one?"

"There were two, but both to the same purpose. The master requested an advance of seventeen thousand pounds for urgent repairs to the engine and boiler. The bank official who inspected the ship was of the opinion that it was in a seaworthy condition, and as such was a good risk. The master had to admit, however, that the hull was insured for twelve thousand pounds only, which meant that the bottomry bond must be limited to that figure. The master then produced bills of lading and insurance certificates for the cargo, so the bank agreed to advance the other five thousand pounds under a second bond."

"What bills of lading did he produce?"

"One for thirty-two crates of machinery consigned to an agent in New Orleans, and valued at thirty thousand pounds; a second for a dozen crates of fine china for a merchant in Memphis, Tennessee, which were valued at six thousand five hundred pounds."

"I see."

"Having decided that it was money for jam, the bank official somewhat uncritically accepted the security offered. In his report he said, in terms, that even if the engine could not be repaired at Charleston, he had no doubt that the vessel could reach New Orleans under sail well before the hurricane season."

"I don't follow the Charleston bit," remarked Bragg.

"The master had expressed the intention of proceeding to Charleston in South Carolina to have repairs carried out. You must understand that there are no facilities in Bermuda for such work."

"But the ship was lost, possibly scuttled. Is that why you are suing for repayment?"

"It is by no means the case that failure to complete a voyage because a ship was scuttled invalidates a bottomry bond. If, for instance, a master raised money for genuine repairs which were in fact carried out; and if thereafter he scuttled the ship without the knowledge of the owners, then there might well be no breach of the terms of the bond."

"You mean that the loan would not be repayable?"

"That is correct. In this case, however, my clients have established that the *Dancing Lady* did not call at Charleston for repairs, or, indeed, anywhere else so far as they have been able to ascertain."

"Perhaps the master discovered that the engine didn't need these expensive repairs after all. What then?"

"I must confess that the position is somewhat obscure," replied Kenyon. "My clients would, naturally, take the view that since the need for which the advance was made did not eventuate, then the loan agreement was void, and the money should be returned."

"Harvey & Crane are saying that you are alleging fraud."

"Yes, indeed. It seems to be accepted that the vessel was scuttled, and we shall argue that the master never had an intention of using the money for the repairs that he alleged were necessary."

"But from what you say, you could only succeed against Harvey & Crane if you could show that they were in on the fraud. You know, of course, that the ship was chartered?"

"Yes, we are aware of that. We shall argue that since a bottomry bond is taken out essentially to save the ship, then the owner of the vessel must be liable for repayment, in despite of any charter."

"And will you succeed?"

Kenyon pursed his lips. "I would say that the outcome is problematical. However, while we have been talking, another line of argument has struck me. After all, the master could have completed the voyage envisaged in the bonds, by calling at New Orleans. In fact, we understand that he sailed beyond that port, and the vessel was lost thereafter. Yes, I think we could contend that the voyage had been constructively completed . . . thank you, sergeant, you have been of great assistance."

"And what about the other bond?"

"Since the master is theoretically pledging the cargo in an attempt to save both the ship and cargo, I would expect that if the court found in our favor, and we were for some reason unable to recover the whole advance from Harvey & Crane, we would be able to recover the balance from the cargo owners."

"It may be of interest to you," said Bragg, "that we have a warrant out for the arrest of Ben Gadd, and we have alerted the police in America and Europe to pick him up if they find him. If we lay our hands on him, I will let you know."

• • •

"I expected to see you before long, sergeant," said Burney, his loose mouth hanging in a smile. "Where is your favorite constable?"

"Investigating the American end of this case."

Burney cocked his head. "I thought it was the senior officers that claimed the perquisites."

"We are saving the taxpayers money, at his expense," replied Bragg. "Don't worry. He can afford it."

"I won't. I am a taxpayer myself. I suppose you have come about Ingham." He indicated the empty shell of a man's body on the marble slab.

"Yes."

"The strange thing is that nature might well have saved your murderer the trouble. Our friend there had advanced cirrhosis of the liver. All this heavy drinking the City people go in for."

"But there is no doubt that he was murdered, I take it?"

"None whatever," beamed the pathologist. "I derived considerable satisfaction from this one. I brought a few of my students up from Bart's this morning, while I was dissecting out the head."

Bragg glanced at the red shapeless mess that had once been a man's face. "I'm glad it has been of use to somebody."

"He provided an interesting, if fairly elementary, exercise in forensic medicine for them. I am grateful."

"Everybody seems to be grateful to me today, but I don't seem to be getting any further forward myself."

"Well, at least we can say that there was nothing casual about the attack. One would deduce that the killer was known to the victim, for he went to some trouble to ensure that he was dead."

"Why do you say that?" asked Bragg.

With a cherubic smile, Burney picked up a probe. "The way I reconstruct the attack, sergeant, is as follows. You will remember the injury to the right eye? I think that was the first blow, and it was probably totally unexpected, for there are no signs of injury on the hands or arms, such as one would find if an attempt had been made to ward off the attack."

"I imagine that Ingham was sitting in his chair, talking to someone perched on the corner of his desk," remarked Bragg.

"That could well be so. It was certainly a sudden, savage, and rather lucky blow."

"Lucky?"

"Yes, because as we proceed, you will realize how easily things might have gone wrong for our murderer. You see here?" He indicated delicately a jagged edge of bone. "That is where the line of the eye-socket should run. The blow was in a downward direction, just missing the frontal bone and crushing the eye-ball to a pulp. There was considerable force behind the blow, because the floor of the orbit—the eye-socket, if you will—has been disrupted downwards into the maxillary sinus."

"And would that kill him?"

"Very probably, in time; but not immediately. It would, however, render him unconscious." Burney gave a ghoulish smile. "Then follows the series of blows to the head, which give me grounds for surmise that the attacker wanted him dead. There are seven in all, delivered with some force, but six of them struck the thicker bones of the cranium, and, while they caused severe contusions, did not fracture the skull. That tells us something about the nature of the weapon used, sergeant."

"I think I may have discovered it."

"Then do not spoil my pleasure by telling me about it . . . The last blow—last in sequence of consideration, but not necessarily the last to be delivered—struck the relatively weak bones of the temple and fractured them. Ingham lived for a time after it, however, and there was considerable bleeding into the cranium from the damaged meningeal artery, which would have compressed the brain and killed him in time." Burney grinned slyly at Bragg.

"So you are telling me that did not kill him either."

"Correct, sergeant. I told you it was interesting." He beckoned Bragg to a side table on which lay a bloody pile of entrails. "This is the answer," he said, pointing with his probe. "Here is the upper part of the windpipe, and the voice box. Now, you see this little bone?"

Bragg swallowed hard. "Yes."

"It is one of the horns of the thyroid cartilage. The only time it is fractured in this way is by the pressure of a thumb."

"Strangulation?" exclaimed Bragg in surprise.

"Without doubt. The conclusion is supported by various

other indicators, such as bruising on the front and back of the neck, and tiny haemmorrhages in the capillaries of the remaining eye.''

"He was certainly for making sure," remarked Bragg pensively. "Can you tell me anything about the attacker?"

"There is an interaction here between the build of the man and the weapon he used. We must assume that he was unable to produce death by repeated blows with the weapon, hence his resort to manual strangulation. We must then proceed on the hypothesis that he could have been of small build, and the weapon adequate, or that the weapon itself was of such a size that it was useless for the task. In testing this, one has to remember that the victim was unconscious throughout."

"And which is it?"

Burney's mouth sagged open in a smile. "The injuries to both the orbit and the temple suggest impact by a hard object, possibly metal, with square corners, about two inches long and half an inch deep. It must have had some kind of projection to act as a handle, but not one long enough to increase by much the force of the blow. I see the wounds as having been made by something like the plinth of an ornament, and the striker as being of no more than average build . . . Well?" he asked expectantly.

"I found a marble statuette under the body. It was blood-stained, and the base would have been about the size you mention."

"That would do very well, sergeant," remarked Burney with relish. "Yes, it would do very well."

Bragg rapped on the door of the shabby, workman's house in Stepney. Coming from the country, he always felt a sense of guilt at seeing these monotonous rows of mean houses and dirty streets. How could one expect anything wholesome or vital to exist in such depressing surroundings? Best tear them all down, and start afresh.

The door opened, and a man's head appeared. "Hello," he said in a cheery voice. "What's this, then? Collecting for charity, are you?"

"Sergeant Bragg, City Police," said Bragg gruffly, waving his warrant-card.

"Very nice," remarked the man.

"Are you Bert Knowles?"

"I am. D'you want to see me?"

"I'd like a few words."

"Come in then, I was just having my supper, I'm on duty in an hour." He ushered Bragg into a sparsely furnished kitchen at the back of the house. "Annie, love," he called to his buxom wife, "give the sergeant a cup of tea, I can see he's parched."

"Am I right in thinking that you are a night-watchman at the West Indies docks?"

"That's right," assented Knowles cheerfully. "The export dock, number three warehouse."

"Is that the one which contains the dock office?"

"That's right."

"Good. I am told that you were on duty throughout January."

"Yes, I was. I got bronchitis at the beginning of February, and I was off for five weeks. Still, I'm all right again now."

"I want you to cast your mind back to the ninth of January, when a freighter called the *Dancing Lady* tied up, right opposite that warehouse."

"A little one, was it?"

"So I am told."

"And a bit battered?"

"I would not be at all surprised."

"Yes, I remember it. I used to try and talk to the serang in his own lingo. He's the boss of the lascars—quite important, too, in their eyes. I was stationed in Bombay for a few years."

"Indian Army?"

"Right. I was a quartermaster-sergeant by the time I came out."

"Good going, that," said Bragg warmly. "I can imagine you keep a keen eye open at the docks."

"It's my job," replied Knowles simply.

"There's a bit of mystery about the ship," went on Bragg. "I will not bore you with the details, because I don't understand them properly myself. The ship loaded its cargo on the tenth—that is according to the dock manager—but it did not sail until noon on the twelfth of January. On the face of it then, they were paying dock fees for no purpose."

"Wait a minute. I remember now. They were still loading her when I came on duty the night before she sailed. There were a lot of crates, of all sizes. They'd had to store one down in number seven warehouse, because it was too big to go in ours . . . And the dockers loading the next ship wouldn't le them bring it down the quay till they'd finished loading theirs It was dark when they brought it up, and they had to rearrange the crates they'd loaded, so as to get it in the hold.''

"Why did they bother to do that, when they had a second hold?" asked Bragg.

"They could have put it aft, certainly. The other cargo wasn't going to take up all that much room."

"The crates of china, you mean?"

"I don't know about that," grinned Knowles. "They drove up in two covered vans that same night—at about three o'clock in the morning. There were two men and a foreman. It must have been just before the ship sailed, because the officers and crew were there."

"So you do not think it was china."

"Well, some of them might have been," replied Knowles cautiously. "There were a couple of square boxes that could have been anything."

"And the others?"

"No mistaking them. There weren't no markings on them or anything like that, but I've seen hundreds like them while I was serving."

"What was in them then?"

"Rifles, sergeant. That's what was in them—rifles."

As his hansom rattled over the setts on its way back to Old Jewry, Bragg tried to re-evaluate what he knew, in the light of Knowles's assertion. That he believed it, there was no shadow of doubt, and he had more experience of such things than most men. No doubt there were other commodities which had to be packed in long rectangular wooden boxes, though for the life of him, Bragg could not think of any. But, in that case, why the secrecy? Why dash in during the night, when the regular dockers were off duty? And why load them at the last possible moment, before the very tide on which the ship would sail? One thing was sure, you didn't pack china in the kind of crates you needed for rifles. Bragg clumped up the stairs, wishing he could have had half an hour with Ingham before his murder and found a yellow telegraph envelope on his desk. He tore at the flap.

"Ah, Bragg," Sir William Sumner came into the room. "I just thought I would see how you were getting on."

"At the moment, sir, I feel that somebody is out to make a monkey of us. Look at this."

The Commissioner took the cable. "The information requested concerning Lebrun Barré et Cie is not available," he translated.

"I thought that was its drift," said Bragg savagely. "That's from the Sûreté. It's a lot of bloody rubbish! It's got to be. Are you telling me that the Sûreté can't find out who owns that company? Somebody has put up the shutters, that's what."

"It certainly looks like that," Sir William agreed uncomfortably.

"I wish John Goddard had his fraud case stuffed up . . ."

"Now Bragg, there's nothing to be gained by getting angry. We must do our best, but once we can demonstrate that we have explored every avenue, then no one can criticize us."

"First the Americans, now the French; we'll be investigating the whole world before long."

"That was Goddard's theory right from the start, wasn't it?" said the Commissioner gloomily. "An international conspiracy to destroy the City . . . We can hardly discontinue our inquiries on the grounds that another foreign country is involved."

"There is one aspect that can only be dealt with at your level, sir," said Bragg.

"What is that?" asked Sir William suspiciously.

"When I went through Ingham's desk, I found a bundle of five bills of lading, for Spode china which was being sent to New Orleans."

"Ingham is the man who was murdered yesterday, isn't he?"

"That's right, sir. I am convinced that he was involved in this business, right up to his neck."

"Very well, go on."

"These bills of lading were not on the office file for the voyage, they were locked away in a desk drawer with some papers relating to the ship's failure to arrive at New Orleans. The office manager swore he had never seen them, and in the ordinary course he should have. Again, these bills should have been sent out—to the shipper, the agent in New Orleans, the consignee in Memphis. We know that Ingham's firm produces a set of six bills as a rule; and we know that one was produced to the Bank of Bermuda by the master, in support of a request for funds of repairs that were never carried out.''

"Are you saying the cargo of china was fictitious, Bragg?''

"I believe you are right, sir. I had a word with the nightwatchman at the West India docks. He says that it was not china in the crates, but rifles.''

Sir William raised his eyebrows in surprise. "And is he reliable, this watchman?''

"I do believe so, sir. He is an ex-Q.M.S. in the Indian Army; he says he saw similar boxes every day of his life.''

"Yes, no doubt he did.''

"I wonder if you could clear up one point for us, sir?''

"What's that?'' asked Sir William doubtfully.

"Could you find out if there were any official shipments of arms made from West India dock in January?''

"Hmn . . . They would know at the War Department, I suppose—unless they were for the navy, and the Admiralty would tell us then, I'm sure. Yes, Bragg, I'll see what I can do.''

CHAPTER _____
_____ TEN

"Are you the gentlemen who have come to see Mr. Stanton?" asked the liveried messenger.

"Yes, we are," replied Goddard.

"Would you come this way, please?"

He led them along a corridor, and ushered them into a large well-furnished room. A desk stood on one side of the fireplace, and by the window was a long polished table.

"If you would be good enough to be seated, gentlemen," said the messenger gravely, "Mr. Stanton will be with you shortly." He gestured toward the chairs around the table, and withdrew.

"What's going on, Hozier?" exclaimed Goddard irritably. "You are secretary of Lloyd's, why did you not insist on knowing, before committing us to this ridiculous waste of time?"

"One is not summoned to the Foreign Office every day, Goddard," replied Hozier in his precise voice. "It would be folly to get off on the wrong foot, by a display of impatience."

"Impatience?" echoed Goddard. "We have been cooling

our heels in that waiting room for half an hour already." He sat down grumpily, and the others followed his example.

"This business will not be to our advantage," observed Whitlock darkly. "The less you have to do with officials of any kind, the better for you."

"Come now, Peter," said Frankis mildly, "we are not buccaneers. We live in a civilized society, and it is natural that the government should want to talk to commercial people."

"What? With an election coming up?" Whitlock snorted derisively.

"It has never happened before, has it?" asked Goddard.

"Not in my years as secretary," replied Hozier, "and I go back a good long way."

At that moment the door opened, and a slim erect man entered.

"My name is Stanton," he said.

Frankis rose to his feet, and the others hesitantly followed suit. Stanton reached the chair at the head of the table, and indicated that they should be seated.

"First, I must apologize for keeping you waiting, gentlemen. I was unexpectedly called to see the Foreign Secretary."

He was a handsome man of around fifty, his clothes good and discreet.

"By way of preamble," he began in a light musical voice, "I should explain that for some years we have followed a policy of occasional informal meetings with the principal industries having interests abroad—concerns like shipping, manufacturing and banking. The advantages are obvious. The officials in the Foreign Office become aware of the difficulties and opportunities in the mercantile area, and can take due account of them when framing policy recommendations to government. We like to feel, also, that an awareness of our national aspirations has helped industry to direct their efforts in harmony with them."

"There is nothing new in this," he went on. "It is merely formalizing a partnership which has evolved over the last century, and which has played an important part in the establishing of colonies, and the expansion of our empire. Every government since the turn of the century has regarded it as of cardinal importance that political and commercial policies should go hand in hand. Up to now, the insurance industry has not been involved in this process. I would not wish you to think that your commercial importance was in any way unrecognized. I personally regard Lloyd's as the third pillar of the City, with the Bank of England, and the Stock Exchange. And the City is beyond doubt the most important commercial center in the world. I have always thought it odd," he observed with a smile, "that the political head of the City—the Lord Mayor—should be rewarded with a baronetcy for mainly ceremonial duties, while the three men who largely control the economic destiny of the empire—the Governor of the Bank of England, the Chairman of the Stock Exchange, and the Chairman of Lloyd's—have no such recognition. However, I am sure that will be remedied, in time."

Stanton glanced down at a sheet of paper in front of him. "For this inaugural meeting it was thought appropriate to invite members from the administration of the Society of Lloyd's, in the persons of Col. Hozier and Mr. Goddard; and also two working underwriters, being Mr. Frankis and Mr. Whitlock—though I gather," he added, "that Mr. Goddard is distinguished in both categories."

Goddard smiled modestly.

"I feel," went on Stanton, "that the reason Lloyd's has not become a part of the consultative process before, is that the world's marine insurance market is situated in London; and that although you have an extensive network of information-gathering centers abroad, you have no significant competitors there, and your foreign customers come to you here. In the context of our preponderant share of the world's shipping, it has been felt that our general open stance on trade has been enough to promote your interests. I would be glad to have your comments on that, and, indeed, to hear of any specific problems you have of a major nature."

The four Lloyd's men shifted uneasily in their chairs, looking at each other.

"I do not believe that we have any serious problems," said Hozier at length. "There is always trouble in actually collecting the premiums, of course, but that is hardly an area the government could intervene in."

Stanton smiled in agreement.

"There is one thing," said Goddard. "We are experiencing a marked increase in both the incidence and size of fraudulent insurance claims—or at least claims which we are convinced are fraudulent." He looked around the table and drew nods of assent from Frankis and Whitlock. "We have decided that we must take action to stem these frauds, and even now, the City police are investigating a case for us. The problem they appear to have encountered is that since the apparent perpetrators of the frauds are abroad, they cannot carry out a complete investigation themselves. Even when they send a detective officer to the foreign country involved, he can only question people by courtesy of the local police. You can imagine that in some countries no great effort would be expanded to arrive at the truth."

Stanton gave a superior smile. "I am sure you realize," he said, "that this is a subject of great delicacy. Every country guards its jurisdiction very jealously. We ourselves would take great exception to, say, Russian policemen coming unheralded to our country and interrogating our citizens. However, I will see what can be done. What is the case you have in mind?"

"It involves the scuttling of a ship called the *Dancing Lady*, and the diversion of her cargo."

"Ah yes. She was bound for New Orleans, was she not?"

"That's right."

"I am glad you reminded me of that. I wanted to have a word with you about it." He leaned back in his chair, and steepling his fingers, put them to his lips in thought. "I fear," he began, "that this is a case where the interests of Her Majesty's Government and the interests of Lloyd's do not appear to march together. And, because of the nature of the area, the potential conflict could be damaging to this country. Central America and the Caribbean together form an extremely volatile and sensitive political area. On the one hand there are the newly emergent nations, formed by rebellion against the Spanish empire. On the other hand we have our own colonies, which are of vital strategic and economic importance to Britain, and which we must keep tranquil and free from revolutionary influences. Naturally, I cannot disclose to you the reasons why the alleged loss of the *Dancing Lady* impinges so nearly on our vital interests; nor would you wish me so to do. I am to say, however, that there is a great deal more at stake than the value of a ship and its cargo. Her Majesty's Government would be greatly obliged if Lloyd's would abandon any resistance to the payment of insurance claims, and withdraw any pressure for police investigations into the circumstances of the loss."

• • •

"It is good of you to come, gentlemen," said Goddard perfunctorily. "You have now had some time to digest this morning's discussion at the Foreign Office."

"Discussion?" echoed Whitlock. "Lecture, more like it. I cannot remember that we contributed anything."

"However that may be," went on Goddard, "it is clear that Her Majesty's Government wants these *Dancing Lady* claims settled without further fuss. What is at stake?"

"The hull and machinery policy is valued at twelve thousand pounds," replied Frankis.

"There is more at stake than money," Whitlock objected.

"Well, let us stick to the money for the moment. What cargo insurances had we?" asked Goddard.

"The cotton-seed mill was insured for thirty thousand pounds," replied Whitlock. "I know of no other cargo—or at least none insured at Lloyd's."

"Those figures are hardly worth losing the goodwill of the government over," remarked Goddard.

"So who are you proposing should pay the claims?" asked Whitlock sardonically. "The Society of Lloyd's?"

"You know perfectly well, Peter, that the Society is only a regulatory body, without any disposable funds."

"Then who pays?"

"During lunch I had a word with Lord Revelstoke, and several members of the committee. It was felt that the syndicates involved in the insurances should pay the claims, in the general interests of Lloyd's."

"That's a nice formula," snorted Whitlock. "'It was felt' . . . Is the committee going to direct us to pay?"

"You know perfectly well there can be no question of that."

"So John and I will not be expelled from Lloyd's if we refuse to pay."

"It would hardly be a matter within the disciplinary code," replied Goddard.

"But, by God, if we do pay we shall be in danger of expulsion."

"You would have the protection of the committee. In practice, it could never happen."

"And how do I explain to my names that I paid out on a large claim when I did not need to?" asked Whitlock.

Goddard's manner lost some of its composure. "The names

need never find out," he said testily. "What are managing agents for, if not to provide a barrier between the underwriter and the members of his syndicate?"

"So it does not matter whether the claim is valid or not, so long as the names are kept in ignorance of it?" persisted Whitlock.

Goddard flushed. "I am not saying that."

"I'm sure you are not, it's just that it sounded a bit like that."

Frankis intervened. "Not everything can be reduced to profit and loss terms, Peter; but it does not mean that there is no benefit to Lloyd's."

Goddard took a deep breath, and resumed in a level voice. "Take it from me that there are occasions, when, for reasons of high policy, a syndicate is asked to pay a claim for the good of all."

"I have never heard of any," asserted Whitlock.

Goddard smiled thinly. "Well, you wouldn't, would you?"

"In my view," said Whitlock emphatically, "if the settlement of these claims is for the good of all, then all should pay."

"There is no machinery that would enable that to be done," replied Goddard. "But let me assure you that if the committee of the Society had funds at its own disposal—funds that were unaccountable—then it would most certainly pay these claims."

Whitlock narrowed his eyes in thought. "It's no good," he said at length. "My responsibility is to act solely in the interests of the members of my own syndicate, and the names on the syndicates who followed my lead. If it were discovered, they would crucify me."

"I would have thought you had your names under better control than that," commented Goddard acidly.

"You could always tell them to resign," Frankis suggested. "I would."

"And what happens about the reinsurances?" asked Whitlock.

"You should make a claim under the contracts, in the normal way," Goddard advised. "That should convince you that the burden is being shared, at least to some extent, by the Lloyd's community at large."

"That is not good enough," said Whitlock. "Some of the reinsurances were placed with insurance companies. There is no way that they have even a moral obligation to pay out because of these claims."

"Surely the companies must also benefit from a harmonious relationship between the government and the insurance industry?" Frankis suggested.

"No," said Whitlock firmly. "What you are asking is dishonorable and I will not do it. I have a witness to the fact that the *Dancing Lady* deviated to Galveston, that the cargo was diverted to someone other than the consignee, and that the ship was subsequently scuttled. By tomorrow evening he will be safely tucked up in the De Keyser Hotel, and on Monday morning he will be in the witness-box giving his evidence to the High Court . . . Blast it! It was you, Goddard, who identified this as a fraud case in the first place."

"I know," said Goddard patiently. "And I have not changed my mind about that. Let me put it to you in this way. The underwriting agreements with the names give the underwriter untrammelled discretion; the maintenance of a fruitful relationship between Lloyd's and the government of the day must be a factor in the underwriter's judgment. No blame could possibly attach to you."

"This government has only a couple of weeks' life in it," replied Whitlock scornfully. "How do we know there will not be a Liberal government in office after the election?"

"God forbid," Frankis murmured.

"It is the departmental officials who are important in this area," replied Goddard irritably. "Surely so much must have become apparent to you as a result of this morning's meeting?"

"I'll tell you what," said Whitlock rising to his feet. "If you, as a member of the committee, will give me a written recommendation that for reasons that cannot be disclosed I should pay out on this claim, then I will do so."

"You know that cannot be done."

"That's it then."

"You always were stubborn, Peter," exclaimed Goddard in exasperation, "but surely even you must realize that we cannot flout the wishes of the government? I have to report to the chairman this evening. I hope that before five o'clock saner counsels will have prevailed, and you will have changed your mind."

CHAPTER ──────────
────────── ELEVEN

"More tea, sir?"

"No thanks, son. I shall just sit here for a bit, so don't keep bothering me."

"Very good, sir."

Bragg was sitting in the palatial tea-salon of the De Keyser hotel. The walls were of polished marble, the furniture and carpets rich, and enormous gilded gaseliers hung from the ceiling. On his left, the windows looked down the river to the half-built Tower Bridge in the distance. If he peered through the palm-tree on his right, he had a good view of the hotel foyer. Any minute he should see Morton arriving with Ryan in tow. Bragg pulled out his watch yet again. They ought to have been here twenty minutes ago, he thought irritably. Another waiter approached him, and he waved him away. His stomach felt full of wind. It must be those blasted cucumber sandwiches; he'd eaten far too many. These places were preposterous. They gave you a great heap of dainty sandwiches like triangles of playing-card stuck together. You could put three in your mouth at once, but you were expected to nibble them delicately, with your little finger cocked in the air. There was a feeble ripple of applause as the trio finished their piece. Even that was a surprise; nobody was listening to them. It was astonishing that anyone was remotely aware they'd stopped playing . . . From what Bragg could see, most of the plates went back to the kitchen practically as full as they'd come out. Would the sandwiches be thrown away? Or would the waiters eat them? He hoped they'd have more sense, or they'd be as full of wind as he was. Mind you, they didn't have to sit still . . . He shifted his position, and a long gurgling rumble came from his belly. A shocked silence fell on the tables around him, and women's faces were turned toward him in indignation and censure. Bragg wanted to shout "It wasn't what you think! Anyway, I missed my lunch and had to make do with those fart-arse fripperies—and I don't give a bugger what you think!" But he gazed at the river, and pretended to be oblivious of it all. You didn't speak your mind in places like this. The music began again, and the women resumed their attempts to talk over it. Music . . . Oh, damn! He'd nearly forgotten . . . It was his birthday on Sunday. If he forgot, he'd be in trouble. Three years ago, he'd made the sort of stupid gesture that always gets you into trouble with women. Mrs. Jenks had been off-color, and she was so bloody miserable, that he'd asked her to come to the music hall to celebrate his birthday. It had cheered her up all right, especially the five port-and-lemons. He'd kidded himself he had a fair chance of getting his leg over when they got back. But she was up the stairs like a scalded cat before he'd got his collar off, and he'd heard her lock her door. And that was that. Except that the next year, she'd been dropping hints for days beforehand; washing his shirt, brushing his clothes, telling him he ought to get his hair cut. So, of course, he'd asked her again; with exactly the same results. And it had become an institution—institutionalized bloody chastity. He pushed two pennies under the rim of his saucer, and strolled into the foyer.

"Who is on at the music halls?" he asked the head porter.

The man's eyes scrutinized his baggy clothes, his collar scrubbed threadbare, his scuffed boots. "Are you a resident in the hotel, sir?" he asked disdainfully.

"No, I'm not, thank Christ," Bragg snarled, pushing his warrant-card under the man's nose.

"Cor!" he exclaimed, relapsing into cockney. "What's up? You here on a case?"

"Yes. I'm investigating who is on at the music halls tomorrow night, look them up, will you?"

The man gave a disbelieving smile, but turned to a typewritten list on the wall of his cubicle. "There's Harry Champion at Collins' . . ."

"No, I don't want to go out of the West End. I'm taking a young woman I have great hopes of," Bragg winked suggestively.

"Oh. Then why not Vesta Tilley at the Empire?"

"She's too namby-pamby for my taste."

"I see. You have got hopes . . . How about Dan Leno and Marie Lloyd at the Oxford?"

"Just the ticket. Thanks, mate."

As he turned away, he heard Morton's voice calling his name, and saw that he was standing by the reception desk with another man. He strode over and shook Morton's hand.

"And you must be Mr. Ryan," he said, holding out his hand. "I gather you have been through a rough time."

"You sure could say that," replied Ryan. He looked fatigued and ill.

"Have you registered yet?"

"Yes. Three zero two. The bell captain's having the bags sent up."

"Then I suggest we go up, too," said Bragg. "Fortunately, they have a hydraulic lift here, so you will not have to walk up the stairs."

"Do I look that bad?" asked Ryan with a grimace.

"You look as if you have had a tiring journey."

"I guess I feel that way, too."

Bragg led the way to the lift cage, and pulled the gate closed behind them.

"Isn't science wonderful?" remarked Morton ironically, as they rose silently upward. He elicited no response. Ryan was slumped against one side of the cage, and Bragg was scrutinizing him closely. The lift stopped abruptly, and Morton led the way to the room. It was comfortable enough, with an armchair, and a view of the river. Ryan took off his coat, and with a sigh of relief slumped into the chair.

"Would you like some tea?" asked Morton.

"I have some bourbon in my bag . . . the top one there. It's not locked."

Morton found the bottle, and mixed him a generous measure.

"No ice, I'm afraid."

"That's fine." Ryan took a gulp. "Thanks, James. Did I need that!"

"Now I want you to listen carefully, Mr. Ryan," said Bragg. "We've got you here safe and reasonably sound, but on no account must you take any risks. We do not want a repetition of what happened to you in New Orleans. You are perfectly safe in the hotel, but if I were you I would lock my door. Get your meals sent up here, and if you need anything, ring the bell. Do you understand?"

"Sure. I'm not feeling like going any place, right now," replied Ryan in a stronger voice.

"Good. Tomorrow morning, at ten o'clock, we will collect you, and take you to the offices of the lawyers acting for Lloyd's. From then on, they will take responsibility for your safety. You must be one of the most precious people in London at the moment. They are going to provide two guards, round the clock, till Monday evening."

"What happens Monday?" asked Ryan.

"You will be giving your evidence in court on Monday. After that, everything you can tell will be public knowledge, and your troubles will be over."

"I think Mr. Ryan should have a chance to recuperate, before he is allowed to go back to America," Morton said.

"No need to worry about that," Bragg assured him. "Lloyd's will be very generous, you may be sure."

"I'm grateful, sergeant," said Ryan.

"I have no doubt that Constable Morton has a full account of what happened."

"Indeed I have," said Morton, "from the stowing away in London docks, to paddling ashore in Mexico on a hatch cover."

"Ah," remarked Bragg. "So that is where they landed the rifles."

"Rifles?" echoed Ryan.

"Yes, rifles," said Bragg firmly. "Don't pretend you know nothing about them. We knew they were on board, it was just a question of where they off-loaded them—and there was never a chance it would be Galveston."

"You could be right, sergeant," said Ryan tiredly. "All I saw was some boxes being unloaded. James knows all about it."

"Did you know they were rifles?" asked Bragg.

"No."

"Did anyone say anything about rifles?"

"No."

"Did anyone mention, in any way, what was in the cargo?"

"No."

"All right. Have a good night's sleep, and we'll see you in the morning."

Morton took his leave of Bragg at the hotel entrance, and walked slowly towards his rooms in Bishopsgate. He had been away for almost eight months. He sauntered along, savouring the half-forgotten atmosphere of bustle and purpose, the narrow streets jammed with hansom cabs and trade vehicles, the streams of clerks going home to the suburbs, the all-pervading smell of horses. He went into the telephone call room, in Cannon Street, and had a brief shouted conversation with his mother. Inevitably, the line was crackling so much that conversation was virtually impossible, but at least she knew he was back in England. She did manage to let him know that Mr. and Mrs. Chambers, who looked after him, had left The Priory for London three days before. Good! He was looking forward to one of his housekeeper's steak and kidney pies.

They were waiting at the top of the stairs when he arrived. They must have heard his key in the street door—or else they had been looking out, and seen him walking along the street. But, of course, his luggage had already been delivered. He gave Mrs. Chambers a warm hug, and shook her husband's hand. They received these gestures of affection with a mixture of pleasure and embarrassment, then retreated into their own quarters.

Morton indulged himself by luxuriating in a hot bath, then spent the evening writing a few letters, and happily poking around his rooms. He went to bed early, and lay awake for a long time, mentally picking up the threads of his old life. The cricket season was in full swing. No doubt he would be expected to play for Kent—though Sergeant Bragg might have other ideas. He was contemptuous of such idle occupations, so he had better not raise the possibility until he had worked assiduously for some weeks . . . He must try to get down to The Priory, as soon as he could. And there were lots of friends he should look up. He did not know how he would be able to pack it all in, but it was good to be home . . .

As soon as he set foot in the office next morning, Morton was hailed by the desk sergeant.

"Well done, young fella-me-lad! That was a cracking inning you played in the last Test. I reckon it won the match for us."

"It was good to get my first century for England, but it was Briggs's bowling that really won the match."

"We were dead proud of you, make no mistake. The Aussies are coming over here next summer, according to the papers. Will you be playing?"

"I think you ought to ask Sergeant Bragg that question," replied Morton with a smile. "Is he in yet?"

"Only just," said the sergeant, with a wink.

Morton climbed the stairs, and found Bragg gloomily contemplating a piece of paper on which he had drawn several small squares, with names underneath them. After Bragg had explained the significance of the diagram, Morton gave him a full account of his investigations in America.

"And who, amongst that lot, are the villains?" Bragg asked.

"I suppose the man to whom the cotton-seed mill was diverted, must be involved."

"Will we ever find him?"

"I think Lieutenant Gregory will do his best, but he has quite an area of the hinterland to cover. At the same time, the mill will hardly be erected outside the coastal strip, where the cotton grows."

Bragg glanced at his watch. "Come on, lad, it's time we got over to pick up Ryan." He took his bowler from the hat-stand and led the way out of the building."

"Are there any other villains in America?" he asked.

"Lieutenant Kinsella half hinted that the New Orleans importers might not be as honest as they make themselves out to be," replied Morton.

"How many business people are?" remarked Bragg. "At this end we are dealing with the aristocracy of wealth, and yet not one of them is being entirely open. But, according to the Commissioner, unless we play it their way, they will see to it that we are absorbed by the Met; so we have to step carefully."

"Could they do that?" asked Morton in surprise.

"According to Sir William, all they need do is cease to oppose it, and it will just happen . . . It's a funny thing, among all these wealthy City gentlemen, the only one I trust is the cargo underwriter, Peter Whitlock. And he is clearly not regarded as a gentleman by the others."

"That can only mean that he is prepared to flout the rules of the club," observed Morton.

"I'm more concerned with finding the person in the club that's prepared to break the law."

"And who is in the running?"

"It's difficult to say, at the moment. The company that owned the ship gives us the bare minimum of information, and that only when we have found it out already. It is beyond doubt that the *Dancing Lady* was a decrepit old bag, and they were probably quite glad to have the insurance money instead."

They stopped while a loaded omnibus passed, its horses straining up the rise, then crossed into Queen Victoria Street. "It's the French company that intrigues me," went on Bragg. "The advance charter-money they paid, almost exactly corresponded to the amount due for the proportion of the charter up to the scuttle. That smells of a precise, official mind to me. You can bet your life it was the French Government that told the Sûreté to shut up. If I'm right, we can expect pressure to close down the case any minute . . . A more fundamental question is the seventeen thousand pounds." Bragg chuckled as Morton grimaced at the pun. "That reminds me, lad, we must find out who owned the other ship that Gadd scuttled, and if it was chartered."

"I will remember," replied Morton. "To me, that bond sounds an excellent reason for scuttling the ship."

"Yes, but who got the money? We'd be a damned sight further forward if we could get our hands on Gadd."

"And where did Ingham fit in?"

"He had to be the linch pin. Nothing could have happened without his knowledge. I would have said that he was the principal scoundrel, if he had not got himself murdered. If only I had been twelve hours earlier . . . One thing's for sure. He was killed because somebody thought he would crack under pressure. So we shall just have to keep pushing until somebody else breaks.''

They entered the foyer of the De Keyser hotel. "What room was it, lad?"

"Three hundred and two," replied Morton.

"Good. I think it's hot enough to go up in the lift."

Moments later, Bragg was rapping on Ryan's door. There was no immediate response, so he knocked more loudly. "Come on, come on," he muttered irritably. He put his ear to the door, but could hear nothing. "The silly bugger has gone out, despite what we told him," he said. "Here lad, run and fetch the chambermaid to unlock the door. We might as well wait in comfort."

Morton soon returned with a gangling girl in a pinafore that was far too wide for her skinny body. She smiled perkily at Bragg, and inserting the key pushed open the door.

"Coo! He must sleep sound," she remarked. "After all your racket."

Ryan was lying fully dressed on the bed, his shoes were placed neatly by the chest of drawers, his bags were still stacked in the corner.

"Right now, young woman," said Bragg, grasping the maid's shoulder and propelling her back into the corridor. "Will you do one more thing for me?"

"My mum said I shouldn't never answer questions like that from a gentleman," she replied cheekily.

"Go on, you baggage," said Bragg with a push, "tell the manager that Sergeant Bragg, of the police, would like a chat with him here . . . Straight away, mind."

He crossed to the bed, and laid his hand on Ryan's cheek.

"Cold," he said. "He has been dead a long time."

"There is a tray here with a plate of cold cuts on it," said Morton. "It looks as if he had his supper sent up, then for some reason lay down without eating it."

"Perhaps he felt unwell . . . But he didn't die in his sleep. His eyes would be closed if he had." Bragg lifted his hand to pull down the lids over the staring eyes, then spun around.

"Come here, lad. Look at this!"

In the shadow of the left lapel of Ryan's jacket there was a small tear. Bragg unbuttoned the coat, and pulled it back. The waistcoat and shirt beneath it were sodden with blood.

"Oh my goodness!" The manager stood in the doorway, fussy-looking in his black morning coat and striped trousers. "Oh, how terrible! The bed will be ruined." He darted forward, and with surprising strength began to roll Ryan's body over.

"There, you see," he cried, "the bedspread is soaked." He ran toward the bell-push, and Bragg caught his arm.

"Do you want to shout it from the housetops that somebody has been murdered in your hotel?" he growled.

The manager's struggles ceased. "No, no. I certainly do not!" he said in alarm. "I'll never be able to let this room again, if it gets out."

"Then do as I say. Send a message to the coroner's office. Tell him that Sergeant Bragg has discovered the body of a murdered man, and is arranging to have it taken to the mortuary. And, most importantly, say I want Professor Burney to look at it."

The manager took a small pad from his inside pocket, and noted down the points.

"And I want a full list of all the guests who have moved out of the hotel since yesterday, with their addresses. Right?"

"Yes, sergeant . . . You will keep it as quiet as possible, won't you? This kind of thing is very bad for trade."

"We will be as discreet as we can. Is there another key for this room?"

"There would be a second key at the reception desk, since the gentleman was alone. And, of course, the chambermaid has her pass key."

"Who was on duty at the reception desk last night?"

"Mr. Perkins."

"Where does he live?"

"I think we might just catch him. He only goes off duty at a quarter past ten."

"Send him up, then. And hurry."

"One can only wonder at the sensibilities of some people," Morton remarked in disgust.

"I expect he is afraid for his job. Now, lad. I want you to interview everybody staying on this floor as soon as you can.

Find out if they saw anything, or heard anything, during last night. We shall have a better idea of the time of the murder after the postmortem, but you can be getting their stories now. And see the hotel staff who were on duty. I am going to stir up old Burney to see if he will give up his weekend in a good cause."

There was a rap at the door, and a white-faced man came in. He studiously avoided looking toward the bed.

"Are you Perkins?" asked Bragg.

"Er . . . Yes, sir," he replied hesitantly.

"You are not going to be much damned good to us," said Bragg roughly. "You don't seem sure of your own name."

"It . . . it was a shock."

"The manager tells me there was a second key with you at the desk last night."

"Yes."

"Did you let it out of your possession at all?"

"No . . . Only to the doctor."

"What doctor?"

"He said Mr. Ryan had sent a message for him to call."

"What time was that?"

"About twenty minutes to two o'clock."

"Did any of the hotel servants take the message to him?"

"He didn't say."

"Did he give his name?"

"No."

"Did he know the room number?"

"No. He asked for Mr. Ryan, and I gave him the key. He said he was sedated, and would not hear his knock."

"You stupid sod!" Bragg cried angrily. "Is that how you do your job? What was he like?"

Perkins flinched away. "How was I to know?" he whined.

"What was he like?"

"Well . . . like a doctor. He was of medium height, and he had on a black top hat and a black cloak . . ."

"His face, man, his face!"

"He didn't have a beard . . . or whiskers to speak of."

"Did you notice the shape of his nose, or the color of his eyes?"

"No. They were just ordinary . . ."

"Is there anything else you remember?" Bragg glared at the hapless clerk.

"No."

"Well, if you do remember anything, you get in touch with me, see?"

"Yes, sir."

"And don't waste any time."

"That should narrow it down a bit," Bragg said excitedly, as the door closed. "How many people knew that Ryan was sick, lad? I told no one."

"I suppose that he might have said so himself, when he had his supper sent up," replied Morton. "Aside from that possibility, the only person who was aware of his condition, to my certain knowledge, is Luigi Rossi, the Lloyd's agent in New Orleans."

"Lloyd's, eh? That doesn't seem likely."

"But if Ryan was attacked there because of the information he gave, then the instigator would undoubtedly know how ill he was."

"Finishing the job properly?" said Bragg pensively. "Well, Lloyd's may have lost their crucial witness, but at least this confirms that we are standing on somebody's corn. We only have to jump about a bit, and when he shouts, grab him . . . Right, get on with your end, and let me know tonight what you found out."

Morton closed the curtains of the room, and locked the door. Then he went down to the reception desk.

"Can you give me a list of the residents on the third floor?" he asked.

The clerk had clearly been alerted by the manager. "What, yesterday or today?" he asked.

"At this moment."

"There's only a handful. Most of our guests are business gentlemen, who go home on Friday."

"Are you saying that there were very few people on that floor last night?"

The clerk produced a floor chart for the previous day, and went through it, stabbing with his pencil at each square.

"There was Mr. . . . . er," he nodded significantly, "in three-oh-two; old Captain Varney and his wife in three-oh-nine; Mr. Woods, in three-one-three—he's gone home this morning . . ."

"You will be giving his address to Sergeant Bragg."

"In three-two-two there is the Rev. Mortimer. He's some-
hing to do with the British and Foreign Bible Society."

"Very sinister," remarked Morton.

"And in three-two-three is Miss Challis. And . . . yes,
hat's the lot."

"Really?" said Morton, heartened. "Do you know if any of
hem are in now?"

The clerk turned and peered at the key rack. "The only one
s Miss Challis, I have two keys for every other room."

"And she is in three-two-three?"

"That's right, sir."

Morton mounted the stairs, and walked past Ryan's room
oward the other end of the hotel. He found the door he was
eeking, and knocked quietly. There was no response. He had a
udden picture of a dear old lady skewered to her bed with a
tiletto, and hammered at the door.

"Just a moment," shouted a muffled voice from inside, "I
m coming."

Morton waited with growing impatience, till at last the door
vas opened, and a pretty tousled head appeared.

"Constable Morton, of the City police," he said, showing
is warrant-card to the young woman. "I would like a word
vith Miss Challis."

"Please come in." She opened her door, and Morton went
n. He looked around the room nonplussed, averting his eyes
om the mound of frilly underwear piled on a chair.

"It was Miss Challis I wanted to . . ." he began lamely.

"I am Dorothea Challis," said the young woman in
musement. "I am sorry if the room is in some disorder. You
nust pretend you have just wandered into your sister's room.
he fact is, I have only just awakened."

"I'm sorry," Morton mumbled. He saw that her shapely
ody was clad in a patterned silk peignoir, thrown over a pink
ightdress.

"I dare say you are thinking, 'What moral turpitude! What
ecadence!' " She perched on the end of the bed, and began to
wing her bare foot like a pendulum. "In fact we had a very
ng and tiring rehearsal last night, so I feel totally justified."

"Ah, I see!" cried Morton, comprehension dawning . . .
But you are beautiful! . . ."

"Pray what is that supposed to mean?" asked Miss Challis
with a ripple of laughter.

"I'm sorry," said Morton. "You must be the soprano who i
appearing at the Royal Opera."

"That is so," she smiled.

"It is just that one has become accustomed to opera singer
built like elephants, trumpeting Wagner."

"You have the most revoltingly perceptive mind. However
I promise you that I shall never become like that."

"What are you singing?" Morton asked eagerly.

"Just the one role, Cherubino, in the Marriage of Figaro.'

"Oh, but that's a wonderful part!" exclaimed Morton. "I an
sure you will carry it off marvelously."

"I am very lucky to be appearing alongside artistes lik
Teleki, Eames, and Bauermeister."

"But why stay here, when you are so far away from Coven
Garden?"

Miss Challis smiled ruefully. "A young lady on her ow
cannot be too careful . . . Sometimes it is better to stay in
quiet respectable hotel, and have a mile or so to travel."

"I am sure that is wise," agreed Morton. "Where do yo
live when you are not singing?"

"The Cathedral Close, Bury-St. Edmonds, will always fin
me . . . Well?"

"Well what?"

"You have not yet explained why you are here, Constabl
Morton," she said firmly.

"I seem to be perpetually apologizing," said Morton with
laugh. "I am afraid you have quite shattered my professiona
sangfroid . . . I have come to see you about a rathe
unpleasant business. The occupant of room number thre
hundred and two was found dead this morning, in somewha
suspicious circumstances."

"Was that the tall man?"

"Did you see him?"

"I saw someone come out of that room."

"At what time was that?"

"I suppose about two o'clock this morning."

"Are you quite sure it was that room?" asked Morton.

"Why yes, it is the one nearest the staircase and the lift.

"You understand that I shall have to write out what you te

me in the form of a statement, and get you to sign it . . .
May I ask why you were at the other end of the corridor at two
o'clock in the morning?"

"Alas! The heavy hand of the law is about to breach my
maidenly modesty," she said with an amused smile. "Despite
present appearances, I am a somewhat fastidious person . . .
There is a water-closet just beyond the staircase."

Morton's face reddened with embarrassment, then he
laughed. "I refuse to apologize again," he said. "The
interesting thing is that you very probably saw the murderer."

Miss Challis gave a theatrical frisson of horror. "How
dreadful!" she cried. "But how exciting! Will you catch him?"

"With your help we may. Do you remember what he looked
like?"

"I was about to step into the corridor, when I saw him, so I
stayed in the closet, and peeped out. I never saw his face. He
came out of the room and locked the door. Then he walked
quickly down the stairs."

"How was he dressed?"

"He was wearing a black cloak, and a top hat."

"Did he look like a doctor?"

She thought for a moment. "Not particularly," she said.
"He certainly was not carrying a bag. In fact, I distinctly
remember that he was holding an ebony stick, with a silver
knob."

"I am most grateful, Miss Challis," Morton murmured as he
completed his notes. "When I have written it all out in
statement form, I will come to see you again, if I may."

"Then you had better call me Dorothea," she said . . .
"You do not seem an ordinary policeman," she added
suspiciously. "Are you sure this is not some kind of hoax?"

"It is no hoax, Dorothea, and I am a very ordinary
policeman indeed—but I shall be at your Marriage."

CHAPTER ─────────
───────── TWELVE

Bragg stared moodily at the people leaving St. Giles's church after early communion; all purified, and ready for another week of gluttony and sloth. Good for them! He hadn't got anywhere near the seven deadly sins last night. With Marie Lloyd on top form, running her pearls lasciviously through her teeth, and now and then giving the gallery a lecherous wink, he'd thought he was on a cert. But she'd done it again! He had bent down to unlace his new boots, and she was gone—barricaded in her bedroom. The worst part of it was, she was as happy as a lark this morning, chattering about the music-hall, and reminding him of the jokes, so she could pretend to be shocked. It was a poor look-out, when a woman of forty turned into a cockteaser. He'd be better off in a hostel . . . But perhaps he had got it wrong, perhaps she fancied a tumble, but didn't want to let herself go too cheap. Blasted women! He was glad to see Morton standing on the corner of Golden Lane. At least he'd have something else to occupy his mind.

They went up the narrow passage by the mortuary, and entered the yard by the back gate. As he tapped on the window of the dissecting-room, Bragg could see that Professor Burney and the coroner were already there. He led the way through the side door, past the grey slate slabs, some of them bearing white-shrouded forms, and tapped on Burney's door.

"Ah, there you are, Bragg," exclaimed Sir Rufus. "I was wondering how long you were going to be. Having got your message, I asked for you as my officer for this homicide also. Is it linked to the murder of that broker fellow?"

"Almost certainly, sir," replied Bragg. "This Ryan man is an American that Constable Morton brought over from New Orleans to give evidence in court tomorrow. He was murdered the same night he got here."

"That was very prompt," Sir Rufus remarked.

"I find it somewhat curious," said Morton. "Whoever knew he was in London must also have known that I accompanied him. It surely must have been self-evident that he had already given his story to me."

"Then it is the court-case that is important to them," said Sir Rufus. "Whatever he has told you, it cannot be accepted as evidence by the court, unless he can be cross-examined on it."

"So they don't care that we know," Bragg commented, "so long as the facts cannot be given in court?"

"That seems about the size of it. What is this case?"

"The man who ordered the diverted cotton-seed mill is suing Lloyd's because they will not pay out on the insurance claim."

"Ah, yes. You told me." The coroner glanced across to the marble slab in the center of the room, where Burney was examining the supine naked body of Ryan.

"I cannot imagine," Morton remarked, "that Jethro Dillard either could or would instigate Ryan's murder . . . though he did threaten to horsewhip me, on very slight acquaintance, for insinuating myself into his daughter's affections."

"He'd have good reason, if I know you," growled Bragg.

"My firm impression," said Morton, "is that he was totally confident of winning his case."

"You were always convinced," said Bragg thoughtfully, "that Ryan was holding something back."

"Yes. But even if I were right, how could the murderer know he had not told me everything?"

"Perhaps the true explanation," said Sir Rufus portentously, "is that we are dealing with a man who is becoming increasingly desperate, and is prepared to kill anyone with knowledge, as a kind of insurance policy."

"Well, gentlemen," Burney interrupted, "I am ready to begin. Since my clerk is not here on this sanctified day, I would be greatly obliged if Constable Morton would make notes for me. Don't worry," he added, "I will describe it in layman's terms, and my clerk can translate it tomorrow."

With a look of dismay, Morton took out his note-book, and stationed himself at Burney's side.

"Right. The subject is male, in his mid-thirties, six feet two-and-a-half inches tall, weight approximately fifteen stone, with a well developed physique. Got that?"

"Yes, sir," said Morton.

"Good. I will deal with the time of death next. I came in at seven o'clock last evening, and made all the necessary notes, so you can relax, constable, for a moment . . . I take it, Sergeant Bragg, that this is one of your principal concerns?" He screwed up his eyes and smiled benevolently.

"Yes, indeed, sir."

"At that time, the lividity staining on the back was well-established, and rigor mortis was complete. I took the internal temperature, and bearing in mind that the body was fully clothed, and had been kept in a closed room on a warm night, I came to the conclusion that death had occurred some seventeen hours previously."

"That means about two o'clock on Saturday morning," remarked Bragg. "Good. It confirms the evidence of an eyewitness."

Burney's mouth sagged open in pleasure. "I expect you would like my views on the murder weapon," he beamed, "and then we can leave the rest till tomorrow."

"That would suit me, sir," said Bragg.

"Right, constable? . . . There is a puncture wound medial to the left nipple, between the third and fourth rib." He took a steel ruler from the side table. "The wound is one inch in length, roughly parallel to the breast-bone, and wider at the top than the bottom . . . That indicates a single-edged knife, sergeant, but a fairly strong one. I shall, of course, preserve the tissue surrounding the wound as a specimen, should we need it."

"You think there may be more killings, Burney?" demanded the coroner.

"I'm only taking up your last remark, Sir Rufus. Murderers often have a favorite weapon. Right, constable?"

"Yes, sir."

"There is a perceptible area of bruising around each end of the wound, which should be helpful to us. It was probably made by impact from the guard of the knife, suggesting that the blade was plunged in to its fullest extent." He picked up a probe, and carefully inserting it into the wound, began to poke around. "The fourth rib has been cut through at this point, which is perhaps not surprising, since at his age it would still be cartilaginous. Still, it argues a vigorous blow, and a very sharp knife." He began to prod downwards. "The direction of the blow is vertical," he went on. "Whether we shall be able to determine the length of the blade is problematic, since it penetrated the chest cavity, but we shall be able to judge better when I have opened him up."

"Was he standing or lying down when he was struck?" asked Bragg.

As Burney pondered for a moment, his smile became oddly shamefaced. "I think the latter," he said. "Had he been in any other than a lying position, the direction of the travel of the weapon would have been different."

Bragg picked up the ruler, and taking up position by the body, made as if to strike, "Like this, do you think?"

"No, the murderer must have been facing the bed-head when he struck . . . In saying that, I am making an assumption that the handle of the knife is shaped to fit the hand, but even if I am wrong, few men would strike a blow with the blade horizontal."

"That was a double bed, wasn't it, constable?"

"I would say so."

"That argues a fairly tall man, to be able to exert the force you speak of, at full stretch," said Bragg.

"Unless, of course, he is left-handed, and struck from the far side of the bed," Burney remarked. "Shall we open him up?" With a sweep of his scalpel he severed the skin from the neck to crotch, then eased back the breast tissue. "There, you see?" He pointed with a bloody finger. "It went through that rib as clean as a whistle."

Morton could feel his mouth dry, and a cold sweat of revulsion breaking out on his forehead. He shook his head at Bragg, and stepped away from the table. Burney did not notice, he was busy snipping away at the rib-cage with what looked like heavy wire-cutters.

"It is a revolting trade you practice, Burney," exclaimed the coroner. "It was the surgical operations that put me off medicine in the end. Of course, in those days, there was no such thing as ether or chloroform. You would give the patients a large dose of laudanum—which they usually vomited up again—then hold them down with straps and your bare hands, while the surgeon went at it like a butcher. We lived perpetually with the surgeon's paradox—the operation was a success, but the patient died. Eventually it sickened me, and I turned to the law, where the blood is metaphorical, and pain felt only in the pocket-book . . . To think," he mused, "if they had brought in anaesthetics a few years earlier, I might be hacking away like Burney there." He consulted his watch. "Well, I must be off. We are forsaking matins this morning, in favor of a picnic on the river at Hampton Court . . . You will let me have your report in due course?"

"By Wednesday at the latest," Burney murmured absently, as Sir Rufus hurried out. "Yes, there is a lot of blood in the chest cavity, so death was not instantaneous . . . I think the external flow of blood came from the severed inter-costal artery behind the damaged rib. The knife went on to penetrate the right ventricle, leading to failure of the heart."

"When we found him, you would have thought he was asleep, if it were not for his eyes," said Bragg.

"I find that surprising," remarked Burney, with a loose smile. "I would have expected some struggle, even an attempt to grapple with his attacker."

"He was still very weak from the attack he had suffered earlier, and the effects of the journey," said Morton from the window. "In addition, I imagine that he took a sleeping draught."

"That could explain it then. Let us hope so, for his sake, though he could not have lived for more than a few moments."

"So what about the weapon?" asked Bragg.

Burney gave his cheshire-cat grin. "A stout single-edged

blade, about six inches in length, with a small guard—say a Bowie knife.''

Bragg arrived early at Old Jewry the following morning, to find Morton already waiting for him.

"What's the matter, lad?" he grunted. "Can you not sleep these mornings?"

"I am trying to impress you, sergeant."

"It's a good thing you told me, then. I might not have noticed. What is all this about?"

"Nothing specific at the moment," replied Morton lightly. "But you never know, someday someone might ask me to play cricket."

"I wonder you are not sick of it," said Bragg. He picked up an envelope from his desk and ripped it open with his thumb. "Now this is interesting," he remarked. "I asked the Commissioner to find out if there were any official shipments of rifles out of London in January. This note says he has been told there were none."

"That rather knocks the idea on the head, then."

"Not necessarily. There could be unofficial ones—maybe perfectly straightforward commercial shipments. Who manufactures rifles, lad? It's more in your line than mine."

Morton pondered awhile. "If the cases described by Ryan and the nightwatchman did in fact contain rifles," he said at length, "then they would almost certainly be military rather than sporting rifles. I think my father would be best able to answer your question."

"Any chance of you popping down to find out?"

"I hardly have time now," Morton demurred. "I have to take statements from the residents at the De Keyser, and get them signed. Then there are all the people who left the hotel that morning to follow up."

"I suppose so."

"If you like, I could telephone him."

"Are we connected up to Kent, now-a-days?"

"Yes. I rang my mother last Friday. The line was very crackly, but we could just about understand one another."

"All right then, have a try. I think that is our best line of inquiry at the moment."

Bragg left the office, and strolled the short distance to the Royal Exchange. The pavements were clogged with people

streaming to work, the Bank crossing jammed solid with
omnibuses and vans and horses. He stood in a doorway and
gazed at it all with affectionate nostalgia. It was over twenty-
one years since, as a new recruit, he had first tried to grapple
with that traffic. There must have been a lot of the country
yokel about him even then, for he believed that the word of the
law, embodied in his brawny person, would be instantly
obeyed. It took him all of ten minutes to realize that this was a
phenomenon with its own rules, that for an hour and a half
each morning, all traffic laws were in suspension as people
tried to get to work at the very last minute. By the stroke of
nine o'clock, it would be stilled as by magic; even now there
was a slackening in the press of people coming by the Mansion
House from Cannon Street station. A gaggle of chattering girls
pushed up the steps past him, and hurried upstairs—probably
typewriters at the office of the insurance company. In a quarter
of an hour the tangle of traffic would have been conjured away,
and the stage would be set for the entry of the principal actors
in the City's arena.

Bragg waited another five minutes, then wandered into
Lloyd's. The great glass-roofed quadrangle, which formed the
trading-floor, seemed unnaturally quiet. The throngs of brokers
had not yet arrived, and the boxes were mainly occupied by
clerks quietly writing up Saturday morning's business. He was
glad to see, however, that Whitlock was at his box, talking to
his deputy.

"You have heard the news about Ryan, I suppose?" Bragg
greeted him.

"Yes, the solicitors sent me a telegraph at home. It's a bit of
a shaker."

"What is happening about the case?" asked Bragg.

"I had dinner with the senior partner, last night. He is
confident that he can get a four-week adjournment this
morning. With any luck, he might get six weeks, which would
effectively mean that the case would not come on until
October, after the vacation. That should give you enough time
to find out what the hell has been going on."

"I cannot imagine I would find another witness to take
Ryan's place. We have a warrant out for the arrest of the
master, but even if we managed to get our hands on him, so far
as you are concerned, he would be a hostile witness."

"All I need is someone who can give evidence of the deviation to Galveston. Short of that, I shall have to pay up, and it will look as if I am just giving in to pressure."

"Pressure? What pressure?" asked Bragg.

"You are not aware of the famous summons to the Foreign Office, then?"

"No."

"Last Thursday, Goddard, Hozier—the secretary of Lloyd's, Frankis and I were invited to see some high official named Stanton. It was all dressed up as a consultative meeting with the insurance industry, but I know better than that. I would never have been asked, or even allowed, to represent Lloyd's in any genuine consultation. My views are too unreliable for that. Of course, it was all handled with the utmost delicacy. The *Dancing Lady* was brought in at the very last moment, as an afterthought—almost by accident, as it were. But that was the real purpose of the meeting, and we were left in no doubt at all that the government wants the claim paid, and all inquiries abandoned."

"In a way, I have been waiting for this," said Bragg slowly. "The charterer of the ship was a French company. At first the French police gave me all the information I asked for, then suddenly someone put up the shutters. It could only be the French government. I have been expecting a directive from the Home Office myself."

"The Foreign Office are much more devious, and they kick you in the teeth with such charm."

"So what happens now?" asked Bragg.

"I have refused to go along with them, on the grounds that it would be a gross breach of trust."

"I cannot understand why you refuse to pay; the more so, now that you have lost your main witness. Everything that has happened seems to be covered by the policy, everybody seems to want the case closed down, your rich backers can stand it. Why fight on?"

"Because I'm not having my arm twisted by that damned committee. The syndicates are all in competition with each other, and the committee is just there to hold the ring. But they take it upon themselves to pontificate about the ethos of Lloyd's, about what is done and what isn't done, as if we were a collection of curates."

"Are you saying that the committee acted in concert with the Foreign Office to ensure that you attended that meeting?" asked Bragg.

"No. I would not go so far. I think Goddard was as unaware of the purpose of the meeting as I was. But they made damned sure that he would toe their line. Stanton promised him a knighthood if we complied. Of course it was done with great finesse; nothing so crude as a bribe. It was almost imperceptible, except to a suspicious character like me; but it was there all right. And he took the bait. The same afternoon he was pushing like mad for me and Frankis to settle. But we shall see. Perhaps your friend Gadd will turn up in the net. Then we would have some fun."

When Morton got to Bragg's lodgings that evening, he was delighted to find that Catherine Marsden was there. She was dressed in a smart blue tailor-made, and a perky little hat. She looked fresh, and graceful, and somehow sparkling with well-being.

"You remember Miss Marsden, I take it," remarked Bragg.

"How could I forget someone at once so beautiful, and so distinguished?" he replied, making to kiss her hand.

"Don't be silly, James," she protested, pushing him away.

"Did you get anything more out of the residents of the hotel?" Bragg asked, as Morton sank grinning into an armchair.

"Are you saying that you have a witness?" asked Catherine, pouncing on his words.

"Why yes," said Morton lightly. "The most ravishingly beautiful opera singer you could ever imagine."

"I don't believe one exists," replied Catherine, her face clouding.

"Oh, but yes! Dorothea Challis, the young soprano. She is quite radiantly lovely."

"She is the one they call the Suffolk mare, isn't she?" asked Catherine sourly.

"I thought that was one of Henry the Eighth's wives."

"I would not know. I never met either of them."

"Would you like to? Dorothea, I mean. I could arrange it."

"No, thank you," Catherine said crossly.

"On a professional basis, of course."

"I cannot think that she would be of interest to anyone. And I can arrange my own interviews." She turned to Bragg. "Can you give me the latest news on the two murders?"

"Well, you can say that the police are exploring a possible link between them."

"Can you put some flesh on that?" Catherine asked briskly.

"You can say that Ryan was to be the main witness in the lawsuit against Lloyd's, resulting from the loss of the *Dancing Lady* . . . They are going to ask for the case to be adjourned. I expect that you will be able to check on that."

"Yes. The *Star's* legal correspondent will know."

"It might be useful to us if you were able to tie in the bottomry business, as well. Maybe you could say that Ryan could have been a useful witness in those proceedings."

"Leave it to me. Is there anything else?"

"Not for publication," said Bragg. "I think that should stir everybody up nicely."

"So there are other developments?" Catherine asked.

"Well hardly 'developments,' more 'ripples,' so far as we are concerned. And that is the interesting part of it, really . . . The Lloyd's people were called to the Foreign Office, and told to close the *Dancing Lady* case down—pay the claims and forget it. In a sense I was not surprised, because of the French companies involved, and the fact that we seem to be treading on sensitive toes. But why is there no pressure on the police to suspend their inquiries? I saw the Commissioner this afternoon, and he says there had not been the remotest suggestion to that effect, from the Home Office or anybody."

"Perhaps the idea is that Lloyd's will call off the dogs, once there is nothing at stake," Morton remarked.

"Well, with two murders on our hands, that would never be a runner in my book."

"Perhaps your informant drew an erroneous conclusion," suggested Catherine.

"It's not likely," replied Bragg. "Peter Whitlock is a very shrewd man. But young Morton here might be right. Whitlock says it was made clear to Goddard that he would get a knighthood, if Lloyd's did as the Foreign Office wanted . . . That's a thought. It seems to be accepted that without Ryan's evidence, Whitlock would be forced to pay up. Would you kill to get a knighthood, lad? You ought to know, if anybody does."

"Not I," smiled Morton. "The most obvious result of having a title is that you get charged twice as much for everything by the tradesmen. But I suppose someone with towering social ambitions might."

"Is that all you have for me?" asked Catherine.

"All for the moment, miss," said Bragg.

She rose to go. "I am sorry that I have not yet discovered who is behind Harvey & Crane Ltd., but the financial editor of the *Star* is going to introduce me to a stockbroker he thinks will know."

Morton sprang to his feet gallantly. "Allow me to escort you home, madam," he said.

"Indeed I will not!" cried Catherine indignantly. "I came here alone, and I can find my way home alone." She marched to the door, and closed it behind her with a bang.

"Our little Miss Marsden seems to have been transformed into Miss Anthrope this evening," Morton said with a mischievous smile. "Or in view of the occasion of her wrath, into a Miss Ogynist."

"If you are not careful," growled Bragg, "you will find that she has become Miss Appropriated."

"What can you mean by that, sergeant?"

"I'll tell you what I mean, lad," said Bragg wrathfully. "I mean that you are twenty-five, and it's time you acted like an adult, instead of flitting from one girl to another because you have no need to settle on one."

"But, sergeant . . ." Morton began with a flippant smile.

"You rich people disgust me." Bragg's lip curled in scorn. "You play around, because you can have all the women you want. Then when you are old, you marry some young bit of stuff; and after two years, you are worn out, and she is having it off with the coachman."

"But I shall have the family line to think of," protested Morton with a grin.

"All right then. So you'll get married for breeding. You'll think no more of her than a pedigree mare."

"At the moment," Morton complained, "everyone seems to be conspiring to get me tied down in matrimony. It's almost as if they are intent on seeing that I have my share of the wedded woe they have experienced . . . I'm sorry, sir,'' he leaned forward with concern on his face, "I should not have said that. It was unforgiveable."

"That's all right, lad," said Bragg gruffly, "It's natural that the young should be wrapped up in their own affairs . . . Anyway, it was all a long time ago, and it's not my place to tell you what you should do." He gazed hard at Morton. "But you know what I think," he said. "Now then, what about those rifles?"

"I telephoned my father," replied Morton soberly. "He says that the only British military rifle worth considering is the Lee-Metford, made in Birmingham."

"What is the railway terminus for Birmingham?"

"Euston, sergeant."

"Right. I'll meet you there at half-past seven tomorrow morning, under the clock. And don't be late."

CHAPTER ———— ———— THIRTEEN

By half past nine next morning, Bragg and Morton had arrived in Birmingham, and were bowling along in a four-wheeler towards the suburb where the factory of the Lee-Metford company was situated.

"It looks just as prosperous as London, and a damned sight cleaner," remarked Bragg.

"This is Liberal radicalism in action," replied Morton. "Joseph Chamberlain was mayor here for several years."

"They were saying at the pub last night that if the Liberals get in at the election, and old Gladstone kicks the bucket, then Chamberlain would become Prime Minister."

"I would not have thought he had a big enough following in the party for that," said Morton. "But looking around here, there seems to be a lot to be said for his brand of politics."

"Oh well, it won't make any difference to the likes of me. Do you think that's the factory, on the right there? . . . Yes, it must be, we are slowing down."

The Lee-Metford works seemed to cover several acres, and consisted of half a dozen single-storied brick workshops,

ominated by the tapering column of a vast chimney. The cab
urned into the yard, under the watchful eye of a uniformed
ateman.

"You had better wait for us, driver," Bragg called. "I can't
ee us getting a cab here easily."

Bragg led the way to a small office, on the right of the gate.
le clanged the bell on the counter, and a thin-faced clerk
ppeared, with black sleeve-protectors on his arms.

"Yes?" he asked.

Bragg showed his warrant card. "Police," he said tersely.
Who is the boss around here?"

"Mr. Dawkes is the office manager," said the man ner-
ously.

"Tell him I want to see him."

The clerk disappeared, and soon came back with a short
arrel of a man, wearing pebble spectacles that magnified his
rown pupils, till his eyes looked like dark craters in his head.

"Mr. Dawkes?" asked Bragg.

"That's me."

"We are making inquiries about some rifles you consigned
January to the West India docks, for the ss Dancing Lady."

Dawkes stared at them owlishly, without saying a word.

"You do remember them, don't you?" asked Bragg.

"I am sorry, but I cannot discuss anything about the business
ith you." Dawkes blinked rapidly. "You will have to see the
orks manager."

"And where is he to be found?"

"Just wait here a moment," Dawkes said, and vanished.

The moment stretched to a quarter of an hour, and although
ragg had been glad at first to stand for a change, he began to
ast his eye around for a spare chair.

"Hey," he muttered, "there is some crockery on that table
ver there. Do you think they would make us a cup of tea?"

"I doubt it," replied Morton. "They are not exactly putting
ut the welcome mat."

Then the door behind them opened, and a young woman
ustled in. She was wearing only a blouse and skirt, and her
air was pulled close around her oval face.

"Well, you were worth waiting for," said Bragg cheerfully.

"That's enough of that," she replied sharply, "I'm a married
oman."

"I don't doubt it, with a nice little waist like that."

"Are you the gentlemen waiting to see Mr. Gosling?"

"If he is the works manager, yes we are."

"Will you follow me, please?"

"I'd follow you anywhere, love."

Her head jerked up, and she strutted indignantly across th[e] yard. Bragg and Morton followed her meekly to a small offic[e] built on to the end of one of the workshops.

"Just wait there a moment," the woman said peremptoril[y] as they crossed the threshold. When she was satisfied that the[y] had indeed halted, she turned and knocked on a door at th[e] other end of the room. There was a murmur from within, an[d] she poked her head inside. Then she opened the door fully, an[d] beckoned. Bragg and Morton trooped through, and she close[d] it quickly behind them.

A man in his mid-forties rose from behind the desk. He wa[s] clean-shaven, and dressed in a dark blue lounging suit and white shirt. He held out his hand to the policemen.

"My name is Gosling, I am the works manager here. [I] gather that you have been making inquiries at the office." H[is] voice was musical and educated, without any of the inflection[s] which would have betrayed a man promoted from the sh[op] floor. He glanced briefly at Bragg's warrant card.

"What have you been doing to our Mrs. Paxton?" he ask[ed] with an amused smile. "Her face is like thunder."

"It's something to do with her being a married woman[," Bragg remarked. "It's funny to find an armaments facto[ry] staffed by Sunday-school teachers."

Gosling laughed. "You are nearer the truth than y[ou] imagine," he said. "One of our directors is convinced th[at] Christians work harder than unbelievers. I suppose he is rig[ht] up to a point."

"Are you a director of the company, sir?" asked Brag[g.]

"No, no." Gosling replied. "My background is in enginee[r]ing. I was production manager here until two years ago, a[nd] now I manage the whole works."

"Are you reponsible for sales and shipment also?"

"Everything. The factory is a self-contained unit. T[he] company has other interests, of course, but this is the on[ly] small-arms plant."

"We are wanting information about a shipment of rifles [in] January," Bragg said.

"Yes. Well, I am afraid I shall have to disappoint you, gentlemen. The company's policy is that all transactions relating to armaments must be kept secret, and in no circumstances whatever may information be given concerning them."

"That cannot apply to the police," Bragg protested.

"I am afraid it does," Gosling said firmly.

"But two men have been murdered and God knows how many more will follow, if we don't get this information."

"I am sorry. You are asking the impossible."

"Can you not even tell us if there was a shipment, without saying what it was, or where it was going?"

"No."

"I shall have to get a search warrant," said Bragg truculently. "Then we would find out."

"Perhaps. But since we are suppliers to the government, you might not find that so easy. You must realize that it is not in the public interest for information about our trading to be bandied about . . . Now would you like to look around the works, while you are here?"

Bragg was about to refuse, but Morton quickly jumped in ahead of him.

"We certainly would," he said warmly.

Bragg trailed through the workshops after Gosling and Morton, resentful of their animated conversation, uninterested in the lines of milling and boring machines, and lathes. Gosling seemed intent on compensating for his enforced lack of courtesy, by going into the minutest detail about every operation that took place in the factory. And Morton was no better; showing a lively interest in everything, and sometimes prolonging a discussion when it seemed to have petered out. At last they bade farewell to Gosling, and climbed into their cab.

"God knows how much this trip will cost us," Bragg grumbled. "Inspector Cotton will be on my back, that's for sure."

"It is all money well spent, sir," said Morton with a smile. "We now know exactly what a Lee-Metford magazine rifle looks like. And perhaps of equal importance, we have seen the cases they are packed in."

"By God! lad," Bragg suddenly ejaculated, "that Gosling had me so irritated, I'm missing the obvious." He stuck his head out of the window. "Driver," he called, "don't take us to the station. Take us to the goods depot." He sat down again with a grim smile. "We'll beat the buggers yet."

The cab set them down outside the main railway goods yard, and Bragg paid the driver.

"Impressive, isn't it?" Morton remarked. The huge cobbled area was a seemingly confused mass of sweating horses and rumbling carts. Yet it was apparent that some inbuilt dynamism kept it swirling purposefully. Vans with goods for consignment came in from the street at the left-hand gate; empty carts, and those which had goods for delivery, came out at the right-hand gate. And weaving in and out of this slow-moving stream were porters with barrows and trolleys, orderlies sweeping up the horse-droppings, perspiring foremen with lists. They looked like black birds trapped in the mechanism of a great clock.

"Goods inwards is on the left," said Bragg. "That's our mark."

They dodged under the heads of a pair of horses nuzzling in their nose-bags, and went through an archway into the gloom of the sorting area. The dispatch foreman on duty was a stocky man with a broad leather belt, and his shirtsleeves rolled up his knotted arms. He wore a mustache that was even bushier than Bragg's.

"If you are on about stolen goods," he said, "you'd better see the Railway Police at New Street."

"It's not quite that," Bragg replied amiably. "We just want to verify that you did, in fact, dispatch a consignment of goods in January."

"Where were they going to?"

"London."

"Well, the records should be here somewhere." He turned, and began to sort through a pile of tattered dispatch books. "What date in January was it?"

"Some time in the first week."

"Right then," he selected two books and came back to the counter with them. "I shall need a description of the goods."

"They were oblong cases from the Lee-Metford factory."

"And we all know what that means," broke in the foreman with a grin. "What was the delivery address?"

"The West India docks, for loading on the *ss Dancing Lady*."

The foreman rapidly turned the pages of the dog-eared book.

Morton was beginning to think that they would draw a blank, when he stopped abruptly.

"Here we are," he announced. "Ten cases were received here on the fourth of January, to be held until we received two further cases. Then all twelve were to be dispatched to London together. I see that they left here on the eleventh of January."

"What about the other cases?" asked Bragg.

The man's finger found a reference, and turned over more pages. "Yes, two cases from Dunbar's to the same destination."

"And do we all know what that means?" asked Bragg with a smile.

"Smokeless-powder cartridges, sergeant. To fit the rifles, I should think."

Catherine Marsden looked with dissatisfaction at her article in the Wednesday edition of the *City Press*. She had been scrupulous in conveying only what Bragg had agreed to. She had even suppressed the temptation to add that the Challis woman was supposed to have seen Ryan's murderer. As a result the paragraph had made up to only two column-inches, and had been tucked away at the bottom of page three. It was inconceivable that more than a handful of readers would ever discover it, surrounded as it was by trivia. She could hardly imagine it stirring things up for Bragg. She wondered irritably if she should write a sensational exposé for Saturday's edition. She had enough information to cause a flutter among a few City dove-cotes, and she would be saying nothing that was not factual. But, of course, it would be bound to put at risk her relationship with Sergeant Bragg, and after an early crusading article in which she had pilloried a City police Inspector, Bragg was her only source of information in the force.

"Why are you sighing, dear?" asked her mother absently. She was reading, as usual, with her book propped up against the toast-rack.

"I was yawning, Mama."

"I am not surprised. I do not know how you keep it up." Mrs. Marsden looked up from her reading with reluctance. "When I was your age, I never got up till ten o'clock during the Season."

"Yes, but you were not a working girl." Catherine saw a reproachful look come over her mother's face, and moved to head off the impending homily.

"What is it you are reading, Mamma?" she asked.

"*Tess of the D'Urbervilles* again," her mother replied. "Hardy is so deliciously gloomy. He writes like the prophet of inexorable doom. I love it."

"Scarcely breakfast-time reading, I would have thought," Catherine remarked.

"Do you know, my dear," her father interrupted from behind *The Times*, "Lady Lanesborough has died. She could hardly have been much over fifty."

"Goodness!" exclaimed Catherine. "What a family I have. One wallowing in vicarious melancholy, while the other is showing decided intimations of mortality, by reading the obituaries over breakfast."

"Not so, young lady." Her father's face appeared briefly from behind the paper. "In my case at least, it has a very practical purpose. When you are a portrait-painter, it is important to keep a very careful eye on the social scene, if you are to prosper. You have not only to be in with the people who are fashionable now, but you have to form an acquaintance with those who are likely to climb to the top in future. Lady Lanesborough was a noted hostess, though, alas, not one of my patronesses. But someone will take her place—the intriguing question is, who?"

"You make it all sound rather parasitic, Daddy. Would you not rather give up portraits, and concentrate on your other paintings? After all, they sell well enough."

"But only because of the portraits. Make no mistake, the portraits are our bread and butter. And with two beautiful and expensive ladies to maintain, I need a steady supply of commissions."

"But I keep myself," Catherine objected.

"Well, let us say," replied her father with a twinkle, "that for a period slightly in excess of one year, your emoluments have enabled you to meet your day-to-day expenses, and buy your clothes—that is if one ignores ball-gowns, and outfits bought for special occasions." He lifted his hand to still her protests. "Do not think that I am ungrateful, or that I in any way belittle your undoubted success in your profession, but what you earn would not go very far in providing you with the style of living we enjoy." He disappeared again behind his paper.

Catherine moistened the tip of her finger, and moodily stabbed at the crumbs of toast on her plate.

"Who was the young man you were dancing with at Lady Ellesmere's ball, dear?" her mother asked.

"The one with the fluffy mustache and the stammer?"

"You are not very complimentary."

"He was all right."

"Who was he, dear?"

"His name is Thomas Tipping," said Catherine with a resigned sigh. "He comes from Christchurch in Hampshire."

"Do we know them, William?"

"The same family as the Gloucestershire Tippings, I think," said her husband. "Distantly related to Lord Warminster."

"Then at least he comes from a good family; and he must be eligible to have been invited at all. Does he live in town?"

"Yes, Mamma, he has rooms at Albany."

Her mother nodded her head approvingly. "Does he do anything?"

"Yes, Mamma, he is a very junior Lloyd's underwriter."

"Then obviously he is not working for his living . . ." Mrs. Marsden pursed her lips judicially. "You could do much worse, dear. Is he . . . interested?"

Catherine gave a snort of exasperation. "Mamma, I am much more concerned with the fact that he is moderately interesting. My involvement goes no further."

"Ah, but it may. You are seeing him again, I hope?"

"Yes. He is taking me to dinner at the Savoy tomorrow night."

"But is that wise, dear?" Mrs. Marsden asked anxiously. "There will be so many people there who matter."

"I can hardly advance our relationship, if I never see him, Mamma."

"I suppose not. But I would not want you to be thought fast . . . You will be discreet, won't you?"

Bragg read the paragraph in the *City Press* with approval.

"A good lass," he remarked, "Reliable. Now, lad, here is what I want you to do. By this evening, everybody we are concerned with will either have read it, or have heard about it. First thing tomorrow morning, you must go round all our suspects. If any of them is missing, find out where he is. If he cannot be accounted for, we will go for a warrant. But we shall have to move smartly. These people would think nothing of popping on a Channel packet, and away.''

"And who, pray, are our suspects?" asked Morton.

"Everybody who seems to have a connection with the case. Goddard, Frankis and Whitlock in Lloyd's, and then Cakebread. You should be able to check up on the first three by just wandering around the floor at the Royal Exchange. Goddard is least likely to be on view, but if he is around, the red-coated messengers will know.''

"And what about Cakebread?"

"Let's put the squeeze on him a bit. Call at the office, and if he is there, make an appointment for us to call and see him next Wednesday. If he asks what it is about, tell him you do not know.''

"Right. And will you keep the appointment?"

"Probably. He will have his lawyer there, of course, but he will have had a week to sweat over it . . . Now here is a list of all the people who left the hotel on the morning of Saturday the eleventh. I want you to split them up on a territorial basis into two lists. Then I will take one, and you the other, and we will ask if any of them has seen anything. While you are doing that, I will bring Sir William up to date.''

The majority of the people on the list proved to live in the midlands and the north. One man was Dutch, and had left for the continent. Bragg decided that in those cases a preliminary interview should be carried out by the local police, and they spent the rest of the day composing telegrams for transmission. This left five people who lived a reasonable train journey from the capital. Bragg allotted three of them to Morton, and took the other two himself. After two hectic days of travel they met on the Friday evening at Bragg's lodgings, and had to admit that they were no further forward. Except for the reception clerk and Dorothea Challis, no one would admit to having seen the murderer; and, of those two witnesses, one described him as of medium height, while the other had said he was tall. So far as the men who had left on the Saturday morning were concerned, two might have fitted the general description of the killer. One was a traveler in leather goods, from Northampton; the other was a landowner, who had been up to London for a banquet. Neither of them appeared in any way to be involved in the world of shipping or marine insurance.

When Morton arrived at Old Jewry next morning, he expected to find a thoroughly dejected Bragg. Instead, he was smoking his pipe, and smiling in satisfaction. He tossed an envelope to Morton.

"There is somebody who can get results," he said.

"Miss Marsden?" asked Morton, recognizing the handwriting.

Bragg nodded. "Read it."

The letter was brief. It told Bragg that according to information from a source she would regard as reliable, Frankis had paid out the claim on the hull insurance of the *Dancing Lady*.

"She is certainly a good jounalist," remarked Morton, handing back the letter.

Bragg seemed about to make a rejoinder, but contented himself with reading the letter again. Then he rose, and knocked out his pipe in the big glass ash tray on his desk.

"I have a fancy to lean on Frankis a bit," he remarked. "We do have the discrepancy between his story and Ingham's, about whether he was told that Gadd was master. And, frankly, since none of our prime suspects made any move after reading the bit in the *City Press*, I don't see there is a fat lot else we can do."

They took a hansom cab to Marble Arch, and got directions to Park Street from the constable on the beat. Grosvenor Mansions was a red-brick block of apartments five stories high, and a hundred yards long. It had been built without mews; evidently the residents were expected to travel around London by cab or underground railway. As they entered the spacious entrance-hall, Morton remembered that Catherine Marsden's home was a mere stone's throw away.

There was a lift opposite the door, and giving a grunt of anticipation, Bragg made a bee-line for it.

"I imagine," said Morton, suppressing a smile, "that number three will be on the ground floor."

Bragg swung around. "Ah yes," he mumbled. "I expect you are right . . . There it is. Come on, lad." He strode across the polished marble, and pressed the electric bell.

After a moment they heard the rattle of a chain being hooked in position, and then the door was opened a crack.

"Yes?" a woman's voice inquired.

"We have come to see Mr. Frankis," Bragg replied.

"Who are you?" asked the voice.

"Police officers."

"Well, he is not here."

"Can we come in?" asked Bragg, presenting his warrant card to the aperture.

The door was closed, the chain rattled once more, and then it was opened wide. A young woman of about thirty stood there. She was wearing a rather drab day-dress, and her mousy hair was scraped up to the top of her head. She wore no jewelry. She looked in alarm at the intimidating size of the two policemen, then stood aside.

"Thank you, miss," said Bragg in a friendly voice. "We wanted a quick word with Mr. Frankis on an insurance matter, and we were not able to let him know we were coming."

The woman took them into a modestly furnished sitting-room. Bragg saw that off the entrance hall, there was an open door to a kitchen. On the other side was a door with opaque glass panels—presumably that was a bathroom. Which meant that the only other door must lead to the sole bedroom of the apartment.

"And who are you, then?" asked Bragg.

"I am Miss Givan, Mr. Frankis's housekeeper."

"There doesn't seem to be a lot of house to keep," Bragg remarked genially.

A dogged look settled on her face, and she looked away.

"You say Mr. Frankis is not here. When will he be back?"

"On Monday evening, about seven o'clock."

"I see. It will hardly wait till then. Do you know where he is now?"

"He is at home," Miss Given said in a small voice.

"And where is home?"

"In Sussex. He comes up on a Monday morning, and goes back on a Friday evening."

"I see. And what would be the address?"

"The Grange, Brookwood, near Liphook."

"Right. Thank you, miss. We will probably go and see him down there."

When they reached the street again, Bragg made to call a cab, then checked. "No," he said. "On second thoughts, it might be wrong to give him the whole weekend to ponder on things. I think we might do better to see him Sunday afternoon. Is that all right with you?"

"I would be very happy, so long as I can play cricket today as a *quid pro quo*."

Bragg smiled. "All right, lad. But mind you, it is not a precedent."

They arrived at Liphook station at one o'clock, and lunched on pork pie and beer at the Railway Hotel. It was a tiny village, and they were forced to bribe the local undertaker to convey them to Brookwood in a black-trimmed coach used for funerals. But, countryman or not, the man had his professional pride, and, having harnessed two coal-black horses to the carriage, he insisted on changing into his black funeral clothes before proceeding. So it was after considerable delay that they set out, and even then they made but slow progress. The horses had a clear understanding of what was an appropriate speed, and, disregarding the urgings of the undertaker and the cracking of the whip, proceeded at a dignified funereal pace, their sable plumes nodding.

Once out of the village, they passed through two or three isolated hamlets, but otherwise they saw no human habitation. The carriage crawled respectfully through heavily wooded country, split by numerous streams. After nearly an hour, they began to ascend a steep hill, and Morton, leaning out of the window, could see the spire of a church at its crest.

"I think we must be almost there," he remarked. "I must say that if I lived so far in the country, I too would stay in town during the week; and that without taking into account the charms of the young miss, who has obviously given her all."

"It's not funny, lad," said Bragg curtly. "What is she going to get out of life? She probably went to Frankis's office as a typewriter, and had her head turned by a few glittering presents. You will know how it is done better than I."

"You make it sound like a bad melodrama, sergeant. I am sure she must have had some say in the outcome. She is not particularly pretty. Perhaps she preferred this to remaining at home with her parents."

"That's the way you people ease your consciences. But what has she to look forward to?"

"I am sure that Frankis would be generous."

Bragg snorted in derision, as the carriage came to a halt, and they heard the undertaker asking for directions. The horses resumed their grave pace, and turning up a graveled drive, they solemnly approached The Grange. At first sight, Morton thought, their grotesque conveyance was perhaps not so incongruous after all; for the house was itself a discordant conjunction of different architectural styles. Built in assertive red brick, it combined an Italianate porch, medieval towers, thrusting Jacobean chimneys, and jutting Elizabethan gables— all within a building a hundred yards by fifty. The whole exuberant extravaganza could only have been conceived by someone with a bizarre sense of fun. It would serve well as a bordello, or a gambling club, but to Morton's mind, would be intolerable to live in.

They got down from their coach, and Bragg tugged on the great brass bell-pull. The door was opened by a smart maid, in a black dress, and crisp white apron and cap. She confirmed that the master was at home, and showed them into a large sitting-room. The walls were covered with wainscot to head height, which was broken now and again by fluted wooden pillars up to the ceiling. Over the mantel was a heavily carved slab of white marble. Heavy oak beams dissected the ceiling into large panels, which were encrusted with Jacobean plaster-work. But at least the room was a simple rectangle, which was an improvement on the fragmented exterior. The furnishings were substantial and rich, the carpet luxurious. Whatever it said about the aesthetic sensibilities of its occupants, the house proclaimed to the world their wealth and social standing.

The door opened with a faint susurration, and a woman entered. She was about thirty-three, a little taller than average, and with an exquisitely proportioned body. Her face was heart-shaped, her eyes green, her hair auburn. Her striking beauty was somehow in harmony with the extravagance of the house. Morton would not have been wholly surprised, had she materialised in a flash of magnesium powder. She was wearing an embroidered cream silk dress, which rustled over the carpet as she came toward them.

"My husband seems to have gone out for a moment," she

said with a welcoming smile. "I imagine he is in the grounds somewhere."

"If you do not mind, madam, we will wait for him," said Bragg.

"Of course. I have sent for some tea." She glanced through a window, where the sombre heads of their horses were visible. "You seem to have applied considerable ingenuity to get here!" Her voice was deep and warm. "If we had known you were coming, we would have sent the dog-cart."

"Since it seems we may be here for some time, it would be a great favor if you would get us back to the station," said Bragg. "I could dismiss our present conveyance, then."

"By all means. An undertaker's carriage is scarcely an agreeable mode of transport."

"Thank you." Bragg went out to pay the driver.

Mrs. Frankis moved closer to Morton. "You came via Liphook, I take it?"

"Yes. It was a most beautiful drive," replied Morton.

"Isn't it?" She looked up at him with a friendly smile. "Do you come from London?" she asked.

"My home is in Kent, near Ashwell. It is on the edge of the downs, so there are nothing like as many trees as you have here."

She seemed to be projecting all her personality at him, to make him feel at ease, and to comprehend what he was saying. Her eyes were fixed on his, and her lips were parted in a half-smile.

"Yes, it is a lovely area," she murmured. "I cannot understand how my husband can bear to stay in London all the week."

There was a click from the doorway, and the maid placed a tea-tray on a low table. Mrs. Frankis laid her hand on Morton's arm, and drew him down into a small settee.

"Do you take milk, constable?" her voice caressed him. "Or would you prefer lemon?"

"Milk, please." Morton was beginning to feel a combination of embarrassment and concupiscence.

"That's got rid of our undertaker," said Bragg breezily, as he re-entered. "I do not think we could have borne a journey back at that pace. I felt like jumping on the box and lambasting those nags with a whip." He took an armchair near Morton, and picked up a cup of tea.

"A cake, sergeant?" Mrs. Frankis leaned forward, and her breast pressed against Morton's arm.

"No, thank you, madam. We had something to eat in Liphook . . . Do you think your husband will be long?"

"I cannot say. Why do not you, sergeant, walk around the grounds to find him? Your constable could stay here, in case he comes back first."

Bragg rose, and crossed to the french-window; beyond was an extensive lawn fringed with trees, and between the leaves he caught the glint of water. He screwed up his eyes.

"I think I can see him, in a boat." Bragg stepped out into the garden, and Morton leapt to his feet. "Thank you for the tea, Mrs. Frankis," he mumbled, and shot out in pursuit.

"That's a hot-arsed one," observed Bragg laconically. "If I hadn't been there, I reckon she would have had you down behind the sofa, by now."

"I have never met anyone like her before," said Morton, with a rueful laugh.

"You'll meet a few before you are finished . . . I won't deny they are tempting. It would be like every day was your birthday, particularly if she was married to some other poor devil." He raised his arm, and returned Frankis's wave.

The underwriter propped his fishing rod against the stern of the tiny boat, and began to row toward the landing stage close by them. He backed water and slid smoothly alongside.

"Hello!" he called. "Nice to see you . . . I have to catch some fish for dinner tonight. We are having the neighbors over." He jerked his head, and through the trees they could see several other houses, which must have been built further down the lane.

"Come aboard," Frankis suggested. "We can talk, then, while I fish."

The two policemen clambered precariously into the little craft, Morton squatting uncomfortably in the bows, while Bragg settled himself in the stern, facing Frankis.

"Quite a stretch of water you have here," Bragg remarked, as Frankis began to pull towards the middle of the lake.

"It was just a rather soggy area of ground, with the river running through it, when we came here. There is a narrow ridge of rock across the bottom end, and the river used to drop down through a cleft to the rocks below. It was quite spectacular, in its way, but I thought of a better idea. I had the ground excavated to form the lake, and built up the ridge to make a weir.'' He turned the boat slightly and pointed to a gap in the trees, where a flimsy chain was outlined against the sky.

Morton shaded his eyes with his hand. ''There is quite a volume of water going over,'' he remarked.

''Yes,'' said Frankis. ''After a really bad storm, the noise of the fall is so great it is difficult to sleep, I lose a good number of my fish then, of course, and have to re-stock. They just get swept down the river.''

''You stock with trout, I suppose?'' Morton remarked.

''Yes. Brown trout mostly, but a few rainbow.'' Frankis began to row towards a stake positioned toward the bottom end of the lake. ''Would you be so good as to tie up, constable?'' he asked.

They glided smoothly up to it, and Morton secured the bow of the boat. Immediately, it swung round in the current, until it was pointing upstream.

''The stake is on the edge of the main stream,'' Frankis explained. ''Trout are lazy animals, and prefer to have their food brought to them by the river. I have always caught my biggest fish here.'' He took up his rod, and, balancing himself against the thwart, began to scan the water. ''There is one taking nymphs over there. Let me see if I can tempt him.'' He began to cast out his line. ''I am afraid I use wet fly when I am fishing for the larder,'' he said, as the line dropped on the surface. He watched intently as it drifted down the current. ''No, he is too wily for this fly, I'll try a different one.'' He reeled in his line, and removed the fly from the trace. ''What is it you wanted to talk to me about?'' he asked.

''I saw Ingham, the broker, before he was killed,'' said Bragg. ''He insisted that he told you Gadd was master of the *Dancing Lady*.''

''Then we will say that he did—*nil nisi bonum*, after all.'' The Latin tag somehow fitted the scholarly face better than the tweed fishing hat. ''Since our conversation, I have looked up the papers on the *Pearl* sinking; and really there was no indication that the ship had been scuttled. The Board of Trade inquiry was purely routine, and the evidence of the master was accepted.'' Frankis selected a dun-colored fly from his hat, and began to tie it on to the trace.

''Were there any other witnesses?'' asked Bragg.

"The other two European officers gave evidence, and they confirmed the master's story."

"What were their names?"

"I cannot recollect. I believe they were referred to in the report by their rank only."

"And did you pay out on the claim?"

"Of course. Even if the Board of Trade had concluded that the *Pearl* had been scuttled, it would still have been a loss covered by the policy." Frankis began to cast his line again.

"I am told that you have paid out on the *Dancing Lady* hull claim," said Bragg. "Is that correct?"

"Yes . . ." replied Frankis, watching his line drift down the stream. "Yes, I paid the claim."

"Why did you do that, when Whitlock is fighting a court case to avoid paying, on precisely the same facts?"

Frankis paused, and began to gather the slack line in his left hand. "You must understand that there is no cohesion amongst the various syndicates at Lloyd's, and it would be undesirable that there should be. Each underwriter has to exercise his own judgment. But the fact that I have paid out in no way undermines Peter Whitlock's position. If he succeeds, then I shall have to put on as brave a face as I can muster." He began to cast again, and Bragg watched with interest.

"What factors influenced your decision?" he asked.

"Purely commercial ones. I personally do not think that Whitlock will succeed in avoiding payment. He is an odd man, and is inclined to find a point of principle in the most obscure circumstance." He began to recover his line again. "It is beyond doubt that barratry is intended to be covered by the Lloyd's policy, and is covered by it. To my way of thinking, it brings discredit on the market when someone tries to take advantage of a minor deviation to avoid paying out. I suppose Whitlock can afford to take a robust attitude . . ." he began to work out his line again till it dropped lightly on the surface. "He writes mainly a cargo account, and cargo is inevitably irregular business. I write mainly hull, and, quite frankly, I cannot afford to take the same view. I have led the insurance of the Green Funnel ships for fifteen years, and, all in all, I have done very well out of it. If I refused to pay this claim, I would never be shown their business again . . . ah," he began to gather in the line with his free hand. "See that big one? Over there by the weed." He jerked his head toward the side of the

ake, and began to cast in that direction. As the line dropped
ently on the water, a dark shape rose to the fly, the surface
impled, and Frankis struck. "Got him!" he cried exultantly.
he line was taut for a second, before the fish began his run.

"The trouble here is the weed," Frankis grunted. "I don't
eem able to get rid of it." The reel screamed as he fought to
eep the trout away from the edge of the lake. He would reel in
ard, the rod arcing under the pressure, then the fish would
reak away again. But each time, the dash would end further
way from the safety of the weed. Finally, the fish seemed to
urrender, and Frankis pulled it in, its back cutting a ripple on
ie surface.

"That's a beauty," said Bragg admiringly, "I never caught
nything approaching that in my whole life."

"I was not aware that you were a fisherman, sergeant," said
rankis.

"I'm not. I used to go out to the local pond as a boy, with a
amboo cane and a bent pin. I caught my biggest fish ever,
/ith that—a six ounce roach! Then I thought I was a real
sherman, and blew my hard-earned money on a rod and reel,
ut I never caught anything worthwhile with it."

"Have you ever tried fly-fishing?" asked Frankis.

"Not for trout. I had a go with my cousin's salmon rod, on
ie river at Wareham, but I didn't catch anything."

"Would you like to try with this?" asked Frankis, holding
ut the butt of the rod. "It is more or less the same. The rod has
springier action, but the technique is identical."

Morton watched temptation and caution chasing each other
ver Bragg's face. "Yes, I would like that," he said emphati-
ally.

Frankis surveyed the trout in his bag. "It would be nice if we
ould get another one, but if we do not, the last one will make
p for it." He dropped onto the stern seat, and Bragg made his
ay forward, gripping the sides of the boat. Then, pressing
gainst the thwart to steady himself, he picked up the rod.

"Take your time, until you have got the feel of the rod,"
rankis advised.

Bragg's first cast was a failure, the line landing in a heap a
ere ten feet from the boat. He reeled it in self-consciously,
d began to cast again, feeding the line out until a con-
derable length followed the swish of the rod-tip through the
r. Then, with a final flick, the line settled gently down. There

was an immediate swirl of water; Bragg jerked the rod up involuntarily, and the fish was hooked. Instead of making for the weeds, this one dived down, and the line went slack.

"Reel in! Reel in!" cried Frankis. "It's coming down river." Bragg brought up the tip of the rod, and started to reel in frantically. He got the line taut, only to have the fish tear most of it off the reel again, as it turned for the weed.

"Make him fight!" cried Frankis. "Try to turn him."

Bragg pivoted, dragging on the rod, and began to reel in again. "I must have lost it," he said. "No, there it is, it's given up . . . It's only a little one," he said disappointedly as it came into sight a short distance away from the boat. At that moment the surface of the water was shattered, and the trout was seized by a gleaming projectile which hurtled back into the river, taking the line with it.

"It's a pike," yelled Frankis in excitement, "an enormous pike!"

"I can't hold it," gasped Bragg. "Here you take it."

Frankis stumbled forward towards Bragg, the boat lurched, and with a startled yell Bragg toppled into the river. He came to the surface struggling and spluttering. "Help!" he cried, "I can't swim."

Frankis seemed frozen in horror. Morton began to drag off his coat and his boots. Bragg was flailing at the surface of the water in an attempt to keep up, but his sodden clothes and the weight of his boots were dragging him down. Morton jumped into the water and began to swim towards him. Immediately, he could feel the pull of the current, and had to tread water to get his bearings. He saw Bragg's anguished face as it disappeared under the surface, and he propelled himself downstream with powerful strokes. He was about to cast around again, when he collided with something beneath him, and felt his left arm seized in a desperate grasp. Bragg hauled himself to the surface and gulped at the air.

"Roll on to your back," Morton shouted. "You will drown us both!"

Bragg turned an uncomprehending face towards the sound and recognizing Morton, wrapped a frenzied arm around his neck. Morton ducked down, and managed to extricate his head, but as he came up again, the panic-stricken Bragg grabbed his shoulder and tried to drag himself upwards. Morton could feel the current swirling them towards the weir

If they did not drown in the next half-minute, they were likely
to be shattered on the rocks below. In desperation, he pulled
sideways, and smashed his fist into Bragg's jaw. The threshing
body went inert, and Morton twisted under it to support it.
There was no question of swimming against the current, the
best he could hope for was to paddle with his feet and edge out
of the main stream . . . But that would take them into the
weed. The weir gave a better chance than that. He lifted his
head. They were now about twenty yards away from it, and
slightly off its center. The current was at its most powerful
here, and would catapult them over to their death. Then he
realized that they were being swept toward one of the
stanchions that held the safety-chain. If he could work over to
the left a little, they had a good chance of striking it square on.
Then if he could wrap himself around it, and hold on, he might
possibly get hold of the chain. At least there was firm footing
there. He began to pump with his feet, going with the current
rather than against it. They were approaching the weir at an
alarming rate, and when he lifted his head he could hear the
roar of the water as it plunged over the brink. He wrapped one
arm around Bragg's chest, and paddled furiously with the
other. Then he felt a jarring shock as his knees struck the inner
surface of the concrete. He felt the current whipping his body
over like a twig, then his shoulder struck the stanchion and he
grabbed at it. For a moment the rush of water threatened to tear
Bragg out of his grasp, then he managed to maneuver and lift
him, until the hollow of his back was against the stanchion,
and he was sitting on the top of the weir.

Now the strain was off him, Morton looked back toward the
boat, Frankis was standing immobile, looking towards the
weir. Morton waved his hand and Frankis came alive. He cast
off the boat and began to row toward the landing-stage. Morton
was aghast at this callousness, then realized the futility of
rowing towards the weir. The flimsy boat would be smashed to
matchwood. But, by the time Frankis got help, his own
strength would have given out, and they would have been
swept over. He looked along the weir. They were about ten
yards from the end, with another stanchion in the middle.
There was nothing for it but to make the attempt. He grasped
the stanchion and pulled himself upward till he was kneeling
on the weir, straddling Bragg's inert body. He then reached up
to the chain. Fortunately it was taut, and would give a secure

support. He raised himself until he was standing on the top of the concrete. The surface was rough, and with care he ought to be able to achieve a kind of equilibrium with the rush of water. He lifted his foot, and felt it being swept away by the current. The only way would be to shuffle forwards, but he could use Bragg as a counterbalance by trailing his legs along the inside face of the dam. He looked upwards at the sky and trees, in a kind of invocation; then working his foot between the stanchion and Bragg's back, he wrapped his left arm around his chest, and with a sudden twist pushed him off the weir. He thought the weight would tear his arm out of its socket as he began to edge along. But at least Bragg's body was breaking the force of the current, and helping him to keep his footing. When he reached the next stanchion, the dam seemed to stretch endlessly before him. He wanted to rest, to prop Bragg up, and release the agonizing pull from his arm. But, if he did, he knew he would never have the strength to start again. He shuffled on, oblivious of everything except the rasp of the concrete, the tug of the chain in his hand, and the inexorable weight that was tearing him apart. He shuffled on mindlessly, until he felt Bragg jerking to get away, pulling him down, down to the rushing torrent. It seemed unfair after all his efforts to want to go back. He felt like weeping with self-pity. Then a petulant anger welled up inside him. With the dregs of his strength, he gave a despairing wrench at his tormentor. Bragg's boots were dislodged from the tree root which had entrapped them, and the two men pitched together on to the earth.

How long he was unconscious, Morton never knew. He remembered hearing Bragg's voice complaining faintly, he remembered rolling off him on to lush grass, before the swirling mists enveloped him again. When he finally came to his senses, a bedraggled Bragg was propped against a tree talking to Frankis. He was helped to his feet; and, while Frankis went for the dog-cart, Bragg and Morton, leaning on each other, struggled up to the house. While they were standing under the Italianate porch, they heard a window opened behind them; and as the trap started down the drive, they were followed by the derisive laughter of the lady with green eyes and auburn hair.

CHAPTER ———— ———— FOURTEEN

"Good mornin', Mr. Wilson." Greg held out his hand with a smile.

The planter rose from his office desk. "Good morning, lieutenant. This is a pleasant surprise. Will you have a cigar?"

Greg took one from the box on the desk, bit off the end, and spat the shred of tobacco through the open window. "The cotton is looking real fine," he remarked.

"Yes. We ought to have a better crop than ever." Wilson eyed Greg warily, as he puffed at the cigar.

"Didn't have much to do this morning," went on Greg. "So I thought I might ride over, and see how things are goin' with you."

"That's a long way to come visiting," replied Wilson. "I can not believe you came over here just to say hello."

"Well," drawled Greg, inspecting the end of his cigar, "I thought I'd like to take a look at this cotton-seed mill of yours."

"Tarnation!" exclaimed Wilson in irritation; then he smiled.

"Well, I suppose it had to come out some time. Would you like to see it?" he asked eagerly. "It's just across the yard."

Greg followed him to a large sun-bleached wooden building, some two hundred yards from the rear of the house. Wilson flung open a door, and in the gloom Greg could see the outlines of a huge piece of plant.

"You are standing now where the cotton-seed will come in," said Wilson. "The bag will be emptied into this hopper, and the conveyor belt will take the seed to the top of the crusher." He pointed towards the beams of the roof. "You see that smaller hopper there? Well, the conveyor empties the seed out into that, and from there it comes down just by gravity . . . That's the crusher," he indicated a massive piece of machinery resting in mid-air on stout brick foundations. "Of course, you cannot see the crushing-heads, because they are inside. The oil and pulp fall to the bottom of it, and the oil goes through a sieve, and runs off into that tank."

"Seems kind of high up for you to get at it," remarked Greg.

"You don't get the idea, lieutenant," Wilson replied buoyantly. "This is not a domestic installation. It is designed so that barrels can be filled on the platform, and then rolled on to a cart. I tell you, everything has been thought out . . . Now, inside the crusher-box is an arm which scrapes across the face of the sieve, and pushes the residue up this slope into the presser. There the remaining oil is squeezed out, and what is left of the seed comes out as a kind of cake, and almost dry. Clever, isn't it?"

"And what do you do with the cake? Eat it?" Greg tittered.

"I see no reason why the hogs shouldn't," replied Wilson seriously. "But I've got a better idea. Come round to the other side."

Greg ducked under the chute from the presser, and saw that this side was festooned with drive-belts in all the directions.

"The mill has its own steam-plant built in," said Wilson triumphantly. "Of course, it hasn't been run for any length of time yet, but I guess if we use the cotton-seed cake for fuel, we will not need much wood in addition." He looked expectantly at Greg for his verdict.

"That sure is a fine piece of machinery," said Greg reflectively, as he led the way back to the yard. "Will it pay?"

"If my neighbors have the sense to use it, I am certain it will. Why, we could even bring a branch of the railroad down, and then it could serve the whole area."

Greg leaned on a fence in the shade, and tossed the butt of his cigar away.

"Why did you bring it in by Dettingers' pier, instead of the port, Mr. Wilson?" he asked.

"Well," replied Wilson uneasily, "I wanted to keep it quiet. I reckoned that if the news got out, somebody might beat me to it. Now the mill is ready and working, I am hoping that everybody will accept it, and send their seed here for crushing, instead of shipping it out to New Orleans."

"That doesn't explain why you didn't use the port—not to my mind, Mr. Wilson."

"Come on, lieutenant. This mill is going to take work away from the port. If they'd discovered what was in the crates, I guess one or two would have found their way to the bottom of the harbour."

"You know, Mr. Wilson," said Greg lazily, "they are sayin' that this mill don't belong to you, and that it was meant to be delivered to New Orleans."

"They are lying, if they say that," retorted Wilson angrily. "Come on, I'll show you." He stalked into the house, and through to his office.

"You know," said Greg, "I would be real glad if you could show me somethin' to prove them wrong."

"I had to surrender the bill of lading to the master, in order to get the goods, but I can describe it."

"Go on."

"Well, it was made out to 'Order,' and endorsed by the manufacturers. It was sent in the ship's mail, in an envelope addressed to me. I just opened the envelope, gave the bill to the master, and they unloaded the crates."

"Seems might complicated, to me," said Greg.

"It was suggested by the agent who got it for me. He knew I wanted to keep it quiet for a time."

"Who was the agent?"

"De Wolf & Fletcher, of New Orleans. I had talked to De Wolf about buying a cotton-seed mill at the beginning of last year, but had not taken it any further. Then in September, he wrote and said he could get hold of one for me. I went over to New Orleans, and clinched the deal."

"Have you nothing to show this mill belongs to you?" asked Greg.

"Indeed I have." Wilson took a box file from the cupboard, and exracted a paper from it. "See, here is a letter from the shippers, Taylor Pendrill & Co., in England. They instructed me to send the money for the mill to an account in New York."

"And did you?"

"I did, on the twenty-third of October. You can check with the bank if you want to."

"Now you know I would not embarrass you by doin' that, Mr. Wilson. Can I see the letter?"

"Sure."

The letter was typed on headed paper, and directed that a sum in dollars, equivalent to the purchase price of £30,000, should be sent to Willam Heath & Co. in New York, for credit to the account of Martin & Co., bankers, of 68 Lombard Street, London.

Greg folded the letter, and handed it back. "Fine, Mr. Wilson," he said. "Then I guess the only folk who are unhappy will be the U.S. Customs; always assumin' they ever get to know about it."

By the time Bragg and Morton had got back to London, their clothes were more or less dry. They had taken a growler at the station, and hopped into it before the driver had a chance to question their dishevelled appearance. Morton had been dropped off at Bishopsgate, and then Bragg had gone on to Tan House Lane. He had crept painfully up the front steps and just unlocked the door, when Mrs. Jenks swooped down on him. At a glance she had taken in his muddied clothes and grazed hands, and had scolded him like a naughty child. Then she had decreed that he should go straight down to the kitchen for a bath. In a trice she had lit the fire under the wash-boiler, and before he could summon up the strength to resist, Bragg was sitting in a steaming hip-bath. She had modestly thrown in some clean underwear, and then insisted on pouring iodine over the ragged abrasions on his shins. He had cursed her wildly and at length, but was in no state to resist; and he had to admit that she had been right. After that ordeal, he had drunk half a bottle of whisky and collapsed into bed.

Next morning he had hobbled into Old Jewry, only to meet the Commissioner in the corridor. He had been compelled to give an account of Sunday's incident, and had been ordered to stay at home until he had recovered. He had spent the rest of the day sitting in the sun in the garden, to Mrs. Jenks's evident disapproval. She clearly felt that this was the grossest form of self-indulgence, and had sniffed reproachfully when he ventured down to the kitchen for his lunch. During the evening Morton had called, and Bragg was uncharitably gratified to see that he was walking stiffly, and shielding his left shoulder. They had relived the previous day's events over a drink, and agreed that their injuries merited a further day of convalescence.

By Tuesday afernoon, Bragg was feeling uncomfortably like a malingerer, and was pleased when, after supper, Catherine Marsden put her head round the door. She looked anxiously at him sitting with his legs propped up on a stool.

"Mrs. Jenks has been telling me about your accident," she said in consternation. "It sounds as if you are lucky to be alive."

"I wouldn't be, if it were not for young Morton. I reckon he will get a medal for bravery."

"Really?" exclaimed Catherine with pleasure.

"It must have taken tremendous courage to risk his life like that."

"These things can happen so quickly," remarked Catherine.

"Well . . . I know this job makes you suspicious of everyone, but I can't make out Frankis. From what Morton says, he just stood in the boat for around three minutes, watching us being swept towards the weir. He didn't even untie the boat to go for help. He didn't move, until Morton waved at him. I cannot understand that. Morton says he must have been immobilised by the shock. Certainly, when he came down after I had recovered consciousness, he seemed perturbed all right . . . I don't know."

"But he could hardly have manufactured an incident like that."

"No, I grant you that. And he would have had to be very quick-thinking to take advantage of it in order to tip me in the river; and, frankly, he does not look capable of that kind of reflex action. But there was another odd thing. As you know, the Foreign Office has been bringing pressure on Lloyd's to settle the *Dancing Lady* claims. When I got your note, I thought it was worth pushing Frankis a bit on it. I asked him why he had settled. He gave me a lecture on the underwriter's discretion, and the pressures of the market, but he never once mentioned Lloyd's or the Foreign Office. I find that curious. It was almost as if he thought we didn't know, and so he was not going to mention it."

"How about letting me write a paragraph for tomorrow's *City Press*?" Catherine suggested.

"I would prefer it if you did no such thing," replied Bragg with a wry smile. "You can do a full column, if Morton gets his medal."

"And is he as incapacitated as you are?"

"He was in a bad way, but you young people are resilient. The last thing he said to me was that he couldn't miss the first night of Marriage."

"Oh," Catherine said flatly. She looked out of the window for a space, without speaking. Then she turned to Bragg. "I found out about Harvey & Crane for you," she said.

"Did you?" exclaimed Bragg. "Good girl!"

"It is owned by the Jacobson family. I ought to say 'clan,' really. They have members in virtually every country in Europe, and in America."

"And are they shipowners?"

"Not according to my informant. He describes them as international financiers. He said that they were actually keeping some governments afloat."

"Now that is interesting. Thank you. It looks as if we will have to re-think our views on this case, yet again."

They relapsed into their own thoughts, Catherine showing no inclination to leave. Suddenly she looked quickly around the room and said, "Are you happy here, Sergeant Bragg?"

For a moment Bragg was at a loss. "Am I happy?" he repeated.

"Are you happy with your life?"

"Goodness me! What a deep question for a summer evening."

"Nevertheless, it would be helpful if you would tell me . . . I find it difficult to discuss serious matters with my family," she added.

Bragg looked at her quizzically. "You are not going to tell me why you, of all people, need help, I suppose?"

"Let us say that it is merely out of human interest."

Bragg looked at her determined face. "All right, I will try . . . If you measure it by what I expected, I suppose you would say this is a disappointment. At twenty-five I had a quarter in the Bishops gate section-house, a pretty young wife, and a baby on the way. I thought then that I had everything I could want. It takes so little to destroy things. The doctor was at great pains to explain that it was a minute microbe, you could barely see under a microscope. I don't know what help that was supposed to be, with both of them dead . . . But life goes on, and you have to go with it. And, as time passes, you begin to realize that it might not have been so rosy as you anticipated. Half the time, it's only because you want things so badly that you think they are worth having." He looked at Catherine pensively. "My wife was a real country girl, brought up in a village with ten houses and a pub. She would never have stuck it here."

"Anyway," he went on somberly. "I made a fresh start here, and I am content enough. I have a comfortable home, even if it isn't my own . . . I could not tell you what happiness is. To me it's something that evaporates as soon as you realize it's there. As I say, I am content, and that is all I expect now."

"Are you content because of living here, or because you hold an interesting and responsible job?"

"You can't carve it up like that, miss. I've got a comfortable way of life that I could never have dreamed of, if I had stayed at home in Turners Puddle. It sounds big-headed, I know, but I've taken the chances that came my way, and gone up in the world at a time when most people are struggling not to be any worse off. I don't mind admitting that I get a lot of satisfaction from that. There have been bad things in my life, but you learn to live with them. There's not a ha'porth of use fighting against circumstance. I remember when I used to drive the cows back into the field after milking. It was the first through the gate that had the good grass, and the one that tried to go off up the lane that got the stick . . . There you are, real market-cross philosophy. I don't suppose it helped at all."

"No," replied Catherine dolefully. "I do not think it has."

* * *

"I hope you realize how privileged you are, being allowed to visit me in my dressing-room." Dorothea Challis was struggling to comb out her hair.

"Then at least my devotion has brought me some slight reward," replied Morton.

"Slight? I would have you know that no one else has been so favored."

Morton smiled mischievously. "I meant slight, in relation to what I hope to receive in the future."

"I refuse to acknowledge that remark, lest you mean something indelicate," Dorothea said sharply.

"I assure you that my adoration is pure beyond understanding."

"It is your persistence that is beyond understanding," replied Dorothea with a smile. "I always thought that policemen were dull, uncommunicative creatures. I did not expect to meet one who could string out for two hours the simple process of procuring my signature on a piece of paper."

"Your beauty confounds my senses," he said lightly. "Nor am I alone. Look at all the bouquets. There is hardly room to move in here for flowers."

"I am sure that you must have sent half of them!"

"I have never known such an ecstatic reception from a first-night audience."

"But not for me," Dorothea protested, the excitement suffusing her face once more.

"Not for you? With four curtain calls to yourself? I tell you, they were enchanted with you."

"What, dressed as a boy? . . . Don't be silly, James."

"Such is the magic of Mozart."

"I wish I could bring some magic to dressing my hair. These wigs leave you looking quite hideous."

"Then stop fishing for compliments, and let us to supper."

Dorothea slipped into her cloak, and Morton followed her through the white-painted subterranean passage under the stage.

"I have not encountered a tunnel like this," he said, "since I went round Newgate prison."

Dorothea laughed. "But think of all the famous feet that have trodden it . . . and been glad to reach the fresh air!"

She pushed through the stage door. "Where are you taking me?" she asked.

"Unless you object extremely, I shall take you away from all your other admirers, so that I can have you to myself."

"Is that fair?" she pouted. "I am an opera singer, not a society beauty. I need to be with people who will praise my singing. All you tell me is how pretty I am."

"Ah, but I shall adulate your arias, rhapsodize over your recitatives, praise your pianissimos, relish your rallentandos . . ."

"Enough, enough!" she cried happily. "Is it far?"

"Just round the corner. May we walk?"

"Don't forget, James, that I have been leaping around in a most unladylike way all evening." She tucked her hand in the crook of his arm.

"This evening was delightful," Morton murmured. "I am torn between the desire to cherish you as a treasure too delicate for this way of life, and an impulse to shout in the streets 'Here is an English soprano equal to any in the world!' . . . Why don't you join the D'Oyly Carte company? We could see you in London all the time then."

"What? Sing Gilbert and Sullivan?" Dorothea asked in astonishment.

"Why not?"

She stopped, hitched her skirts over her ankles, and did a coy pirouette.

> *"Three little maids from school are we,*
> *Pert as a school girl well can be,*
> *Filled to the brim with girlish glee,*
> *Three little maids from school."*

she sang in a mincing voice.

"James," she said, "you are a Philistine."

CHAPTER FIFTEEN

When they got to the shipowners' office, Bragg and Morton found that Pocklington was there before them. Cakebread's face was haggard, but the solicitor had the contented look of a man who was going to be well paid for doing nothing.

"It is no use asking for more information," he said urbanely. "You already have all that the company is prepared to give."

"I have not come to ask," said Bragg firmly. "I've come to demand. Here is a search warrant for these and any other premises occupied by the company." He flung the document on the desk.

Pocklington perused it carefully. "It only relates to information relevant to the loss of the *Dancing Lady*," he said. "You are not entitled to any other."

"That is all we are interested in, at the moment," replied Bragg. "Now are you going to cooperate, or do I have to shut down the offices and bring in a team of detectives to find what I am looking for?"

Pocklington turned to Cakebread, who had gone an unpleasant shade of gray.

"It would be inconvenient . . ." Cakebread muttered.

"My advice to the company, then, is this," said Pocklington. "They should cooperate insofar as they will make available to you any documents and information relating to the last voyage of that ship, but they will take steps to insure that you are not given access to information in files and ledgers which relates to other vessels."

"You can cover everything else up, if you want to," said Bragg. "I am not interested in it."

"We would further require that any examination should take place in this office."

"I am going to look at them now, whether you like it or not," said Bragg truculently.

Pocklington looked across at Cakebread, who inclined his head.

"What have you got on that last voyage?" Bragg demanded.

"Not very much," Cakebread said tremulously. He went to a cupboard, and returned with a thin file. "Here is the charter party with Michel Tissier et Cie."

"I think I saw the draft in Ingham's office. Were there any changes?"

"I do not think so. He said it was in the usual form."

"What else?"

"Well, nothing."

"Nothing?" Bragg exclaimed angrily.

"We would normally have a voyage account prepared by the ship's husband, but for one reason or another Taylor Pendrill have not sent it yet."

"I would have thought Ingham's murder was a very powerful reason," said Bragg brutally. "Will the figures be in their offices?"

"The expense figures should be."

"Oh, yes. I wanted to ask you about the charter income," Bragg said. "It worked out very nicely for you, didn't it, that the advance was precisely equal to the hire charge earned by the company up to the date the ship was scuttled?"

"That is a wholly unwarranted aspersion, sergeant," said Pocklington. "And you must know it."

"Must I? How would you explain it, Mr. Pocklington? Would you say it was all pure chance?"

"It is at least possible."

"Would you like to tell me what the odds are against it happening? You would need a sheet of paper a yard across to write them down."

"I assure you," Cakebread quavered, "that no one in this company had anything to do with settling the advance. That was done by Mr. Ingham, and embodied in the charter party. I was unaware of the coincidence until you pointed it out."

"It was no coincidence," said Bragg roughly. "Somebody had it worked out. Have you got anything else?"

"No."

Bragg scowled. "Right, let me see the ledger."

"Could you please explain its relevance to the warrant?" asked the solicitor courteously.

"It contains the asset account for the company's ships."

"I fail to see how that would provide information relevant to the loss of the *Dancing Lady*," Pocklington said.

"It's simple," replied Bragg. "The ship was an asset of the company. It was lost, and now it is an asset no longer."

Pocklington smiled. "We could argue over that interpretation for a week," he said.

"I have no time for arguments," said Bragg. "Where is Mr. Jacobson? I will serve the warrant on him personally."

Cakebread's mouth dropped open in surprise. "I, er . . . he is away in France," he mumbled.

"In France, is he?" Bragg snarled. "Right, clear everybody out! Give me the keys to the office, and keep clear of it till I tell you to come back."

"Are you not being somewhat precipitate, sergeant?" asked Pocklington.

"Precipitate?" Bragg sprang to his feet, towering over the solicitor. "Two men have been murdered already in this case, I and my constable were nearly killed last Sunday, and he could be next." He flung out his arm in the direction of Cakebread. "Believe it or not, sir, we have a responsibility to protect the public, even when they are being obstructive."

"I see." Pocklington pondered for a moment. "Then, without conceding the principle, I would advise the company to accept that the search warrant extends to the account book you require."

Cakebread crossed wearily to the cupboard, and brought out a large leather-bound ledger. He opened it, turned a few pages, then pushed it across to Bragg.

As he scrutinized it, a fierce smile spread across Bragg's
ce. "So this is what you have been hiding, is it? You knew
mned well that the *Dancing Lady* is in the company's
counts at a value of two thousand pounds. You have just
en paid out twelve thousand by Lloyd's. In my book, you
ade a profit of ten thousand pounds because that ship was
uttled." He glared angrily at Cakebread. "Are you still
ying you knew nothing about it?"

We have stopped buggering about, Mr. Gosling," said
agg.

"There's the search warrant you thought we couldn't get.
ou have caused us a lot of trouble, but it's got to stop."

"So long as I can plead *force majeur*," replied Gosling,
rusing the warrant, "then I am perfectly willing to give you
e information you need."

Bragg sat down, somewhat deflated. "Right. Now, we know
at you sent ten cases of rifles to London to be loaded onto the
 Dancing Lady, at the West India docks. They arrived at
rmingham goods depot on the fourth of January, so presum-
ly they left the factory on the same day. I want to know how
any guns there were, who they were being consigned to, and
ere they were going."

Gosling rang a bell and Mrs. Paxton strutted in. Gosling sent
r to the dispatch office for the necessary documents.

"You saw for yourself how they are packed," he remarked.
f there were ten cases, there would be forty rifles."

"Is that a representative shipment?" asked Morton.

"There really is no such thing. One could take an average,
t that would be meaningless. If the War Department were re-
uipping a regiment, we could well ship several hundred rifles
one time. At the moment, consignments are smaller merely
cause we are delivering the arms as quickly as we can make
m."

"There is a big demand for them?"

"Very healthy indeed, if that is the right word! Without
due modesty, it is an outstanding weapon . . . Ah, here we
." Mrs. Paxton placed a dispatch book on the desk, already
ened at the relevant page, and departed disapprovingly.

"The information you gave me seems to be correct," said
sling. "Forty Lee-Metford magazine rifles were consigned

via the *ss Dancing Lady*, for delivery to the Garrison
Commander in Guadeloupe."

"Where is that?" asked Bragg.

"In the tropics somewhere," said Gosling vaguely.

"It is in the Caribbean," said Morton, "and it is a French
colony."

"French?" Bragg turned to Gosling. "Why would the
French be buying rifles from you? They have guns of their
own."

"But none as good," replied Gosling with a complacent
smile. "Until two years ago, the French army was wholly
equipped with the old Lebel tube-magazine rifle. It was good in
its way, and reliable. But what matters nowadays is the rate of
fire, and the Lebel is desperately slow. Recently, they have
developed the Berthier carbine, which has a box magazine. But
that is designed for mounted troops, and their requirements are
very different from those of the infantry."

"Are you saying that it is no match for the Lee-Metford?"
asked Bragg.

"As an infantry weapon, certainly not. Its magazine holds
only three rounds, compared to our ten, so there is no
comparison in the rate of fire that can be achieved. If you add
to that the fact that the Lee-Metford has superior rifling and a
longer barrel, which gives greater accuracy, the French rifle
really cannot compete with ours."

"That does not explain why the French should buy it, all the
same."

"We decided at the time that they had bought them for
evaluation," said Gosling. "It would make sense for them to
carry it out in the colonies, so that the Paris newspapers would
not become aware of it."

"This case is like trying to grasp a fistful of quicksilver,"
Bragg complained. They were sitting in his office next
morning, and Bragg had his charts spread out in front of him.

"Yesterday morning, when we found out about the profit on
the insurance, it looked like Harvey & Crane were the villains.
Yet, when we went up to Lee-Metfords, and found out where
the rifles had been consigned to, the French side of it seemed to
hold the answers." He fumbled in his pocket, and pulled out
his tobacco pouch. "It's a mess is this case."

"Perhaps they are not separate, but different pieces of the same puzzle, and we have not yet found the connecting piece," said Morton.

"You could be right, lad," Bragg mused. "I'm not over-keen on Jacobson being in France. Suppose Michel Tissier et Cie is a part of the international Jacobson empire?"

"I suppose it would be possible," replied Morton. "But we must not lose sight of the fact that the rifles were not taken to Guadeloupe, but ended up in Mexico."

"Another diversion of cargo, do you think? Or was Guadeloupe just a blind?"

There was a knock at the door, and a young constable put a letter on Bragg's desk. "This was sent to you by hand, sir," he said.

"Thanks, son," Bragg tore open the envelope in a preoccupied manner, and glanced at the letter inside.

"Oh, God!" he exclaimed, his eyes riveted to the page. "Frankis has been murdered . . . This is a note from Whitlock. He says he has confirmed the rumor with Frankis's deputy. He was killed at home in Brookwood. The police at Chichester are in charge of inquiries." He tossed the note over to Morton. "It can't be a coincidence, it just can't . . . First Ingham, and now Frankis. It seems that every time we lean on somebody, he gets the chop. Whoever is at the center of this web, is totally ruthless."

"It seems to confirm that Frankis was part of the conspiracy," remarked Morton, putting down the letter. "Also, it adds some substance to your notion that Frankis deliberately tried to drown you."

"The bastard . . . Well, suspicion seems to have swung back to Lloyd's, with closing down the *Dancing Lady* case as the central motive."

"But why kill Frankis?" asked Morton. "He was not being obstructive, he had already paid out the claim."

"He was killed because he knew too much. I want you to go over to the Royal Exchange, and warn Whitlock to take precautions. At the same time, find out where he has been recently—he could easily be our man. I shall go to the Commissioner, and ask him to get permission from the West Sussex Chief Constable for us to go down and poke around. He should be able to do that by telegraph before lunchtime. And I think we will take Professor Burney down with us, as well. I don't reckon much to these country police-surgeons.''

Sir William Sumner proved to be unexpectedly robust, and by one o'clock Bragg, Morton, and Burney were entrained for Chichester.

"Did I see that you were limping, sergeant?" Burney asked, with his lopsided grin.

"I went swimming over a waterfall."

"You want to get some good horse-embrocation, and rub it well into the muscles. It will have you skipping like a lamb in no time.''

"It would have me jumping over the moon," said Bragg wryly. "Surely you can do better than that, sir? I was hoping you would prescribe some medicine for me.''

"Medicine? Good heavens, medicine would be no help at all!" exclaimed Burney in perturbation. "There are only three medicines that work. There is a red bottle for nerves, a brown bottle for a cough, and a white bottle for a bad stomach. Everything else is a mere placebo. You would be just as well off with a nostrum from the quack at the market stall.''

"But surely medicine has advanced since you were trained?" asked Bragg with a straight face.

"That would be a totally unwarranted conclusion, sergeant. The day that I find myself working only for you ruffians, I might be prepared to agree that medicine has advanced.''

"Well, if that is all there is to medicine, sir, I wonder that it takes so long to train as a doctor.''

"It would never do to allow people to realize it, sergeant. Once they knew, everybody would want to be a doctor, and then no one would make any money.''

They arrived at Chichester police station at three o'clock, and asked for the officer in charge of the Frankis case. They were shown to the office of Inspector Jardine. He was a grizzled, disagreeable-looking man.

"I expect you have been told by your Chief Constable that we would be coming down," said Bragg.

"Yes. I do not understand why. I cannot see what good it will do," Jardine replied ungraciously.

"We are interested in the case, because we think this death might be one of a series. We want to try and see if there is a pattern.''

"It looks like a break-in that went wrong. Robbery, I shouldn't wonder," said Jardine.

"What was taken?" asked Bragg.

"The wife couldn't say that anything had been taken. But naturally, she was a bit upset . . . The french window was open in the drawing room. It looked as if the catch had been forced."

"I wonder," replied Bragg. "I noticed that it was defective, on Sunday."

"Well, if you know all about it, I'm surprised you needed to come down," said Jardine unpleasantly.

"It seemed to me it would be helpful if we pooled our knowledge, sir," said Bragg patiently.

"I don't want you City lot complicating a straightforward case, just to make a name for yourselves . . . Mr. Frankis clearly surprised an intruder, and was killed when he tried to detain him."

"How was he killed, sir?"

"Stabbed in the chest."

"I have brought Dr. Burney with me. I would like him to be present at the postmortem examination."

"I can't see that is necessary," said Jardine sourly. "Our police surgeon is perfectly competent."

"I do not doubt it. But Dr. Burney is Professor of Pathology at St. Bartholomew's Hospital. He is a leading authority in his field, and has written a standard work on forensic medicine. I am sure your man would not object to his presence."

"I can't think he needs lessons at his age."

"The advantage from our point of view," Bragg persevered, "is that Dr. Burney has carried out the autopsy on both the other murders that we think are connected. Because of that, he might pick up something your man might overlook."

"I keep telling you," said Jardine stolidly, "it is a simple case of unpremeditated murder by an intruder."

"You cannot have many more years to do, can you, sir?" asked Bragg pleasantly.

"No, two and a half," said Jardine, nonplussed by the change of topic.

"You see, sir, I seem to have two options open to me. The first is to make a formal complaint about your obstructiveness to your Chief Constable, through our Commissioner. The other is to see to it that the national newspapers get hold of it. In either case," he smiled, "I would not lay much odds on your drawing your pension."

"You dare to threaten me, sergeant?" spluttered Jardine.

"You misunderstand, sir. It is not a threat. I am only taking you into my confidence, in the way that I would like to be taken into yours."

Jardine glared at Bragg, his jaw set hard. Then he rang a bell, and a uniformed constable came in. "Take Dr. Burney down to the mortuary," he ordered. "Tell the police surgeon he has my permission to assist at the Frankis postmortem."

"Thank you, sir," said Bragg, when the two had gone out. "Have you any idea of the time of death?"

"Mrs. Frankis discovered the body," said Jardine grudgingly. "She came in at half past ten, and found him on the floor of the study."

"Where had she been?"

"Next door. They had been having a dinner party, at which she was a guest."

"Who lives next door?"

"The Sorensons. He is one of our Justices of the Peace."

"Then he should be able to give a clear account of anything he saw."

"Not necessarily. We find that if we have any business with him, we need to get there in the morning."

"Why is that?" asked Bragg.

"Well, let's say that he is a connoisseur of wine."

"Did Mrs. Frankis know her husband was coming home?"

"Apparently not."

"I see. Do you know who else was at the party?"

"No."

"Would it be possible to find out?" asked Bragg.

"It might."

"You said that there was no sign of disturbance, which suggested that the intruder had only just gained entrance."

"That is correct."

"Where was the body lying?"

"On the right of the desk. The chair was pushed back, as if Frankis had just got up to investigate."

"I see. So it suggests that the intruder came into the room and attacked him?"

"I, er . . . yes," said Jardine uncertainly.

"Was there anything on the desk?"

"A blotter, and a silver inkstand."

"Anything else?"

"Yes. There was book open on the blotter."

"What book was that?"

"I can't say, for certain. I remember it had a picture of a steam yacht on the open page."

"Where is Mrs. Frankis now?"

"She said she was going to her people."

"Where is that?"

"I have no idea. She will be back for the funeral on Saturday."

"I suppose everything has been tidied up now?"

"There is no point in you going up there," said Jardine with renewed aggression. "The house is locked up."

"Well, thank you, sir," said Bragg, getting to his feet. "You have been most helpful."

Bragg and Morton had to kick their heels for an hour before Burney emerged from the mortuary. He greeted the policemen with his usual loose smile.

"I had a good day, in the end," he assured them.

"The local man treated you well, then?"

"It was all most gratifying. He even allowed me to get my hands in at the crucial stage."

"I'm glad that the medical profession sticks together better than the police," said Bragg. "Well, what did you find?"

"My interest was limited to the wounds, of course. I have left him to do the routine investigation, but he has promised to let me know if anything startling emerges from it."

"When did he die?"

"The police-surgeon calculates the time of death at between nine and nine-thirty on Tuesday evening, and on the data he produced, I would concur."

"About an hour before his wife found him," murmured Bragg, "and halfway through a dinner party . . . And what about the weapon?"

"There were several stab wounds in the chest, any one of which would have caused rapid death. They were probably the result of blows delivered while Frankis was standing, or beginning to collapse."

"It suggests a certain frenzy about the attack, then?" remarked Bragg.

Burney considered for a moment. "Yes, I think that is a reasonable conclusion."

"And the weapon?"

"Oh, he's our man, all right," said Burney with a satisfied smirk. "I had with me the puncture-specimen taken from Ryan. There is no doubt it was the same knife."

When they reached London, Bragg and Morton took a hansom to Park Street. Miss Givan answered the door with her customary caution.

"Sergeant Bragg and Constable Morton again, miss," said Bragg equably.

She released the door, and took them into the sitting room.

"Mr. Frankis is not back yet," she said.

"When did he leave?"

"He said yesterday morning that he was going to go down to the house, when he left the office. He said he would catch the last train back, but he must have missed it."

"He was down there on Monday morning. Why would he need to go back again the next night?"

"He said he had to meet someone . . . he said it was very important," she added wistfully.

"Did he say who it was?" asked Bragg.

"No."

"Have you any idea who it might have been?"

"No."

"Or what the meeting might have been about?"

"No . . . Why are you asking me all these questions? Can't you wait till he comes? He is bound to be in before long."

"I am afraid Mr. Frankis will not be coming again," said Bragg quietly.

A look of dejection settled on her face. "I knew she would get him back," she said. "He always swore it was all over between them, but she could twist him round . . . oh, no!" she took in the gravity of Bragg's expression. "You are not talking about that, are you?"

"Mr. Frankis was found dead in his study late last night. He had been murdered."

She dropped onto a chair, her face stony, her eyes staring.

"So, anything you can tell us would be helpful," said Bragg gently.

"I can tell you she led him a proper dance," she said in a

rd voice. "She spent every copper of his she could get her
nds on, and mocked him while she was doing it . . . And
e wasn't a good wife to him. She flaunted her lovers
actically under his nose . . . It was different between him
d me," Miss Givan looked defiantly at Bragg. "We loved
ch other. We would have been married, only she would never
vorce him . . . He told me so."

"Why was that?" asked Morton sympathetically.

"He was too good a catch, that's why. When he married that
oman, he was a rich man. He spent endlessly to impress her
d her friends—houses, yachts, racing, parties . . . He's
ld her that he has no money left, that the house is mortgaged
d he has borrowed from the bank, but she won't believe him.
nd here am I, putting up with this . . ." Her voice faltered,
d a wail of comprehension escaped her.

"I suppose this is rented?" said Morton.

"Yes," she sobbed.

"I think the best thing is for you to get your things together,
d go back to your parents' home. We will try to keep you out
this mess."

"But I loved him . . ." she cried tearfully.

"I'm sure you did, but people will be coming here, and you
ll only get hurt."

"The constable is right, miss," said Bragg in a fatherly
ice. "Why not go and pack, while we have a look around."

"John always said . . ." the girl began hesitantly, "he said
at if anything ever happened to him, I was to go to his office
Birchin Lane, and ask for the package in the safe with my
me on it. He said there would be money there, to see me
ght."

"Don't worry about that, miss," said Bragg kindly. "We
all be going in tomorrow morning. Just write out your
rents' address, and we will see that you get it."

"I told you that Frankis would be generous," Morton said,
they walked to the cab rank.

"You are naive, lad," Bragg snorted. "Like as not it was
st a tale. Even if he did put some money there at first, I bet
's had to borrow from it every time his wife wanted a new
nket. If he really intended to be generous, why didn't he give
r the money outright? I tell you, it will not surprise me if all
find in the packet is an I.O.U."

CHAPTER ——————
—————— SIXTEE

When Bragg and Morton arrived at the Birchin Lane offic
they found the reception area deserted. Morton looked arou
for a bell, but there was none; then Bragg rapped on the de:
with a ruler. Neither expedient produced a result. It was n
until the telephone began to ring insistently that the receptioni
appeared.

"Just a minute," she said, "I shall have to answer this.

Morton judged that the call was from one of her friend
from the look of apprehension and excitement that spread ov
her face as she talked. Then Bragg cleared his throat noisil
and she regretfully replaced the ear-piece.

"Is Mr. Frankis's deputy in, miss?" Bragg enquired.

"Mr. Hannah? Yes. Will you come this way?"

The deputy's own room was empty, and they found him
Frankis's, staring glumly into a cupboard full of files.

"So you are the boss now?" Bragg remarked.

"I should not think so. Not for long. They will probab
appoint a new underwriter to the syndicate," he replied.

"What is that lot?" asked Bragg.

"Papers relating to the major risks we have written. Someone has got to sit down and assimilate all that."

"Can you get me out the papers on the *Dancing Lady*, please?"

"That is the Green Funnel Line, isn't it?"

"Yes."

Hannah ran his fingers along the top shelf and extracted a fat file, which he carried to the desk. Its contents were divided into numerous sub-files, and he handed one to Bragg.

"Thanks . . . Oh, and can I have the key to this safe?"

The underwriter disappeared, and Bragg seated himself at the opulent desk and opened the file. Its contents consisted mainly of jottings about earlier voyages, with notes on the premium rating, and the percentage written. So far as he could see, there was nothing to suggest that any previous claims had been made in relation to the ship.

"This is an interesting one," he remarked. "The insurance was due to be renewed as from the first of January, and it looks as if Frankis had said in the previous year that he would not renew again without a survey. This is a letter from Harvey & Crane, asking that the survey should be postponed for three months because of the charter. There is a note on the bottom of the letter indicating that Frankis agreed to this."

"What is the date of the letter?" Morton asked.

"The fifteenth of December last year."

"It seems to fit in with the letter that Ingham received from Michel Tissier et Cie, asking him to fix a charter."

"Yes . . ." Bragg chewed at the end of his untidy mustache. "Yes. But it is also interesting in the context of the shipowners. Suppose they decided in December to get rid of the *Dancing Lady*. They could hardly take it a few miles off the coast, and say it had been sunk by a freak storm. And yet, by the time they got it far enough away, the insurance cover would have expired."

"I see. And without a survey, which could have involved a heavy repair bill, the insurance would not have been renewed."

"It is the three months that bothers me," said Bragg. "Like the precise advance of the charter monies—just enough to cover what they were about."

"You are forgetting," Morton remarked, "that the postponement of survey is part of the theory that the shipowners scuttled the ship. The advance charter payment belongs to the theory that it was scuttled in furtherance of some obscure activity of the French.''

"No, I am not forgetting that. I begin to feel that this Jacobson man is the link between them. If I could make out half a case for charging him, I'd try to get him extradited from France.''

Hannah came in, dropped a large key on the desk, and went out again without speaking.

"Not a happy man, that,'' said Bragg with a grin. "I expect he has his shovel full at the moment. Now, let's see what is in the safe.''

On the bottom shelf was a large velvet bag, with the name of Asprey's, the jewellers, embroidered on it.

"The Bohemian Miss Givan's unmarriage-portion?'' asked Morton flippantly.

Bragg untied the string with a scowl, and drew out a tarnished silver cup. From the engraving, it appeared to be a trophy won at a sailing regatta in eighteen seventy-four.

"Why would he want to keep a thing like that in the safe?'' Bragg wondered. "It cannot be worth very much.''

"Perhaps it pre-dates the era of the green-eyed goddess?''

"Very likely.'' Bragg picked a bulky file from the top shelf, and took it over to the desk. "It's a whole pile of legal documents,'' he exclaimed. "There's enough red tape to rig a ship.''

"The bundle at the top is obviously the deeds of the Brookwood house,'' observed Morton. "And here is a mort-gage on it . . . and a second-mortgage . . . So Miss Gi-van's information was reliable.''

Bragg took the remaining folder from the safe. It contained the lease of the Grosvenor Mansions flat, and an insurance policy. He then groped into the back of the bottom shelf, and brought out a crumpled brown-paper parcel. Its flaccid outline bore traces of repeated sealing and resealing with gummed tape.

"Miss Cicely Givan,'' Bragg read the superscription. "So there is your generous jointure,'' he said scornfully. "Open it up, lad. We can't give it to her like that. She loved him, remember.''

"But if we were to give it to her as it is," replied Morton, "she might see him in a different light."

"It's her self-respect I'm concerned with. Open it."

Morton tore open the packet and counted out ten five-pound notes.

"Fifty quid?" said Bragg sardonically. "A fat lot of seeing right that will do. I thought he was a conceited sod when I first met him, but now I despise him." He pushed the notes into an envelope, and sealed it. "You won't break your arm carrying this lot to Islington."

"I am puzzled by this insurance policy, sir," Morton said slowly. "It has been issued by the Royal Exchange Assurance Company, the assured is John Frankis, and it has something to do with the *Dancing Lady*."

"Let me see, lad." Bragg glanced at the document. "Go and get that underwriter chap. He will be able to sort it out quicker than we can."

"Have you seen this before?" Bragg greeted him.

Hannah looked at the policy in surprise. "No. It was Mr. Frankis's private safe."

"Tell us what it is all about."

"Well, it is . . ." a look of incredulity spread over his features as he read. "This is a most extraordinary thing," he said in a troubled voice. "It is an insurance policy relating to that last voyage of the *Dancing Lady*."

"Yes, we know that," said Bragg irritably. "What is its effect?"

"It means that any financial loss Mr. Frankis should suffer, by reason of a claim being made against the Lloyd's syndicate, would be reimbursed by the insurance company."

"Is that a normal thing to do?"

"By no means. It removes all element of risk. In effect, so far as Mr. Frankis's share was concerned, it negates the syndicate's insurance transaction."

"So he knew the ship was going to be lost?"

"I very much fear that it would appear so."

"This was the insurance transaction you forgot to reinsure, isn't it?" asked Bragg.

"Is that what he told you? I was specifically instructed to exclude it from our reinsurance programme."

"Why would he do that, if he knew the ship was going to sink?"

"Perhaps he felt it was unethical, to spread a predetermined loss over Lloyd's as a whole," said Hannah with a wry smile. "Though I doubt if the other names on this syndicate will see it in the same light."

As Catherine pushed open the door of the Ship Registry, Rappaport's face lit up with delight.

"I have not been privileged to have one of the fair sex call on me for, I should say, five years," he chirped. "This is a rare pleasure." He plucked a handkerchief from his pocket, and darting across to a chair, began flapping at the dust. "There you are," he inclined his head courteously until Catherine had sat down.

"And how can I be of service to you, young lady?" he said, perching himself on the corner of the table.

"My name is Catherine Marsden. I am a journalist on the *City Press* and a correspondent for the *Star*."

"Are you indeed? That is very good," said Rappaport warmly. "I like to see young people getting on."

"I am gathering together material for an article on the marine insurance frauds that seem to be the topic of the hour."

"Yes, it is very worrying; yet scarcely a national paper has even bothered to mention it. I suppose it is all these election speeches."

"I want to concentrate on two ships which are alleged to have been scuttled." Catherine consulted her notebook. "The first is the *Pearl* in eighteen eighty-eight. I need to know the name of the owners of the ship."

"I can save you a shilling on that one," said Rappaport with a delighted smile. "It was one of the Curwen Line ships, registered in Southhampton.

"Who owned it?"

"Why, the Curwen family trust, like all the vessels of the line."

"I see. Do you know where the trust is located?"

"In Fenchurch Buildings, Fenchurch Street."

"Thank you." Catherine noted the address. "The other ship is the *Dancing Lady*. I need to know rather more about that one, so I had better pay my fee." She placed a shilling on the table.

"Let me give you a receipt," Rappaport said.

"There is no need, thank you . . . I understand that the name of a ship's master is endorsed on the Certificate of Registry."

"You understand correctly, young lady."

"What I am trying to establish is the date on which Ben Gadd was appointed master of the *Dancing Lady.*"

"That will be in the file, not the register." Rappaport went over to the cupboard, and took a folder to the window. "I do wish the light was better, here," he said peering short-sightedly at the documents. "Are you sure the master's name was Gadd?"

"Quite sure," said Catherine firmly. "We know he must have been appointed by the twelfth of January, because the ship sailed on that date."

"I see. According to our records, the master was a man called Moxon. Perhaps we have some post not yet connected to the file," he said brightly. "Just a moment." He scurried out.

Catherine examined the room carefully, in case she should decide to write a paragraph on it. She noted the meticulous way in which the archives were kept; books of uniform height on each shelf, their spines precisely level. Even Rappaport's pen was laid exactly parallel with the edge of the table. She savored the fusty smell of the old leather bindings. Perhaps she ought to write a full article on the Ship Registry. There was scope for a series on the institutions of the City. She must mention it to the editor, Mr. Tranter, when she got back.

"I was quite right," Rappaport gave a wheezy laugh. "I sometimes think we would be better off if we had young lady clerks in the office. I am sure you would not keep letters unfiled for six months . . . Now, where are we?" He brought a letter up to his nose, and looked at it myopically. "No, it's the other one," he muttered. "Ah, yes. We have a letter from Taylor Pendrill & Co., dated the thirtieth of January, to tell us that Benjamin Gadd had been appointed master on the twentieth of December previously."

"That seems to fit in with what I have already been told," said Catherine, jotting down the date in her notebook.

"Is there anything else?" he asked.

"Well, I know that the ship is owned by Harvey & Crane."

"That is where you would be wrong, young lady," said Rappaport triumphantly. "I have a letter here from that company, saying that it has sold the vessel to a company called D.W. Wallis Ltd. They say the bill of sale will follow . . . that's odd . . . very odd." His head bobbed up and down as he scrutinized the particulars again. "The letter is dated the twenty-sixth of January, but, according to our stamp, it was only received by us on the seventeenth of June." He held out the letter, and Catherine could see the clear impression of a "received" stamp on the bottom.

"Is there any possibility that the stamp was put on long after it was received, in error?" she asked.

"Oh, no," said Rappaport happily. "That is a job I do myself."

Bragg had barely got back to Old Jewry, when he received a summons from the Commissioner. He found Sir William flanked by Chief Inspector Forbes on one side, and Inspector Cotton on the other. He glanced round, to see if anyone else was there, but it was evidently for his benefit alone. So the intention was to overawe him. Well, well!

"Sit down, Bragg," the Commissioner directed. "There has been a development in the insurance fraud case, which rather complicates matters," he went on uncomfortably. "This morning I received a letter from Lord Revelstoke, the chairman of Lloyd's, indicating that we should abandon our investigations."

"Did he give a reason, sir?" asked Bragg.

"He says the committee now takes the view that the prolongation of our inquiries is creating an adverse trading climate. It seems people are beginning to feel that Lloyd's might refuse to pay out on genuine claims."

"Well, that is an about-turn for you," said Bragg bitterly. "It's Goddard, of course."

"How do you mean, Bragg?"

"Revelstoke is a banker, he knows no more about insurance than my hat. He just does what Goddard tells him."

"Even so, we cannot disregard the wishes of so distinguished a City figure."

"But Goddard is one of our suspects," exclaimed Bragg.

DEATH OF A DANCING LADY

With a flash of his teeth, Chief Inspector Forbes intervened. "Are you referring to the notion that he might have murdered Frankis, because he had been promised an honor?" he asked with a patronizing smile. "I find that exceedingly flimsy, Bragg."

"Well, sir," replied Bragg doggedly, "it is beyond doubt that both Ingham and Frankis knew their attacker. Professor Burney says that neither of them put up any resistance."

"Professor Burney is going beyond his proper role," said Forbes curtly. "It is for him to provide the medical evidence, and for the police to draw inferences."

"Nevertheless, he has great experience," said Bragg.

"I do not see that it is the inevitable conclusion." Forbes had recovered his complacency. "After all, surprise is the essence of most violent assaults."

"At the same time," Bragg persisted, "it is a fact that Goddard was known to both Ingham and Frankis."

Forbes twisted the waxed ends of his mustache. "But am I not right in thinking," he asked with a condescending smile, "that the method of attack was different in each case. The first murder was by a blunt instrument, was it not? And the second by stabbing with a knife."

"Yes, sir," Bragg mumbled.

Inspector Cotton jumped in to administer the coup de grâce. "In any case," he said sarcastically, "Ingham was murdered long before there was any question of Goddard's being offered a knighthood."

Bragg tried to shift his ground. "I am saying that the two murders are connected . . ."

"It's no use, Bragg," the Commissioner interrupted. "Lloyd's constrained us to undertake these investigations, and I have to regard this letter as an injunction that it would be perilous to disregard." He held up his hand to still Bragg's protests. "That is not to say that I am prepared to overlook the two murders which have occurred within the City. Investigation of those will continue in a normal fashion, and if they fortuitously produce information on the insurance fraud, so much the better." Sir William's smile seemed foxy under his mustache.

"Thank you, sir," said Bragg.

"I have decided, however, to make certain tactical changes.

Up to now, the thrust of your inquiries has been towards the alleged fraud, and the murders have been investigated only so far as they were incidental to those inquiries. After our discussion this morning, it is obvious that this was wrong. Henceforward, therefore, each murder will be regarded as separate and distinct, and will be investigated as such. I am bringing in Inspector Cotton to coordinate the operation, since he is more attuned to the political dimension of our situation.''

"Yes, sir.''

"You and Constable Morton are detailed to investigate the murder of Ryan, and give such assitance as the Sussex police may need to complete their inquiries into the murder of Frankis. You will report to Inspector Cotton. Is that clear?''

"Yes, sir.''

"Then you may go.''

Bragg marched back to his room angrily. "The bastards,'' he exclaimed. "Not only are we under Cotton's thumb, they have even fixed it so that stupid sod Jardine can walk all over us.''

"So it has happened?'' remarked Morton.

"Yes. We are limited to Ryan, and to assisting the Sussex police on Frankis. So much for your heroism, lad.''

Morton shrugged. "We ought to have ample scope to get where we want.''

The duty-sergeant popped his head around the door, and held out an envelope. "This just came for you by hand, Joe.''

"Thanks, Bill.''

"Had you on the mat, have they?''

"Why, no.'' Bragg said slowly. "The Commissioner and the C.I. and Inspector Cotton were consulting me over a difficult problem.''

"The problem being Joe Bragg, eh?'' The sergeant grinned, and departed.

Bragg looked at the envelope. "There's one thing,'' he remarked, "the Commissioner has no jurisdiction over what Miss Marsden can investigate.'' He tore open the envelope. "Let's see what she has for us this time . . . Well, I'm damned! Harvey & Crane have sold the *Dancing Lady* to a company called D.W. Wallis Ltd.''

"How could they sell a ship that no longer exists?'' asked Morton.

"There seems to be some jiggery-pokery about the date,''

said Bragg, tossing the letter to Morton. "To me it smells of a bit of crafty footwork by old Cakebread. Pass me that telephone directory, lad." He riffled quickly through the pages. "Here we are, 'Wallis D.W. Ltd., 3 Ironmonger Lane.' Why, it's just round the corner."

"They are mainly professional offices there," said Morton. "Anyway, I do not see how we could inquire into that transaction within the terms laid down by Sir William."

"Sod that lot! They'll never know. Come on, lad."

Morton was right. Number three was occupied by a firm of accountants.

"It must be the company's registered office," said Morton, "although it is odd to give that address in the directory, rather than the business address."

"Like as not, it has no business," growled Bragg, perusing the board in the hall containing the names of companies with registered offices there.

"Look," said Morton. "At the bottom, there it is . . . It seems as if it has been added recently."

"Good!" said Bragg with satisfaction. "And have you noticed what is up there?" He pointed to the top of the board.

"Harvey & Crane Ltd.! What a coincidence."

"It is no coincidence, lad. They have just shifted the ship out of the way, into another company of theirs. Let us see what we can find out."

They went into a ground-floor office, where a rotund young woman sat knitting.

"You are quite sure it will be a boy, then?" said Bragg good humoredly, nodding at the ball of blue wool.

The woman gave a self-conscious smile. "It is what my husband would want," she said.

"You will be giving up work, then?"

"At the end of the week. It can't come soon enough for me."

"We are looking for the department dealing with changes in shareholdings," Bragg said easily.

"All the secretarial matters are on the top floor," she said, starting to her feet.

"Don't worry, love, we will find our own way."

The young woman subsided gratefully. "I don't know if anyone will be there," she said. "They may all be out to lunch."

"If they are, then we will come back this afternoon."

Her prediction was all too accurate; the top floor was deserted. Bragg closed the door behind them. "Here, lad, put your foot against that. Don't let anybody in . . . Now, where are we?" He crossed to a shelf filled with ledgers. "Let's hope they are alphabetical . . . Valley Coal, Vulcan Foundry, Woolwich . . . Blast! It's not here."

"Try under D," Morton suggested. "They may be pernickety."

Bragg strode to the other end of the shelf. "A bull's-eye," he called softly, as he took a volume to the desk. "It's a new company," he said. "Only registered last October." He flipped over the pages. "Guess who is one of the shareholders?" he chuckled. "Our old friend Nathaniel Cakebread! No mistaking him! He has only one share; the bulk of them are in the name of a Philippe Jacobson, with an address in Paris. What do you think of that, eh?"

"That was a most magnificent performance," said Morton warmly. "I shall never hear that music without thinking of tonight. You were superb."

Dorothea gave a gratified laugh. "I'm tired," she said. "It is so draining."

"What will you do now that it is over?"

"I cannot tell." She looked round her dressing-room as if to memorize every detail. "The critics were very kind to me. I would hope to be offered other parts."

"The impresarios ought to be throwing themselves at your feet."

"At the moment I would just like to get away from it, and relax. You have no idea, James, of the intensity of the work involved, learning the part, rehearsing every day for weeks—and all for two performances."

"I hope you will let me see you?" said Morton earnestly.

"Who knows?" she said coquettishly. "Why should I?"

"My devotion shall answer for me." He stood up, and placing his hand on his heart theatrically, began to sing:

> *"Voi, che sapete che cosa è amor,*
> *Donna, vedi, s'io l'ho nel cor,*
> *Donna, vedi, s'io l'ho nel cor."*

Dorothea cocked her head on one side, and pursed her lips. "The lady sees not love in your heart," she said, "but a dangerous fascination with an illusion."

"Nonsense," Morton protested.

"If you spent much time in my company, you would discover that I am a selfish, ambitious cross-patch," she said with a smile.

"I would willingly put it to the test."

"It seems," Dorothea said musingly, "that I have found what every artiste desires—a wealthy patron."

"Don't be flippant, I am serious."

"And I . . . am not." She gazed at the handsome face, and sighed. "You are a curious person, James, so young and eager, so untouched by life. I suppose it was inevitable, given your background and upbringing. It still surprises me to think of you as a policeman."

"That is the result of a rather priggish spasm, when I came down from Cambridge. I wanted my life to be significant, and it was the best I could do. I sometimes feel it has not worked out very well."

"Then why do you stay?"

"I suppose it is out of regard for Sergeant Bragg. We could hardly be more different, and yet I like him immensely."

"Need that keep you in the police force?"

"I suppose not. It is just that he inspires a personal loyalty. I admire his concern for other people, particularly for the vulnerable; I respect his integrity, especially when, as at the moment, he is being pressed to do something he regards as wrong; and at times he irritates me with his homilies. I imagine it is much like being married—to a sea-lion."

Dorothea gave a ripple of laughter. "But I would want you to do something useful with your life," she pouted.

"Then why not music? Why not opera?" he said eagerly. "You remember I told you about the medieval hall at The Priory? We could turn it into a theater. It would be perfect. I can just see you singing *Lucia di Lammermoor* there. People would flock to hear you."

"An opera house in the depths of the Kent countryside! Don't be absurd, James; no one would go to opera, except in London."

"It is only an hour from town. We could arrange special

trains, and engage a fleet of carriages to bring them from Hollingbourne station.''

"I am beginning to get caught up in your illusion myself.''

"Then at least come down to see it.''

"I am not sure that I can . . . When would it be?''

"Why not tomorrow?'' Morton suggested urgently. "I will come for you.''

"Very well.'' Dorothea gave a resigned smile. "But not before noon!''

CHAPTER ──────
────── SEVENTEEN

When Morton arrived at the office next morning, he found Bragg studying a long telegram.

"It is from your friend Lieutenant Gregory—he sends his regards."

"What has he discovered?" asked Morton.

"A man called Wilson bought the mill through the agency of De Wolf & Fletcher. He paid for it last October, was given a bill of lading when the ship put in to Galveston, and took possession of the goods. Just like that."

"So far as he is concerned, then, it was a perfectly genuine transaction?"

"More than that, lad. I'm no commercial lawyer, but if the bill of lading was made out to "Order," and endorsed by Thurgood & Jackson, then whoever presents it to the master first has an indisputable title to the goods."

Morton whistled. "Poor Jethro Dillard," he murmured. "His litigation is likely to be expensive."

"So that makes two people that De Wolf sold this plant to, Dillard and Wilson. And, in each case, Taylor Pendrill & Co. were also involved."

"You always said that Ingham was at the center of the conspiracy."

"Yes. But he was not the prime mover, or he would still be alive."

"Does the cable give us any lead we can follow up here?"

Bragg tossed the telegram to Morton. "Yes, I suppose it does . . . It is obvious that the Wilson transaction is the illicit one. Dillard paid Thurgood & Jackson direct—you examined the receipt yourself. You will see that Ingham instructed Wilson to pay the money to a bank in New York, for the credit of the account of an English bank."

"Ah, yes," said Morton. "That is presumably a general account maintained by the English bank, and the money would be moved on to the intended recipient."

Bragg pulled out his watch. "It's Saturday morning, so the bank will shut at noon. Still, I think we just have time to pop down to Lombard Street. Come on, lad."

Bragg set a fast pace, striding grimly on without speaking. Morton mentally reviewed the facts of the case, and idly wondered how Bragg could relate this to the Ryan murder, rather than the Lloyd's insurance claim. No doubt he was untroubled by the distinction.

Bragg pushed through the inner door of the banking hall, and marched up to the counter. "Manager, please," he said curtly.

"I will see if he is available," the clerk replied. "I think he may have a customer with him."

Bragg waved his warrant-card under the clerk's nose. "City police," he said. "What's his name, son?"

"Mr. Brook is the manager here."

"Well, tell him to hurry up, if he wants to get home today."

The clerk disappeared, and Bragg prowled restlessly around. "Bloody banks," he growled, "they will take you to the House of Lords, before they will give you any information about a client. And we have not got that sort of time . . . What's the betting he will have gone home?"

But Bragg had completed no more than two further perambulations of the marble floor, when the clerk reappeared.

"Will you come this way, please?" he said.

They followed him down a passage and up two flights of stairs, where he tapped deferentially on a heavy oak door.

There was a muffled shout from within, and the clerk ushered them inside. A tall man was standing behind an immense mahogany desk. His mottled red face bore a look of reproof, and he disregarded Bragg's proffered hand.

"There is no need to be so high-handed with my staff, sergeant," he said in a carefully modulated tone which suggested that he had spent the last five minutes rehearsing.

"We shall see, shall we not, Mr. Brook," replied Bragg tersely. "We want some information from you about a case that already involves three murders, with God knows how many more to come if we don't solve it."

"What kind of information is it that you are seeking?" asked Brook icily.

"The destination of some monies that were credited to your account with William Heath & Co. in New York."

Brook drew himself up haughtily. "I am afraid that I could not possibly give you any such information."

"That's not true," said Bragg brusquely. "The information must be here. What you mean is that you will not give it to me."

Brook allowed himself an acidulate smile. "If that is the way you prefer it, yes."

"And you refuse to give the information, even though that refusal could mean somebody will die?" asked Bragg roughly.

Brook's face remained implacable. "The policy of Martin's bank forbids any disclosure of information concerning a customer's affairs, without either the consent of the customer, or due legal process."

"All right," cried Bragg angrily, "you shall have your legal process. I expected you would take this line, and I have a Justice of the Peace standing by to sign a search warrant." He tossed to the door. "I shall be back in an hour; and Constable Morton will stay with you to make sure the books don't take a walk."

"If he stays with me for an hour," said Brook smugly, "he will find himself in Finchley, and you will find the bank locked."

"That's all right, sir," said Bragg amiably. "The search warrant will authorize us to break into the premises if necessary. The trouble then is, that when we have finished the search, we can't lock up again. Still, in view of your bank's policy, I expect the directors would understand why the bank had remained unsecured over the weekend."

Brook's face went an apoplectic shade of puce; disbelief was rapidly succeeded by apprehension, then alarm. He sank into his chair, his hands gripping its arms. For a long moment he sat with head bowed, as if trying to control his emotions. Then he looked up. "What is it you want to know?" he asked bleakly.

"The dollar equivalent of thirty thousand pounds was remitted from Galveston to Heath's for credit to your account, on the twenty-third of October last year. In turn you would transfer it over here and credit it to your customer's account. We want to see that account."

"It will not be easy to identify," Brook said dully. "There are scores of transactions on the Heath account every month."

"No doubt," said Bragg mildly. "But I expect we shall find that there are very few that involve the transmission of money belonging to a customer."

Brook reached out his hand, and pushed an electric bell. Almost immediately a clerk appeared.

"Bring me the Heath account for last October," he ordered peremptorily. They maintained an angry silence until he reappeared, bearing a thick ledger, which he deposited on the desk and made to leave.

"Don't go," rapped out Brook. "I shall need you."

The startled clerk looked uneasily at the two policemen, then took up a position by the door.

"What was the dollar exchange-rate last October, Hunter?" demanded Brook.

"It er . . . it was between four point eight, and four point nine all month, sir."

"Right." Brook made a rapid calculation on a pad, then began to turn the pages of the ledger, running his finger down the columns of figures. Then he paused, and closed the book. "Bring me the account of Michel Tissier et Cie, Hunter," he said.

This time the silence extended itself for a full five minutes, with Brook glowering resentfully at the policemen, and Bragg looking relaxed and amiable. Then the clerk reappeared with another ledger.

"I put a marker in the page, sir," he said.

"Right. You may go now." Brook waited until the door had closed, before opening the book.

"I would prefer it if you could refrain from actually examining the account . . ." he mumbled.

"We would be perfectly content for you to tell us what is there," replied Bragg heartily.

"What is it you wish to know?"

"When was the account opened?"

"On the twelfth of October last year," replied Brook.

"Who are the signatories?"

"M. Raoul Boniface, and a M. Jacques Fabry, both with addresses in Paris."

"What references did you take up?" asked Bragg.

"We proceeded on the recommendation of the Banque de Paris alone."

"I see. And what are the transactions through the account?"

"There are only two. The thirty thousand pounds was credited to the account on the first of November. We then received instructions to transfer out the French franc equivalent of twenty thousand pounds, and that was done on the seventh of November."

"It went through pretty smartly," Bragg commented. "And what happened to the rest of the money?"

"It remains in the account."

"Does it now? . . . And the twenty thousand, where did that go to?"

Brook closed the ledger with a bang. "It was transmitted to the account of Lebrun Barré et Cie, with the Banque de Paris."

There was a spring in Bragg's step as they walked back to Old Jewry, and from time to time he would chuckle to himself.

"I think that was the more reprehensible exhibition of duplicity ever seen in the square mile," remarked Morton finally.

"Duplicity? Where's the duplicity?"

"I am quite sure you had made no arrangements to obtain a search-warrant, and I doubt if you would have been given one had you tried."

"Ah, but he wasn't to know that," Bragg said. "I thought at one stage we would never pull it off. But fear is a powerful force, if you can use it to your advantage."

"I suppose we have made progress," said Morton doubtfully.

"Of course we have, lad. There is now a definite link

between the company that chartered the ship, and the money raised by the illicit disposal of the cargo."

"But where do the rifles come in?"

"We don't know yet. Perhaps they are quite separate, but I tell you something, I would give a great deal to have an hour's chat with Jacobson of Harvey & Crane."

"A man came to see you, Joe," called the desk sergeant. "He said he would wait, so I put him in your room."

Bragg leapt up the stairs, flung open the door, then checked. Standing by the window was a bulky man in his early fifties, with close-cropped hair, and a heavy florid face.

"Major Redman!" exclaimed Bragg in surprise.

"Ah, Sergeant Bragg." Redman's cold gray eyes glanced across, to take in Morton's presence. "I understand that you have been making inquiries concerning the loss of a ship called the *Dancing Lady*," he said in an incisive, military tone.

"That is so," replied Bragg cautiously. "Why is the head of Special Branch interested in that?"

"It is merely a professional interest, you may be sure."

"There is nothing political about it, so far as I can make out," said Bragg. "It's just a fraud case with complications."

"Complications?" repeated Redman.

"Like three murders."

"Oh, those," said the major disinterestedly. "Well now, Bragg, when our paths last crossed, you chose to disregard what I said. As a result, you spent a great deal of time and effort to no avail. I hope that this time you will act more sensibly."

"Oh?"

"My branch has been making inquiries which, to a certain extent, have duplicated yours. Our inquiries have now been concluded, and I have to tell you that yours must be suspended forthwith."

"Very well," said Bragg quietly.

Redman looked surprised at the sudden capitulation. "That includes terminating the inquiries into the three deaths."

"Ah, that is different," said Bragg firmly. "You know I cannot do that."

"All right, man, close them down as rapidly as is decently possible," said Redman testily.

"As soon as I have the murderer in handcuffs, I will stop investigating."

"You will never achieve it, sergeant, you have my word for that. Believe me, adequate justice has been done in this case."

"And what does adequate amount to in your vocabulary?" asked Bragg.

"Appropriate to all the circumstances," Redman replied crisply.

"There is only one justice appropriate to murder, in my book, and that is dangling at the end of a hangman's noose."

"As I said earlier, that philosophy did not avail you last time. I had hoped you would now realize that there are more important things than the panoply of the criminal courts."

"Such as?"

"The greater good of the nation."

"And who determines what that is?" asked Bragg. "You?"

Redman shrugged, and picked up his hat from the table. "You will only cause further death, if you insist on proceeding," he said.

"I am quite prepared to take that chance, Major Redman."

Morton bounded up the steps of the De Keyser Hotel, and strode elatedly across to the reception desk. In two hours, Dorothea and he would be at The Priory, exploring the ancient buildings, strolling around the gardens. She was bound to love it. Somehow its atmosphere seeped into your bones, displacing other loyalties, overlaying other experiences. He leaned against the counter, while the clerk dealt with an elderly gentleman who was fussing about his baggage.

Morton was sure that his mother would like Dorothea. None of the girls he had introduced to his family had had her sparkling personality, her confidence, her aura of achievement. She, if any, would be accepted as a worthy daughter-in-law. He day-dreamed about throngs of opera-goers strolling the lawns of The Priory, chattering eagerly about the brilliant way Miss Challis sang *Lucia* . . .

"Can I help you, sir?"

"Yes. Is Miss Challis in, do you know?"

"Miss Challis has left, sir."

"She arranged to meet me here at noon. When will she be back?"

"I'm sorry, sir. Miss Challis has left the hotel."

"You mean she is not staying here any longer?" aske● Morton incredulously.

"That is so, sir. She left this morning with Signor Bevig● nani."

"Bevignani? That's the conductor!" Morton blurted out.

"I believe that is so, sir."

"Where did they go?"

"I am afraid I could not tell you that."

Morton fished out his warrant-card. "City Police," h● rapped out. "Where did they go to?"

The clerk beckoned to the head porter. "George," he asked "Where were Signor Bevignani and Miss Challis going to?"

"Austria," replied the porter cheerfully. "I can't remembe● the hotel, but it was somewhere in Salzburg."

"What room did he occupy here?" Morton demanded.

The clerk turned through his register. "Two hundred an● four," he said.

Morton raced up the stairs, his mind in a turmoil. The roo● was near the stairwell, its door standing ajar. It was large opulently furnished, and had a sumptuous double bed . . So that was it. The girl he was infatuated with, who had sai● she was too fastidious to use a chamber-pot, had been creeping back from her lover's bed in the small hours. Well, she ha● warned him she was ambitious. For all her sneers at *Th● Mikado*, she had no more morals than a chorus-girl.

Filled with a sudden revulsion, he flung himself downstairs and out into the street.

Morton spent a restless night. It seemed that ever since h● set foot in his uncle's house in Boston, he had been engaged i● a prolonged exercise of self-criticism. He was becomin● thoroughly irritated by it all. Most of his acquaintances spen● their time idling around, womanizing, going to the races gambling—spending thoroughly worthless lives. He at leas● had tried to do something useful and responsible; but apparent● ly it was not enough. The very fact that he had made an effor● seemed perversely to justify people's preaching at him. T● uncle Josh he was a moral weakling, a cross between a leec● and a profligate, when he could be building a mountain o● money. Sergeant Bragg thought of him as immature, avoidin● the responsibilities an adult should rush to embrace. Eve●

Dorothea, his flawed jewel, had said he was "young" and "untouched by life." Well, she had been touched by it all right. For her to spurn him, and join in the general carping, was insupportable . . . In an attempt to salve his hurt pride, he half convinced himself that the Dorothea episode was merely an attempt to assert his own wishes, against this chorus of detractors. Confound it! To the man in the street, or at least to the thousands who followed cricket, he was nothing short of a hero. Why should he trouble himself about the criticism? Why not carry on like any other young socialite? . . . The trouble was that he really had become enamored of Dorothea. He seemed incapable of engaging in an inconsequential affair. Perhaps he was too serious a person. He either held back, out of respect for the lady, or became ridiculously infatuated. And he profited from neither. Sergeant Bragg was wrong in comparing him to a butterfly flitting from flower to eager flower. He was more like an assiduous bee probing for nectar, only to have the flower close up on him. Of course, the sergeant's solution was to have him settle down; to pair him off with Catherine Marsden. But he was well wide of the mark there. She was one of the new breed of woman, embattled against the inequality of the sexes, scornful of submissiveness, case-hardened against dalliance. She would cheerfully leave you to change the baby's diaper, because she wanted to go to a suffragist meeting. Morton turned angrily toward the wall, and tried to empty his mind; but light was beginning to seep around the curtains before he fell asleep.

He was awakened by Chambers, shaking his shoulder.

"Wake up, master James. There is a gentleman to see you."

"Tell him to go away," Morton mumbled.

"It is one of your colleagues; he seems very agitated."

"Sergeant Bragg?" asked Morton dully.

"I believe it is he," said Chambers.

"Oh, all right. Give him some coffee, while I shave."

Chambers returned to the sitting room, where Bragg was pacing up and down.

"Master James begs you to take breakfast with him, sir. He will be only a moment."

"Breakfast!" exclaimed Bragg irascibly. "There's no time for that."

"In view of the haste," went on Chambers equably, "my

wife will hardly be able to do justice to the occasion. However, she can manage grilled bacon, devilled kidneys, fried eggs—and there is kedgeree, if you are so inclined."

"Hmn," Bragg grunted. "Well, perhaps we need not hurry, after all."

He was halfway through his breakfast, when Morton entered, looking worn and unhappy. He waved away the food, and took only a cup of coffee to the table.

"I had better tell you," he said contritely, "that Dorothea Challis has skipped to the Continent."

"Has she, now?" replied Bragg, his mouth full of crisp bacon.

"She left the De Keyser early yesterday morning, en route for Salzburg."

"Without telling you, eh?"

Morton nodded dejectedly.

"You ought to try some of these kidneys," said Bragg. "They're a damned sight better than Stoke's Chop House . . . And why would she go there?"

"It is Mozart's birthplace. There is an annual festival there, about this time."

"Will she be singing in it?"

"I expect so."

"Well, then," said Bragg, pushing away his plate, "we shall know where to find her. I know you set great store by her, but I never saw her as a make-or-break witness. She confirmed the reception clerk's story, insofar as she saw someone closing Ryan's door; but since the man asked for Ryan's key, the jury would be able to draw the inference that he went there. She would not have been able to identify the murderer, because she didn't see his face. Indeed, defending counsel might be able to make something out of the differing opinions as to his height. I'm sure both Miss Challis and Perkins saw the same man, it's just that someone who appeared tall to a smallish woman would seem of average height to a man."

"I ought to have been able to detain her," said Morton.

"How? She's a free woman. She has not committed any offense that I know of; and we can't compel witnesses to stay in England on the off-chance we shall find somebody for them to identify." Bragg smiled. "Never mind, lad, if we need her, you can go and fetch her back."

"No, thank you!"

"Well, if that is all the breakfast you are having, we ought to be off. We have bigger fish to fry than Miss Challis."

"Such as?"

"Such as Ben Gadd," replied Bragg with a triumphant smile.

"No wonder you are looking pleased with life."

"The river police picked him up last night, in a pub in Millwall. We ought to get a few answers out of him."

They took a hansom to Wapping and went into the Thames Police station.

"We've come to see Gadd," Bragg said to the duty sergeant. "Thanks for picking him up."

"Always glad to do a favor for the Swell Mob," replied the sergeant with a grin. "He doesn't look like your usual run of villains, though he's not a man you would introduce to your sister. He keeps asking to see a solicitor. I've just fobbed him off till you arrived. He's your pigeon."

He took them down a short flight of steps, unlocked a heavy iron grille, then pushed aside the cover over the peephole in a stout door. Bragg looked in. Gadd was sitting on the corner of the bed staring angrily at the barred window. He was squat, with powerful shoulders. His neck was short and thick, his large head thrust forward. His whole mien was one of menace. If there was any validity at all in physiognomy, then Ryan and the others were right to be wary of him. The sergeant unlocked the door, and Bragg and Morton went in.

Gadd sprang to his feet. "About time, too," he said pugnaciously. "I've been asking for you since six o'clock last night . . . The police have arrested me on some sort of trumped-up charge—I don't even know what it is—and they've held me here all night. I want you to get me out."

Bragg observed him gravely, in silence.

"Do you hear me?" exclaimed Gadd wrathfully. "Go for a *habeas corpus* or something, only get me out of here!"

Bragg remained immobile, and slowly a look of suspicion spread over Gadd's face. "You are not solicitors at all, are you?" he exclaimed. "You're more stinking police!"

"Solicitors don't work on a Sunday," remarked Bragg affably. "We do. Sergeant Bragg and Constable Morton of the City Police."

"Is it you that are responsible for having me arrested?"

"That's right."

"On what grounds?" asked Gadd truculently.

"Well, it goes back a long way," said Bragg in a conversational tone. "Back to the *Pearl*, four years ago. You see, we think you scuttled that ship."

"The loss of the *Pearl* was the subject of a Board of Trade inquiry," replied Gadd curtly, "and I was exonerated."

"Yes, I know," said Bragg slowly. "A tornado, wasn't it? You ought to have been given a medal for getting all your crew off—and all your valuables . . ."

"What is the charge against me?" Gadd demanded angrily.

"You are charged under section forty-six of the Malicious Injuries Act, in that you did injure Harvey & Crane Ltd. by unlawfully scuttling the *ss Dancing Lady*, one of their ships."

"I did no such thing! The ship was lost in a storm."

"Another tornado?" inquired Bragg equably. "It doesn't sound so convincing second time around, does it? Particularly when all the crew was saved again."

Gadd gave Bragg a look of concentrated malice, and said nothing.

"You will also be charged with offenses relating to the criminal diversion of cargo from New Orleans to Galveston."

"You are just bluffing!" sneered Gadd. "You can't prove a thing."

"The most serious charge," went on Bragg amiably, "is the attempted murder of Patrick Ryan, a stowaway on the *Dancing Lady*."

"The attempted murder . . . ?"

"Yes. You left him locked in his cabin. But he didn't go down with the *Dancing Lady*; he escaped."

"It's not true," cried Gadd venomously. "The storm hit us suddenly. There wasn't time for everybody to get to the boats . . ."

"That isn't how he tells it. We've brought him here to London, and he has given us a full account of everything that happened. He was very bitter about finding the remaining lifeboat staved in . . . Yes, in some ways, I think you should be grateful to be safe in here."

"I am saying nothing."

"There's not much we are asking of you. You would swing on what we know already. Attempted murder is a capital offense . . . Have you ever seen a man hanged, captain?"

"No." Gadd's voice had become hoarse.

"I thought you might have. Don't you hang sailors from the yard-arm anymore? It's a nasty business, though they do say the weeks of waiting to be topped is the worst part . . ."

"What do you want?" exclaimed Gadd malevolently. "I don't need any lectures from the likes of you."

"We know you were only a catspaw in this affair," remarked Bragg. "We still have a few gaps in the story. If you helped us to fill them, we might be able to make things easier for you . . . I might even be able to persuade my boss to let you turn Queen's evidence; then you'd walk away scot-free."

Gadd peered at Bragg mistrustfully. "How do I know you would keep your word?" he asked.

"You don't," replied Bragg candidly. "But since you are certain to swing otherwise, you might as well take the chance."

"All right."

"I must first warn you that what you say will be taken down, and may be given in evidence. Do you understand?"

"Yes."

"Then let us begin. When did you first become involved in smuggling arms and ammunition into foreign countries?"

Gadd's head jerked up in surprise, and some of the tension went from his features. "Well, if you know about that," he said, "I might as well tell you the lot. I'll be out of here by tomorrow, then."

"In that case, you make a statement, and we will clear up any difficulties as we go along."

"I've had my master's ticket for fourteen years or more," Gadd began. "I have always had small tramp steamers, sailing mainly to South America and the Gulf. Occasionally, I have carried passengers that have had to be landed in some deserted creek, and no questions asked. With a lascar crew, and the right officers it can be done, and I was paid well for it. Then came the *Pearl*. This was something altogether different. I was called to a government office, where I met two men."

"Can you remember where the office was?" asked Bragg.

"No. They sent a cab for me, and took me back again. I never had the address. It was in the Holborn area."

"What were the two men like?" asked Morton.

"The boss-man was a big chap, with short hair and a mustache. I reckon he was a soldier of sorts."

"Did he have a red face?" asked Bragg.

"Yes. Looked as if he might have seen service in India."

"The other man?" prompted Morton.

"I didn't take much notice of him. He looked like any other civil servant," said Gadd contemptuously.

"Did you hear the name Redman at all?" asked Bragg.

"No. I did not hear any names."

"All right. Go on."

"Anyway, I was asked if I was prepared to be part of a much more important operation. I said I would, if the price was right. This time I was to take command of the *Pearl*. She had been chartered from a British company for a voyage to the Gulf. She was to sail in ballast, except for a small amount of very important cargo."

"Where did you pick up this cargo?" asked Bragg.

"Cherbourg. We sailed straight across to British Honduras, then up the coast, till we were off the Yucatán peninsula of Mexico. There we transferred our cargo into boats that rowed out to the ship."

"Who was manning the boats?" asked Morton.

"Mexican Indians. Only one of them had any English at all."

"What did the cargo consist of?"

"Are you asking me what I saw, or what I think?" asked Gadd.

"Both."

"They were oblong cases, about five foot long, and there were fifty of them. There were no markings on them, but the mate, who was an ex-navy man, reckoned they contained rifles."

"And what then?" asked Bragg.

"We steamed back down the coast, as I had been ordered, and at dawn we scuttled the ship, and rowed ashore."

"Why scuttle the ship?" asked Bragg. "Why was this so different from rowing a passenger ashore, then sailing on?"

"Look," said Gadd irritably. "I'm telling you what happened. I wasn't allowed to ask questions."

"But you must have wondered about it," Bragg persisted.

"I think it was just to keep it secret. I was told to recruit the minimum number of officers, and only men who could be trusted to keep their mouths shut."

"What about the crew?"

"They were lascars anyway, so nobody would take much notice of what they said. But I think the reason for scuttling the ship was that the crew would be landed in British Honduras, and would disperse there . . . Perhaps they had already arranged for them to be engaged for a voyage to China, or somewhere—I don't know."

"And how much were you paid for this public service?" asked Bragg.

"Two thousand pounds."

"My God! That's a king's ransom."

"I had to square the officers, and give something to the serang out of it," said Gadd defiantly.

"And how was it paid?"

"I was given five hundred pounds in advance, and the rest when I got back to England."

"What then?"

"Nothing of that kind, until the *Dancing Lady*."

"When were you approached about that?"

"It would be in the middle of November, last year."

"Who gave you your instructions this time? The same two?"

"The soldier-chap didn't come this time, it was only his number one."

"Was this operation similar to the other?"

"More or less."

"There were differences, though," remarked Bragg. "This time the rifles were loaded in London, and you had other cargo. Why was that?"

"I cannot say. I just followed my orders."

"Were you ordered to off-load the machinery at Galveston?" asked Morton.

"Yes."

"Even though the bills of lading showed it was destined for New Orleans?"

"Yes."

"The bill of lading for china was just a blind, I take it," remarked Bragg.

"Yes. I had it in case I had to put into port anywhere—for the customs."

"Who gave it to you?"

"The ship's husband. He gave me my orders regarding the cargo."

"Including the rifles?"

"Yes."

"Did he provide you with insurance documents to cover the supposed crates of china?"

"Yes."

"So what were your orders for this operation?"

"I was to sail to Galveston, and when I had landed the machinery, I was to go down the coast to a place just south of Tampico, in Mexico."

"Yes, off Poza Rica, we know."

Gadd raised his eyebrows, but said nothing.

"And again," went on Bragg, "boats came from the shore, and the arms were lowered into them."

"Yes."

"What kind of people were in the boats this time?"

"Mexican Indians."

"And what happened then?"

"I steamed out to sea, and scuttled the ship."

"Only this time, you left Ryan to go down with it."

"I tell you it was an oversight," Gadd expostulated.

"That is not how it appeared to him," said Bragg somberly.

"Look. I was given complete discretion to do anything—anything at all—to insure the success of the operation. I have the full protection of the British Government. When they hear about this, you'll be walking the plank, sergeant."

"Maybe," said Bragg dryly. "So we have two ships scuttled, and you say it was under orders, each time."

"Why would I do it, otherwise? I had nothing to gain by it."

"Lloyd's had a lot to lose, though," said Morton.

Gadd shrugged. "I expect it was made up to them in another way," he said.

"With this second operation, you departed from your instructions, didn't you?" said Morton.

"How do you mean?" asked Gadd suspiciously.

"You did not sail straight for the Caribbean."

"No, I had to put in for repairs, on the way."

"Where was that?" asked Morton.

"Bermuda."

"And did you get the ship repaired there?"

"No, there were no facilities for it."

"Were you not aware of that already?"

"No," replied Gadd. "I had never sailed into Hamilton before."

"On a voyage to the Caribbean, you would normally sail down the coast of Spain to pick up the trade winds. Can you explain why you were in the vicinity of Bermuda at all?" asked Morton.

"I knew nothing about the ship," replied Gadd. "But as soon as I asked for full steam, I knew she was liable to break down. I was still in the English Channel, but I had been forbidden to put into a British port, once I had cleared London."

"But why Bermuda?"

"If you had ever tried getting work done in a Portuguese or Spanish yard, you would not ask. Bermuda is a British colony, and I thought I would be better off there."

"But you were not," said Morton.

"No, but the American ports were no great distance away."

"Being a British colony," remarked Bragg, "it was that much easier to raise money on a bottomry bond, though."

Gadd's eyes narrowed, and he did not reply.

"Were you instructed to call at Bermuda and ask for the seventeen thousand?" asked Bragg.

"No. It was needed to complete the voyage."

"But you didn't call at Charleston, as you had indicated."

"Yes, I did," said Gadd angrily.

"And did you have the repairs done there?"

"No. I could see the yards were full, and I had a time-table to keep to."

"So where did you have the repairs done?"

"Mobile," replied Gadd defiantly.

"I see," said Bragg. "And how much were you paid for your services, this time?"

"Three thousand pounds."

Bragg whistled. "Why the difference, compared with the *Pearl*?"

"I said I would not do it otherwise. It meant the end of my career at sea. Even if the Board of Trade brought it off as a loss through the perils of the sea, some people would be sceptical. And anyway, nobody would sail with me again. I would be regarded as unlucky.''

"And how was it paid this time?"

"I did not get an advance. It was all payable after the operation was completed. That is why I am here now.''

"To collect?"

"Yes."

"And who is going to pay you?"

"Mr. Slocum.''

"Who is he?"

"I don't know. I was told to write to him and he would get in touch with me.''

"What is his address?"

Gadd took out his pocket-book, and passed over a grubby piece of paper on which the name Slocum, and an address in the City, had been written.

"You won't be needing this, will you?" asked Bragg.

"Well, I wrote on Friday night.''

"Then I will keep it for the moment . . . By the way, where were you on the night of Friday the tenth of June?"

"The tenth? . . . Why that's over five weeks ago . . . Let me think . . . Yes, I was in Amsterdam.''

"Can you prove that?" asked Bragg.

"Yes.'' Gadd gave a fierce smile. "I was in chokey—for being involved in a punch-up. You can check with the Dutch police.''

"Right. Well, I will see what I can do for you, in view of your cooperation,'' said Bragg, rapping at the door to summon the duty sergeant.

"But what about getting me released?" protested Gadd. "I've been here long enough!"

"If you have any sense,'' remarked Bragg, "you will plead with them to keep you here. Everybody else connected with this business has found himself on a mortuary slab—and double quick.''

CHAPTER _____

_____ EIGHTEEN

Bragg was reviewing the case with Morton next morning, when he received a summons to the offices of Harvey & Crane Ltd. When they arrived, they were taken upstairs, and shown into a large well-furnished room. An elegantly dressed man in his mid-thirties rose to greet them.

"My name is Michael Jacobson," he said, holding out his hand. "I believe you already know our Mr. Cakebread."

The manager nodded briefly to them. His face was shrunken, his neck scrawny.

"I have asked you to come here," went on Jacobson, "because I feel it is desirable to clear up certain misunderstandings and stupidities that have occurred." His glance fell coldly on Cakebread. "Your constable need not take notes. I will have a full statement prepared for you, if you decide it is necessary."

Morton put away his notebook, and settled back in his chair.

"I feel that the best way to approach the subject is for me to give you some general information, before we move on to the specific." Jacobson was dark-haired, and slightly balding, but not obviously semitic.

"I have been made aware of your inquiries here, concerning the *Dancing Lady*," he continued in a relaxed manner. "And am prepared to believe that they will not have rested there. You may, therefore, have already discovered much of what I am about to tell you. I hope, however, that you will bear with me and regard it as a voluntary statement made by the company." He smiled engagingly.

"First, let me apologize for the way in which you have been received by Mr. Cakebread, and our solicitor. It appears t have been discourteous, and, if so, that was certainly unneces sary . . . Now to the detail. I belong to a family wit branches in many countries. You could call us financiers an merchants, and we tend to work together as one. Occasionally we indulge ourselves in other areas, by way of light relief. was thus that we took over the assets of the Green Funnel line We knew nothing at all about shipping, but the firm wa bankrupt, no one was interested in taking it over, and we wer able to secure the assets at a knockdown price.

"In one sense, it was speculation," he went on. "But w were able to sell off the newer ships in the Far East, at goo prices; so that whatever happened, we would still be in pocket We therefore decided to run the rest of the fleet for a time to se what we could make of it. Should the venture be a failure, w could sell the remaining ships for scrap, and lose very little We were therefore somewhat light-hearted about it, and tha was perhaps reprehensible. Since there was a distinct possibil ty that we would not continue the venture for more than a few years, we did not set up a large office to run it. We transferre the ships to Harvey & Crane, and asked Mr. Cakebread, one our most trusted and experienced managers, to run it."

Morton glanced at Cakebread. He did not seem eith flattered or relieved by the reference.

"The actual management of the fleet was left to Tayl Pendrill & Co., who had acted as husbands to the ships f many years. I gather that Mr. Ingham, the principal of the fir is unhappily no longer with us." He looked inquiringly Bragg.

"Are you saying, sir," asked Bragg, "that you went in this with your eyes open? That where an experienced shippir firm had failed, you hoped to succeed?"

"It was not the wild speculation that you imply, sergean

We took the purely financial view that whatever capital loss there was in the enterprise had already occurred. We were thus getting value for our money, in the short term. I should add, however, that we have come to the conclusion over the last few months that the business is not viable, and we shall be disposing of it shortly. I would naturally like you to treat that as a communication made in confidence."

"So far as it is not relevant to any charges, I will do so," said Bragg.

"Then I can feel easy in my mind, sergeant," said Jacobson with a smile. "So that, then, was the management structure of the business. Mr. Cakebread, totally inexperienced in shipping matters, being in nominal control, and under the tutelage of Ingham."

"All I had was a sheaf of notes kept by the previous owners," interrupted Cakebread plaintively.

Jacobson's eyes flickered across to him, and he subsided.

"To turn specifically to the *Dancing Lady*," said Jacobson, "this was a genuine arms-length charter for the voyage to New Orleans."

"Do you confirm," asked Bragg, "that neither Michel Tissier et Cie nor Lebrun Barré et Cie have anything at all to do with Jacobson companies in any part of the world?"

"I do give you that assurance, sergeant."

"Why did you ask for the Lloyd's survey to be postponed?" asked Bragg.

"I was not aware that such a request had been made," said Jacobson, turning to Cakebread.

"It was Ingham who suggested it," said Cakebread nervously. "He said there would not be time for any necessary repairs, if we were to accept the charter. He cleared it with the Lloyd's underwriter. My letter was a formality."

"You will see," said Jacobson, "that Mr. Cakebread was constrained by his ignorance of shipping, to do as Ingham proposed. If Ingham did not draw his attention to an administrative requirement, then the likelihood was that it would not be dealt with. However, we go too fast. The point I want to emphasize at the moment is that our involvement with the ill-fated voyage to New Orleans was no more than that we chartered our ship in good faith to the French company, through the agency of a reputable ship broker."

"You made a profit of ten thousand pounds on the insurance, though," said Bragg firmly.

"Yes, but a book profit only. The ship was put in the books of Harvey & Crane at a proportion of the cost of the whole fleet to us. I said that we bought them very cheaply, and the two thousand pounds was a reasonable estimate of what the *Dancing Lady* had cost us. That, of course, is all we are required to do from an accounting point of view. But the market value of the ship was considerably in excess of what we had paid. Ingham advised us to insure for twelve thousand pounds, and since one is not allowed to make a profit out of insurance, that must have been an accurate estimate of its value. Certainly Lloyd's accepted that figure."

"Well, if everything is as aboveboard as you say, why did Mr. Cakebread whistle up the solicitor as soon as we appeared?"

"I think," replied Jacobson, "that we must be charitable, and attribute the initial lack of openness to a natural apprehension at the sudden appearance of the police." He looked anything but charitable, Morton thought. "Thereafter, I must acknowledge that it is a case of a little knowledge being a dangerous thing. In his natural anxiety to insure that everything required by law had been observed, Mr. Cakebread reviewed his papers. It was then that he found—or rather rediscovered—a letter from me, to the effect that the *Dancing Lady* had been sold to an associate company on the twenty-sixth of January."

"To D.W. Wallis Ltd.," Bragg murmured.

"Exactly." Jacobson smiled in approbation. "Now, Mr. Cakebread is a director of the purchasing company, and I feel that he would wish to tell you himself what transpired."

Cakebread was clearly taken aback. "I should never have been expected to cope with it all," he whined. "Ingham was dead, and I was left all on my own." He looked to Jacobson for assistance, but he was scrutinizing his fingernails.

"Come on, sir," said Bragg encouragingly. "You will feel better when you have got it off your chest."

"It was the middle of June when I found the letter. I looked in the file of notes I had inherited from the Green Funnel line people, and found out that we should have notified the sale to the Ship Registry . . . Then I saw a note summarizing the requirements before a vessel can fly the British flag . . ." His voice faded, and he gulped for air.

"And what gave you concern about that?" asked Bragg quietly.

With an effort, Cakebread began to speak again. "A ship can be on the British register if it is owned by a company registered in Britain," he said. "But in such a case the company has to conduct its business from Britain . . . D.W. Wallis Ltd. is certainly registered in Britain, but it trades in Martinique."

"So you had discovered that it should have been taken off the register in January," remarked Bragg. "What then?"

"I was very worried, and I looked through the file to see if there was anything that would tell me what to do . . . I found an extract from the Shipping Acts, saying that any ship wrongfully flying the British flag was liable to confiscation . . ." Cakebread's voice had risen to an anguished wail.

"So what did you do?" asked Bragg.

"I wrote a letter to the Ship Registry about the sale, and . . . and I dated it the twenty-sixth of January."

"What did you do that for?"

"It was my responsibility, even though I know next to nothing about ships. I felt I had to try to retrieve the position."

"But the *Dancing Lady* had been scuttled for four months by then," exclaimed Bragg irritably.

"Well, they might have been able to take the insurance money. Anyway, no one could be sure the ship had been lost."

"Did you tell the solicitor about this?"

"No. I felt it was best to take no further action until Mr. Jacobson came back."

"You bloody silly old man!" said Bragg with slow emphasis. "Two men might still be alive, if you had made a clean breast of it, instead of buggering about."

"Quite," said Jacobson. "The irony of it all is that the legislation is aimed at foreign ships which masquerade as British. The most that the company would have faced was a trifling pecuniary penalty."

"This is an important operation," said Inspector Cotton forcefully. "Make no mistake about that. Just because I have chosen to forego the support of our uniformed brethren, it is not something you can take casually. I want you to demonstrate that the detective division can take a serious case right to its conclusion; without handing half the credit to the uniformed boys, because they made the arrest."

It was four o'clock in the morning. Even now the temperature was still in the mid-fifties; it was humid and thundery, and exceedingly uncomfortable. The windows and door of Cotton's room were flung wide open, but this produced no discernible draught. The twenty or so policemen crammed in there were sweating and restive.

"It is not only a serious case," continued Cotton, "it is a dangerous case. The man we are after is called Slocum. He has certainly killed twice, if not three times. When you are approaching him, watch out for his knife."

"What does he look like, sir?" asked a man by the fireplace.

"The only person who has seen his face, described him as ordinary looking. He is medium to tall in height, and certainly not old. Our witness took him for a doctor, if that is any help . . . Now, by good luck, we have obtained the address he is staying at. We are going to surround it, and detain anyone at all on the premises. It doesn't matter if one is dressed as a Mother Superior, they all go in the bag. Right?" There was a general murmur of assent.

Cotton turned to a street plan pinned on the wall. "The house we are turning over is number seven, Seacoal Lane—here." He pointed with a ruler. "The big problem is the railway viaduct which runs parallel with the fronts of the houses. Three of the arches are thoroughfares, and they will have to be sealed off. Sergeant Green, you take two of your men, and see to that."

"Right, sir."

"Being a corner house, number seven does not have an exit from its yard, but it does have windows onto Bishop's Court. I want two men in the open ground beyond Bishop's Court to intercept him if he flees that way. Jones and Bracken, you look lively lads, you take that on."

The two constables grinned at each other.

"It is always possible that he might run back down Bishop's Court, and get onto Old Bailey through the pub at the bottom. I want two men by the entrance to the pub. Simmons and Gracey, you'll do for that . . . Sergeant Bragg and Constable Morton will be up on the viaduct . . ."

"A real post of honor," muttered Bragg.

"What's that?" Cotton jerked around.

"I said that it was very astute, sir."

Cotton glared at Bragg, then resumed his instructions.
"They will be able to see the whole area from there. If our man
gets onto the roof they will warn us, and tell us where he is
heading. You can see that he could make for Fleet Lane in the
south, Old Bailey to the east, Green Arbor Court and Holborn
Viaduct to the north, and the railway to the west. If he should
climb up onto the railway, Sergeant Bragg will apprehend him.
Sergeant Roker, I want you to take all the men I have not given
specific posts, and place them in a screen all the way around
that block."

"Very good, sir."

"Sergeant Bliss, you and constables Park and Mandell will
come with me, to enter the premises. There is a tobacconist's
shop on the ground floor, with two stories of living accommo-
dation above. The lock on the street door should not be too
difficult to break. I went in yesterday for some cigarettes, and
had a good look around. There is a door at the back of the shop
which seems to communicate with a storeroom-cum-kitchen.
The stairs will be in there. So we break in, through the shop,
up the stairs and catch him in bed. All right?"

Sergeant Bliss nodded. He did not look overjoyed at being
chosen for the initial assault.

Cotton pulled out his watch. "It is now twenty past four,"
he said. "I want to go in at five o'clock on the dot, so you have
plenty of time to take up your positions. Now, remember, it is
getting light. I have not informed Second Divison, so don't
excite the suspicions of the constables on the beat. Go in ones
and twos, and go by different streets. Sergeant Bragg, you had
better leave first. The best way onto the viaduct is from
Ludgate Hill station. You will find there is a siding opposite
Seacoal Lane, so there should be no possibility of your meeting
your just deserts from a passing train." Cotton gave a token
smile, but there was hostility in his eyes. "Right. I shall walk
round the block at ten minutes to five, to see that you are all at
your posts . . . Then we shall take him."

By the time Bragg and Morton reached their vantage point,
the pearl gray of the sky was tinged with blue. They took up
position in front of a signal gantry, so that they would not be
silhouetted against the sky. They were just above the level of
the roofs opposite, and surprisingly close. Morton felt that
given a good run up, he could have jumped across. It could not

be easy to sleep so near to a railway line. Not that there was
any traffic at the moment, but engines had been getting up
steam in the station.

All seemed quiet in the house. The windows on the top story
were flung wide open, and the drawn curtains sucked gently in
and out with the first intimations of a breeze. By cracking his
ears, Morton could hear someone snoring rhythmically. Everything looked normal and innocent; the sun staining the horizon
yellow foretold another blazing hot day. Morton looked at his
watch. Seven minutes to five. Inspector Cotton should have
started his round by now. He leaned over the low wall, and saw
that Cotton had just turned into the bottom of Seacoal Lane,
accompanied by Sergeant Bliss and the constables. Excitement
began to grow in the pit of his stomach.

"Rotten bastard," muttered Bragg, by his side. "By rights
it's us that ought to be there, not them. You noticed he didn't
give us a ha'porth of credit for finding the address. He made it
sound like he'd won it at a game of dominoes."

"You are surely not concerned at that?" remarked Morton.
"So long as Slocum is captured, what does it matter?"

"It matters between me and Cotton, lad. He's out to get me,
any time, any way. He'd give his right arm, before he would let
me have any credit. Why do you think we are up here?
Anybody else, and I wouldn't mind. But Cotton . . ."

The subject of Bragg's diatribe had reached the shop door,
and was gesticulating to one of the constables to kick it in.
Suddenly, he stretched out a restraining arm, and lifted his
head. In the distance Morton could hear the sound of a train
approaching. At least Cotton had his wits about him. The noise
of the engine would cover the assault on the door. But someone
else had heard the engine also. The bedroom curtains were
pulled apart, and the head of a middle-aged woman appeared.
She had on a cream flannel nightdress and her hair was done up
in curl papers. Bragg and Morton shrank back against the
gantry and froze. She pushed her head out of the window, and
looked up at the sky. Apparently content with the auguries, she
leaned out and watched the advancing train. For an instant all
movement seemed suspended, then as the train coasted behind
Bragg and Morton, she saw them. She was close enough for
them to see the look of puzzlement on her face, then there
came a sharp crack from below. Her head jerked down, and she
began to screech.

"Help! Police! Burglars!" she yelled. Then she ducked inside and reappeared with a police rattle. She began to swing it vigorously, still yelling at the top of her voice. Then she was joined by a tousled man, who blew piercingly on a whistle.

Down below Constable Park was hurling himself at the shop door in a desperate effort to break it in.

"There!" screeched the woman. "You see the one at the back?" She flung out an arm in Cotton's direction. "He's the one that was nosing around yesterday. I told you he was up to no good! Police! Help!"

Above the hubbub, Morton could hear Cotton shouting something about opening the door, then suddenly two uniformed constables came sprinting around the corner. Their impetus knocked Park and Mandell flying, and in a trice they had seized Cotton, and twisted his arms behind him. At the click of the handcuffs, Bragg uttered a guffaw of delight. The newcomers pushed Cotton roughly into the gutter, and pounced on Mandell. Above the hideous clatter of the rattle could be heard the sound of police whistles, converging on the spot. They now had the cuffs on Mandell, and were chasing Park up the street. Cotton rolled over, and levering himself to his knees glanced about him. Then to Morton's astonishment, he tumbled to his feet, and began to run.

"Come on, lad," said Bragg gleefully. "It's time we took charge." He began to run down the railway track.

By the time they reached the shop, a group of five puzzled and angry constables from Second Division were listening to Mandell's protestations. So far as they could see, all the other detectives had stuck dutifully to their posts. The proprietors of the shop were no longer shattering the peace of the morning, but, in company with the other inhabitants of the street, were leaning out of their window watching the proceedings.

"Hello, Jock," Bragg addressed a paunchy constable. "This is a right cock-up. Surely you were warned about this raid?"

"If we were, nobody mentioned it to me, Joe."

"Nor me," chorused the others.

"Well, let's try to salvage what we can," said Bragg. "Will you persuade these good people to come down and open the door. There's no use in my trying."

After prolonged negotiations, the man withdrew from the bedroom window, and shortly after the door was opened a crack.

"I am Sergeant Bragg of the City Police." He pushed h warrant-card at the peering face. "If you don't believe me, as that well-fed constable over there."

"What you doin', breakin' into my shop?" said the ma truculently, opening the door wide.

"There has been a mixup, which need not concern you, said Bragg shortly.

"It bleedin' concerns me, when you start batterin' my doo down. I shall complain . . ."

"You do that, sir. It is your right as a citizen. Now, what your name?"

"Daniel Sawyer."

"Is that your wife at the window?"

"Yes."

"Is there anybody else in the house?"

"No."

"Do you mind if we come in to verify what you have said?

The man looked doubtful. "As long as you don't start tearin the bleedin' place apart again." He stood aside.

The back room on the ground floor was used as a storeroom and gave on to a small yard totally enclosed by the walls of th other houses. There was no way out there. On the story abov was a comfortable living room and a kitchen. On the top stor was the bedroom occupied by the Sawyers, and a small room the back crammed with junk. They examined each roo rapidly but carefully, watched by a glowering Sawyer. The was no attic, and no skylight.

"Right," said Bragg. "That all appears to be in order. No then, have you ever heard of a man called Slocum?"

"Slocum, Slocum . . ." the man repeated. "I shall have look in my book."

"Your book?" asked Bragg.

"Yes. I receive letters here for people. Sometimes I have send them on, sometimes they call for them—when they thin of it." He took a battered notebook from a drawer in th counter and began to turn the pages.

"No, I haven't a forwarding address for him." He turned the back of the book. "Ah, here he is. Mr. Slocum. He's one them that calls for his letters."

"What is he like?" demanded Bragg.

"I can't rightly say," replied Sawyer vaguely. "I see so many folk."

"What can you tell me about him?"

Sawyer turned back to his book. "He came in last January and paid me ten shillings—that's for the whole year. I can't recollect seein' him since."

"Have any letters arrived for him in that time?"

Sawyer took a bundle from the depths of the drawer, and taking off the elastic band, began to flip through them. "Just the one," he said, removing a letter from the pile.

Bragg grabbed it, and tore open the envelope.

"Here, you can't do that!" exclaimed Sawyer in outrage.

"Can't I?" He read the note and replaced it in the envelope. "It's from our friend Gadd," he remarked, then turned to Sawyer. "I am seizing that letter as vital evidence in a triple murder case. I am not able to say what your position is, having been the recipient of this communication. But if I were you, I would not make any fuss about what happened here this morning."

"There's no doubt about it, Bragg. You will have to let him go."

Bragg and Morton had gone to the coroner's chambers in the Temple to report on the failure of the morning's operation. Sir Rufus was standing in his habitual posture, his left hand clutching the lapel of his morning coat, the other flung out theatrically, warming his backside at a nonexistent fire.

"Whatever be the moral rights and wrongs of it, Gadd's fate will be determined by the law. You need not concern yourself about crawling around the squalid dregs of officialdom, looking for the fellow who is alleged to have given him *carte blanche* to do whatever he liked. The plain fact of the matter is that after the twenty-sixth of January the *Dancing Lady* was not a British ship. That it was still on the register is immaterial. And since it was not a British ship, British law cannot apply to it. You might as well tear up your warrant."

"What law would apply, sir?" asked Bragg.

"I cannot say, Bragg. It is rather outside my field . . . French law, possibly, if the ship was trading from Martinique."

"The French police are looking for him on our behalf. Could

we not quietly take him over there, and give him into their custody?"

"Some day, Bragg," observed Sir Rufus portentously, "your Machiavellian maneuvers will be your undoing. In this case, such a stratagem would avail you nothing. Their interest in Gadd depends wholly on the warrant you have issued. With that invalid, and therefore no deportation proceedings possible, the French police would not support your dubious machinations."

"I suppose not . . ." said Bragg slowly. "Dear God!"

"Does that invocation denote some flash of inspiration on your part, sergeant?" asked the coroner.

"The twenty-sixth was even before the ship called at Bermuda."

"Ah, the barratry business. Are you any further forward there?"

"He was very cagey. He finally admitted borrowing the seventeen thousand pounds, but he still claims it was spent on repairs to the ship. We pressed him on where they were carried out, and he said the shipyards at Charleston were full, so he went to Mobile."

"You have made no inquiries as to the truth of that?"

"No. I suppose we ought to do so. Blast it! We shall have every state of America involved in this case before long."

"It is, nevertheless, a more profitable line of inquiry," said Sir Rufus thoughtfully. "Bermuda is a British colony, so British law applies there. If what you suspect is true, he might possibly be charged with fraud."

"I think he kept the bottomry money himself, all right," said Bragg. "He was paid two thousand pounds for the *Pearl*. And although he maintained it would put him on the beach for ever, it was only upped to three thousand for the *Dancing Lady*. But twenty thousand pounds would be a very comfortable sum to retire on."

"But with Ryan dead," observed Sir Rufus, "you will have an uphill task . . . Is there any possibility that Gadd murdered Ryan, do you think?"

"Both Constable Morton and I got a clear impression that he had no idea Ryan had escaped from the ship. He also claims he was in police custody in Amsterdam at the time of Ryan's death. Indeed, he acts as if he believes he is still alive."

"Then Slocum is still your only lead?"

"It seems so," said Bragg dispiritedly. "If that is his real name. I reckon he is one of Major Redman's crew."

"You will get nothing from those Special Branch black-guards, Bragg . . . Incidentally, I have reason to believe that you were less than frank with me concerning the attempt to apprehend the Slocum person."

"Indeed, sir?"

"Word has it that there was something of an imbroglio. How did that occur?"

"Inspector Cotton has a weakness for taking all the credit, and he decided not to involve the uniformed branch." Bragg smiled contentedly. "They decided to involve themselves, however, and we last saw the Inspector fleeing from the scene in handcuffs. I hear that he got them taken off at Snow Hill police station, and he promptly reported sick with an injured head."

"Dear, dear," remarked the coroner solicitously. "Nothing serious I hope."

"He will be back again," said Bragg sardonically, "when' his pride has healed."

Bragg could not conceal his despondency as they walked through the quiet quadrangles towards Fleet Street.

"I reckon we have come to the end of the line, lad," he said. "There is no point in confronting Redman. He would never hand over one of his men . . . This bloody case is like a ball of wool the cat's got at."

"There is one stray end we might pull on, sir," said Morton.

"What's that?"

"We did not follow up Frankis's insurance policy with the Royal Exchange Assurance."

"That's true. We might as well go along."

They took a hansom, and jogged gently along toward the City. Their cab had taken up station behind a brewer's dray, laden with great barrels of beer. The very sight of it made Bragg feel thirsty. He looked at his watch. Eleven o'clock . . . a bit early to start drinking; best leave it an hour. The driver deposited them at the bottom of Cornhill, and they strolled around the back of the Royal Exchange to the company's office.

"The marine underwriter?" repeated a bespectacled clerk.
"That would be Mr. Upton. Just wait here a moment."

He soon returned, and showed them to a small office
overlooking the Bank of England. Upton proved to be bald and
stringy, with a protuberant Adam's apple.

"We are making some inquiries concerning Mr. John
Frankis, the Lloyd's underwriter. You knew him, I believe."

"Yes, yes. His death was a terrible shock. He will be a great
loss to the insurance world, he was quite brilliant." His voice
was light and creaking.

"We understand that he entered into an insurance contract
with your company, dealing with a ship called the *Dancing
Lady*."

"Yes. I remember it well. If I may say so, it was an instance
where his judgment was totally vindicated."

"Why do you say that?" asked Bragg.

"It appears that he was under some pressure—I think it was
from the Lloyd's committee—to lead the insurance on the
vessel. The previous year he had said he would not renew
without a survey, and he was reluctant to go back on that. He
was, however, constrained to do so, but in view of his instincts
about the matter, he asked me to write a personal stop-loss
policy for him."

"You appear to have respected his judgment a great deal,"
remarked Bragg. "Why, in that case, were you prepared to
comply with his request?"

Upton smiled deprecatingly. "In the context of the accounts
I write, the amount at stake was insignificant. And in a way I
felt honored to be asked to perform this service for him. There
was, of course, the added inducement that he said he would
give me some of the syndicate's reinsurances."

"I see," said Bragg dryly. "So it was good business all
around."

"Is this a normal kind of policy?" asked Morton.

"By no means." Upton swallowed, and his Adam's apple
leapt wildly up and down. "I had to ask Frankis for the
wording. I keep it as a precedent, but I suppose I shall only
ever write those two."

"Two?" repeated Morton. "Was there another?"

"Yes. Frankis gave me the details. I wrote them both at the
same time."

"Who was the other assured?" asked Bragg.

"I really cannot remember. Is it important?"

Bragg curbed his excitement. ' Yes," he said quietly. "It is absolutely vital."

"I shall have to get my notebook." Upton crossed to a cupboard, and came back with a small volume. "Let me see, it was toward the end of last December, as I recollect."

"That would be correct, sir," said Bragg.

Upton turned the pages. "Yes, here is the entry for the Frankis policy, so the other would be immediately after it . . . It was a man called Stanton—Phillip Stanton."

"What is his address?" asked Bragg urgently.

"We do not retain the proposal forms in this office, once the policy is issued. I could find out his address for you, but it would take a day or two."

"Never mind, thanks."

Bragg flung himself downstairs and plunged across Cornhill regardless of the clattering hooves. Morton, less reckless, caught up with him outside Frankis's Birchin Lane office. They raced up the stairs and burst into the outer office. The pretty receptionist was red-eyed and harassed.

"What's the matter, love?" asked Bragg.

"We've been burgled," she said with a sniff. "All the cupboards and desks broken into, and everything scattered all over the floor . . ."

"Where is Mr. Hannah?"

"In Mr. Frankis's room." The recollection of his death triggered off more tears, and Bragg marched down the corridor without her. They found Hannah sitting in gloomy incomprehension at the desk. The floor was littered with bundles of papers that had been untied, glanced at, then disregarded. In the corner of the room, the door of the safe stood open. Bragg crossed over to it, and unearthed the silver cup from under a pile of papers.

"So they were not after valuables," he remarked. "I suppose you cannot say if anything is missing?"

"Since I did not know what was here in the first place," replied Hannah with some asperity, "I cannot see how I am expected to know what has been taken."

"The safe was opened with the key," said Bragg. "Where was it kept?"

"In a locked key-cupboard in the general office. The cupboard has been broken open."

"Who knew it was there?"

"All the staff, certainly . . . But then they also knew that the key to the cupboard was under the flower vase on the windowsill."

"I think we know the culprit," said Bragg. "I gather one of the names on your syndicate is a Mr. Phillip Stanton."

"Yes. He was Frankis's cousin."

"Was he now? Can you give me his address?"

Hannah rummaged among the mounds of documents, and uncovered a blue volume with the gilt insignia of Lloyd's on the front cover. He turned the pages rapidly.

"It is Three Albemarle Crescent, SW."

"Thanks." Bragg strode from the room, and ran down the stairs. He hailed a passing growler, and they were soon cantering down the Embankment.

"Stanton is likely to be at work, now," Bragg remarked.

"But why are you so sure he is our man?" asked Morton.

"At the moment it's a gut feeling. I cannot hazard a guess at the motive—it might be some high-powered official business. But the minute I heard he was Frankis's cousin, I was certain."

"Why?"

"You remember that Goddard and Frankis and Whitlock were called to the Foreign Office?"

"Yes."

"Whitlock was very suspicious of the whole proceeding. He felt it had been set up to compel him to settle the cargo claim. Now, when he described it to me, he said nothing to indicate that Frankis and Stanton knew each other. Come to think of it, he was very critical about the way in which Frankis stood up obsequiously, when Stanton entered the room . . . The meeting was very carefully staged, and unless I am much mistaken, Stanton was the stage manager."

The cab stopped outside the Venetian Renaissance pile of the Foreign Office, and Bragg asked the doorman to direct them to Stanton's room.

"That's on the first floor, gentlemen, number eighty-seven," he said. "If you take the left-hand staircase, and go along the

corridor, you will find an inquiry room on the left-hand side.
They will see you right."

They ascended the impressive balustraded staircase, and,
turning down the corridor, tiptoed past the inquiry office. They
crept down the corridor until they came to room eighty-seven.
The door was slightly ajar, and, through the crack, they could
see a solidly built man sitting at the desk.

"He will fit the bill," whispered Bragg. "Right, lad, we
take him first, and ask questions later . . . Ready?"

Morton nodded, and they crashed through the door into the
room. The man, startled, half-swiveled away from the desk,
but was sent flying to the floor. Morton twisted his arms behind
him, and Bragg snapped on the handcuffs.

"Phillip Stanton," gasped Bragg. "You are under arrest for
complicity in the murder of John Frankis and of Patrick Ryan. I
must warn you that anything you say will be taken down, and
may be used in evidence."

The man remained still, stretched out on the carpet, his head
twisted uncomfortably to one side.

"Oh God," he cried dazedly, "I'm not Stanton!" He seemed
near to tears.

"Who are you, then?" demanded Bragg.

"Pringle, Matthew Pringle . . . Stanton retired last Saturday."

Bragg lugged him to his feet. "Can you prove this?" he
asked fiercely.

"If you will take these obscene manacles off, I can."

Bragg unlocked the handcuffs, and Pringle walked painfully
to his desk. "Look," he said, indicating a number of files with
his name printed on the front. "Here," he dived angrily into
his pocket, and drew out a letter addressed to Matthew Pringle,
with an address in Bayswater. "That's from my bank manager," he glared at Bragg. "Read it, if you must."

"Where is Stanton, then?" asked Bragg roughly.

"How do I know?" replied Pringle wrathfully. "I've told
you he has retired . . . Who the devil are you, anyway,
bursting in here, and assaulting me in this fashion?"

"Oh, sod off!" cried Bragg in exasperation, and rushed out
of the room. They pounded down the grand staircase, jostling
startled clerks, and hurled themselves onto the street. A

hansom cab was just discharging a fare, and they directed the driver to hurry them to Albemarle Crescent.

It turned out to be a short curving street of small terraced houses. Bragg rang the bell of number three, shuffling his feet impatiently. There was no reply. He rang several times more, then led the way down the area steps.

"The lock on this door will not be so strong," he remarked, "and the noise won't travel. Right, lad, break it open."

Morton threw his shoulder at the door, and on the fourth attempt there was a splintering crash, and he was projected headlong into the basement kitchen. Bragg restrained him momentarily, listening carefully. "Don't forget he is handy with a knife," he warned. But all remained quiet.

They made a rapid search of the house. It was austerely furnished, rigorously tidy—and empty. Only the unmade bed gave any indication that it was inhabited.

"I suppose we had better wait here, till he comes back," said Morton.

"I can't think of anything else . . . Yes, I can. What do you imagine he was after at Birchin Lane? The Royal Exchange policy! He would have destroyed his own, but as long as Frankis's was in existence, there was still the danger that he might be drawn into our investigations. He didn't find it, because we had it; but he won't know that. Come on, lad. It's us for Liphook again."

It was mid-afternoon before they got there, and Bragg was fuming at the delay. They hurried out of the station yard, and down to the undertaker's. A smart pony and gig was standing outside, and as they approached, the undertaker emerged from the shop.

"Ah," he said regretfully. "You will be wanting to go to Brookwood, I dare say. I am sorry, but I cannot take you today. I am on my way to Cold Ash . . . Dick Giles might take you in his farm cart."

Bragg swung up into the gig, and took the reins.

"Here!" exclaimed the undertaker, "what are you about?"

"Police," shouted Bragg, beckoning Morton to join him. "I'm commandeering it for the afternoon."

"You can't do that!" the undertaker expostulated. "I have to go and measure Alf Doddings for his coffin."

"Then go in your bloody hearse," snarled Bragg, and, flicking the horse with the whip, they set off at a canter.

The horse was a sprightly young colt, and in twenty minutes they were turning up the drive leading to The Grange.

"Hello," exclaimed Bragg, "there's a trap by the front door."

"And another under the chestnut tree," Morton added.

"I don't like the look of this," muttered Bragg, as he hitched the pony to a sapling. He marched around to the back of the house, and found the french window standing open. They entered the sitting room, the blinds drawn, the furniture shrouded in dust-sheets.

"He will be in the study, if anywhere," said Bragg, cautiously opening the door. They began to creep down the gloomy corridor.

"Oh, Christ!" Bragg stopped abruptly. Sitting at his ease on a chair outside the study door was Major Redman, contentedly puffing his pipe.

"What the bloody hell are you doing here?" asked Bragg belligerently.

"I told you," replied Redman mildly, "that if you persisted, you would only cause more death." He nodded toward the study.

Bragg pushed past him, and flung open the door. A man was sitting in the chair by the desk. There was a ragged hole in his right temple. The left side of his head had been blown away. On the floor by the body was a heavy-caliber service revolver.

"It would appear to be suicide." Redman was leaning against the door jamb. "From the general confusion, one supposes he was looking for something; and when he failed to find it, he killed himself."

"Is that Phillip Stanton?" asked Bragg.

Redman nodded.

Bragg peered at the black powder marks around the wound. "Yes," he said icily, "that's what it looks like, all right. But I would like to know whose finger pulled the trigger."

Catherine walked to the edge of the pavement again, and looked down the street, but she could not see him. Back by the wall again, she took his note out of her handbag.

Catherine
Meet me at five by the
Crown and Anchor, Fleet Street, and we will
have some tea.
      All will be revealed!!
        James.

Well, it was not quite five o'clock . . . She really ought to
have been late, and let him do the waiting. She read the note
again, then pushed it back into her handbag. Somehow the
strong regular handwriting irritated her. It was too assertive,
too confident of achieving what it wanted. And indeed, she had
been here—five minutes early. It was a pity, she thought, that in
all her dealings with young men, there was an underlying
eroticism, a suggestiveness—and not only young men. She had
sometimes caught even Mr. Tranter looking at her speculatively. Why could they not treat you like one of them? She took out
Morton's note again. It looked perfectly innocent, of course.
That was the rejoinder of the music hall comedians to the Mrs.
Grundys of the world—it was all in the mind. If you could
identify a double entendre, you were not pure enough to be
corrupted anyway. She tossed her head irritably, and a man
lurching out of the pub gave her a lubricious look. What a
place to suggest for a meeting! Had he no sensibilities at all?
She began to walk toward the corner. If she protested, he
would no doubt retort that it was an obvious landmark. She
turned, and began to walk back. If she went as far as the pillar
box beyond the pub, she would be visible whichever direction
he was coming from. And she wouldn't look as if she were
waiting for him. It would seem that she was just arriving—or
perhaps better still, as if having arrived and discovered he was
not there, was declining to wait.

She stood by the pillar box, looking in every direction, then
began to stroll back to the corner. The trouble with men was
that they had no idea how humiliating it was to be accosted. It
was bad enough to have to enter into ordinary social dalliance
with people one did not particularly wish to encourage, but a
brutal approach in the street . . . She stood at the corner for a
moment, then began her slow walk back.

And, of course, he would come dashing up, all breathless,
with his bubbling charm, and his disarming smile. And she

would forgive him . . . and because she had forgiven him, he would be just as thoughtless next time. If women were less supine, less prepared to fawn on men like him, they might be treated with real consideration, instead of the empty etiquette that restricted their lives.

"Ere, what d'you think you're on?"

A woman in a red hat was glaring at her threateningly, her arms akimbo.

"I'm sorry," said Catherine, "I don't understand . . ."

"Bugger off . . . This is my beat."

Catherine took in the rouge and the lip salve, the provocatively short skirts.

"If you don't bugger off, my bloke'll cut your face. How'd you like that, eh? . . ."

Catherine gave a screech of alarm, and, gathering up her skirts, fled down the street. She dashed into a tea shop for sanctuary, and took a table at the back, out of sight.

"You had a turn, love?" asked the waitress, in a bored voice.

"No. Something rather unpleasant happened outside."

"An accident?" she inquired hopefully.

"No, I was threatened."

"Ah, men are rotten, aren't they? Tea, love?"

"Please."

As her panic subsided, Catherine's indignation grew. She had never felt so degraded, so soiled . . . And if she complained that it was his fault, he would only laugh it off . . . But it was the last thing she could tell him—that she had been mistaken for a prostitute, and by a practicing one moreover . . . Oddly enough, from what little she could recollect, the woman had been quite pretty.

"Ah, there you are!" Morton was hastening toward her with a rueful smile. "I'm sorry I'm late. I was just sneaking out of the office, when I bumped into the Commissioner, and it was, 'How are you getting on, my boy?' I had to endure it." He looked around. "The service is not very good here, today."

"It is hardly surprising, she has been on her feet all day," said Catherine tartly.

"Ah. You are in your working-woman mood today. Well, perhaps I should be thankful; you might have left me high and dry, otherwise."

"Tea, dear?" inquired the waitress.

"Yes, please—and a Bath bun." Morton smiled cheerfully, but the waitress did not respond.

"I hear that your Suffolk mare has galloped off to Salzburg, with her stallion." Catherine remarked pointedly.

Morton looked up, then smiled innocently. "She had the most seductive voice," he replied lightly.

It was as if he had bared his breast to receive the obvious riposte, thought Catherine. No doubt he would protest that his involvement with the Challis woman had been purely platonic. Well, she would not give him the satisfaction of thinking he had deceived her.

The waitress brought Morton his tea, and he began to eat his sticky bun with relish.

"You know," he looked up quizzically, "our mutual friends seem to think that we would make a very good couple."

Catherine was taken aback by this unexpected frontal assault. "I hate the word 'couple'," she said coolly. "It has such a coarse Shakespearian ring to it. 'Pair' sounds much better," she added, then mentally kicked herself for having knocked the ball back into his court.

"You have not answered my question," he said smiling.

"I was not aware that you had asked one. And, anyway, I do not believe we have any mutual friends," she said flatly.

He pulled a comical face. "I have barely seen you for eight months," he complained, "and you promptly knock me over the head."

"You are so lacking in consideraton, James."

"What harm have I ever done you?" he protested.

"I am not thinking of myself. You have been back in England now for over a month, and even though you have not seen your parents since last October, you have not yet visited them . . . But I noticed that you have played cricket."

"What is wrong with cricket?" he asked sharply.

"Nothing. It's just a game—to most people."

"Are you suggesting that I am immature—an emotional cripple?"

"No, not a cripple," Catherine paused to consider. "Perhaps 'lightweight' would be more accurate."

Morton seemed to contain his irritation with an effort. "I play cricket because I enjoy it," he said didactically. "I enjoy

because I am good at it. I go on tours for England because I am
better at it than most other people. Why should you despise
that any more than your father's painting?"

"I do not understand the significance of that last remark,"
said Catherine.

"My cricketing skill stems from a totally fortuitous ability to
coordinate hand and eye. I see a cricket ball hurtling toward
me. I seem to know where it will pitch, how high it will bounce
and I can get my bat in position in time to hit it."

Catherine's smile held a tinge of disdain. "What has that to
do with painting?" she asked.

"It is the same mechanical process," Morton said crossly.
"Your father can see the texture of the cheek of some society
woman, the gleam of her personality. I doubt if he sees them
differently from anyone else, though he probably sees them
more clearly. And he can mix his paints to the exact colors, and
apply them to the canvas with his brushes, *et voilà* a
masterpiece; admired by the kind of people you respect."

"There is much more to painting than that," said Catherine
scornfully. "You have to have a real insight into people, a
sensitivity . . ."

"To hell with your sensitivity," exclaimed Morton angrily.
"I prefer to be respected by earthy, ordinary people, who earn
their living by the sweat of their brow, and watch cricket as one
of their few relaxations. You can keep your smarmy slithering
socialites, and may you be happy with your choice."

"I think," said Catherine icily, "that you had better give me
the information you proposed to give me, and then you can get
me a cab."

CHAPTER ————— ————— NINETEEN

Lord Rosebery, the Foreign Secretary in the incoming Liberal administration snipped the end of his cigar with a gold cutter, and settled back in his chair.

"In the normal course of politics, one would welcome the opportunity to discredit the opposing party," he said with an impish smile. "However, my brief sojourn at the Foreign Office in 'eighty-six has engendered a certain caution, not to say sympathy. I have therefore felt it best to deal with the Stanton affair informally, outside the record, and with none but the four of us present."

In his mid-forties, Rosebery was handsome and well-groomed. His warm voice, and the sly humor lurking behind every utterance, led some to regard him as too lacking in gravity for high office.

"My hope is that, by each sharing his personal knowledge, we shall arrive at an understanding of this most extraordinary episode. I must first, however, obtain from each of you a solemn undertaking that no word of what passes within these walls will be in any way communicated to any other person . . . I should add, Sir William, that the Home Office is in as complete an ignorance concerning the matter, as the proverbial man on the Clapham omnibus."

"Then I give you my assurance that it shall go no further, sir," said the Commissioner.

"Sergeant Bragg?"

"I, too, sir."

"Major Redman?"

"You have my word, your lordship."

"Very well." Rosebery lit his cigar in a leisurely fashion, as if giving himself time for thought.

"Phillip Stanton had a brilliant mind," he began. "There is no doubt about it; a scholar of Eton and Balliol, that sort of thing. He came from a family that has produced many great public servants over the years, and there was every reason to suppose that he would emulate their example. In some ways, he fell short of those expectations. Perhaps the Foreign Office was not the right niche for him; he might have made a better academic. He was a personable enough man, but a little too introspective for us, and far from gregarious. These defects of personality prevented his climbing the ambassadorial tree, but his analytical and cognitive powers insured rapid advancement at home, nevertheless. By eighteen eighty-three he was holding a very important post as deputy to the head of the Central America and Caribbean section. As such he was closely involved in the formulation of British foreign policy in the area." He tapped his cigar on the cut-glass ash-tray.

"In those days," Lord Rosebery went on, "we and the French were considerably disturbed by the aggressive expansionist policies of the United States. The annexation of Texas, the conquest of vast tracts of Mexican territory, the interference in Cuba, all these threatened to overturn the established balance of power in the region. It seemed, indeed, that America was intending to absorb Mexico totally, and perhaps continue southwards through Central America. Their overt support for the corrupt regime of President Díaz of Mexico was interpreted as a statagem to provide a pretext for future expansion. Accordingly, Great Britain and France, those traditional enemies, determined to make common cause, and to contain the American expansionism by supporting disaffected elements in Mexico.

"In eighteen eighty-eight," he went on, "a shipment
arms was sent to rebel Indians in Yucatán, the southernmo
province of Mexico. It was hoped that this would kindle
brush-fire that would sweep north, and oust the Díaz regime.
the event, the project was an abysmal failure. Indeed, it left
in a far worse position than before, for the United Stat
became aware of what we had done, and made it clear that the
would not tolerate such adventurism in future. They demand
blood, and, to placate them, the head of the Central America
section was retired. He was replaced, not by Stanton, who w
tarred with the same brush, but by someone from anoth
section. As we could not afford to lose Stanton's experien
also, he was retained as the number two. It was an unhap
state of affairs, of course, though he seemed to have accepted
with praiseworthy generosity. We now know that he nurtured
resentment, fortified by intellectual arrogance, and was total
unwilling to accept the new direction that foreign policy in th
region had taken. He seems to have conceived a plan to w
back his own prestige, and reorient British foreign policy a
stroke." Discovering that his cigar had gone out, Lo
Rosebery placed it in the ash-tray.

"At the end of March, this year, our Ambassador
Washington was summoned to see the Secretary of State. I
was informed of a most astonishing occurrence. It appears th
along the Gulf Coast of Mexico is a string of oil-wells whi
are owned by American companies, and manned by Americ
personnel. Each well is surrounded by a substantial stockad
and is well defended from the generally hostile natives. Duri
the night of the first of March, a white man approached one
those stockades near Poza Rica. He called out that he was
American, and asked them to open the gates and let him in

"That would be Ryan," said Bragg.

"I see. At all events the guard accepted that he was inde
what he claimed, and opened the gate. Thereupon, the ma
Ryan, dropped flat on his face, and a fusillade of shots rang
from the darkness. The guard tried to secure the entran
again, but was hit and mortally wounded. The stockade w
rushed by armed Indians, but by this time the other America
had been alerted, and there was some resistance. The upshot
it was that everyone in the stockade was butchered, an
storage tank set on fire. The blaze alerted government troo

and American prospectors, and they hurried to the scene. The only man still alive was the guard on the gate, who had been left for dead. He was able to give an account of the attack, though unfortunately he later died in hospital . . . Our Ambassador expressed a friendly but disinterested concern. The Secretary of State then took him to a side table, and, whisking away a cloth like a conjurer, revealed a military rifle. It had been found in the stockade at Poza Rica . . . and it was a new Lee-Metford.''

Rosebery paused dramatically, and re-lit his cigar. ''Naturally,'' he continued, ''the Americans accused us of perpetrating a repetition of the Yucatán incident, and threatened to break off diplomatic relations. We were able to assure them that Her Majesty's Government was not involved in any way, and would not countenance such an unfriendly action against United States property. Largely through the intervention of the American Ambassador to the Court of St. James, they accepted our assurances, and there the matter lay . . . Until, that is, we became aware that Sir William was making inquiries about shipments of rifles from London. Someone then had a rare flash of inspiration, and asked the Americans for the serial number of the weapon they had recovered. It proved to be one of a batch sent ostensibly to Guadeloupe, or the *ss Dancing Lady* in January. As our relations with the French were by no means cordial, it was at least possible that this was one of their devious impostures. Lord Salisbury therefore instructed Special Branch to make inquiries into the affair . . . I think that Major Redman should take up the story now.''

Redman sat bolt upright, and cleared his throat. ''I started my investigations by going to Paris, to see the head of the Sûreté. Rumors of the affair had already reached them, and I had great difficulty in obtaining any information at all.''

''They would not tell us anything worthwhile, either,'' remarked Sir William.

Redman gave the Commissioner a glance of contempt. ''I had, however, already discovered that the rifles had been ordered from Lee-Metford by a French company, Lebrun Barré et Cie, and paid for in advance.''

''We missed a trick there,'' mumbled Bragg.

Redman's grey eyes rested coldly on Bragg for a moment. ''Beyond confirming what I already knew, I obtained little

information from the French. I did, however, form the opinion
that they had had no prior knowledge of the operation, and that
they were as concerned as we were not to upset the Americans.
I then went back to the Yucatán affair, and looking through the
papers, I was struck by several similarities. In that case, the *ss
Pearl* had been chartered by Michel Tissier et Cie, the master
was Gadd, and he was appointed by the charterer for that
voyage. Since we knew that the Yucatán business was jointly
set on foot by the British and French governments, it was
evident that Michel Tissier and Lebrun Barré were companies
used by the French government for covert activities. I went to
Paris again, and confronted them with this information. They
then admitted that they had made available these facilities,
believing that they were assisting a British government
operation. Since this was, as we know, untrue, I went back to
my Yucatán papers. I had learned from the *City Press* that the
insurance of the *Dancing Lady* had been placed at Lloyd's, and
been led by the Frankis syndicate. I found, to my surprise, that
he had also led the insurance of the *Pearl*. In the latter case,
there had been a sub rosa subvention to Lloyd's out of
government funds, to compensate for the claim which had been
paid. To judge by the fuss being made by Lloyd's, the same
procedure did not seem to have been followed for the *Dancing
Lady*. That was interesting in itself, since it confirmed the
unofficial nature of the enterprise.

"By this time, of course," Redman went on, "there had
been three murders, and the City Police were buzzing around
as if someone had stolen their queen. All the evidence pointed
to the involvement of Stanton in the affair. I therefore
challenged him, and he made a full confession." Redman
stopped speaking, and folded his arms across his chest.

"What about the murders, then?" asked Bragg gruffly.

"Ingham was killed by Frankis. He was a new element in
the conspiracy. Apart from the fact that he chartered the ship, I
cannot conceive his function. However, he told Frankis that the
police were pressing him very hard, and were sure to find out
about it all. So Frankis battered him to death."

"And Frankis knew when Ryan was coming to London, and
where he was staying," said Bragg. "He obviously told
Stanton, and, posing as a doctor, Stanton stabbed Ryan to
death."

"That is correct. It was a risky thing to do, but having achieved it, they began to feel secure. Unfortunately, it had the effect of drawing Sergeant Bragg's attentions to Frankis himself. He made a valiant attempt to remove the threat, and the sergeant at once, by drowning him; but this ended in failure. He conveyed this information to Stanton, and arranged to meet him at the Brookwood house. Stanton was part of the social circle down there. In addition to being Frankis's cousin, he was having an affair with his wife."

"Mrs. Frankis would appreciate a slow come," muttered Bragg.

"What?"

"Nothing."

"They were both at a dinner party next door. Stanton simply walked across the lawn while the men were at their port, stabbed Frankis, and walked back again to join the ladies."

"Was Mrs. Frankis involved at all?" asked Sir William.

"Not from what Stanton said, and I don't think he was protecting her."

"Well, at least a few things fall into place for me, now," remarked Bragg. "Neither Frankis nor Stanton was a wealthy man, and their big problem must have been to get funds to prime the pump. They managed it by selling the cotton-seed mill twice over. I take it that De Wolf is one of your agents in the Caribbean, and would do as Stanton instructed him?"

Lord Rosebery narrowed his eyes, then nodded.

"That was why they needed Ingham," went on Bragg, "to obtain the real cargo; to give a bill of lading and an insurance certificate for fictitious cargo, to cover the armaments; and to keep the shipowners happy. The money paid by Wilson, who actually received the mill, was passed ultimately to Lebrun Barré to buy the rifles. At least, most of it was. There is ten thousand pounds, still in a Martin's account, that was presumably going to be split between the conspirators. Somebody ought to be able to claim it."

"It should be that Shreveport planter," said Sir William. "He is the one who comes worst out of it."

"Unless you can count in Goddard," said Bragg with a grin. "I doubt if he will get his knighthood now."

Lord Rosebery pulled out his watch. "Well, gentlemen, I have a horse running in the three-thirty at Epsom. So, if there are no more questions . . ."

"We still need to know who killed Stanton," said Bragg.

"Ah yes, Stanton," remarked Rosebery urbanely. "Once he had admitted this escapade, there could be no question of retaining him in the Service. We therefore came to an agreement with him; we would retire him on full pay, and he would keep his mouth shut. Unfortunately, we were unable to call off the police, and it seemed probable that you would discover the truth. That would have involved a trial, and the whole sorry episode would have become public. Stanton was an honorable man, and he well knew the damage that would cause to Britain's standing in the world. He must have realized there was only one course open to him, which would enable him to keep his agreement with us. Phillip Stanton committed suicide," said Lord Rosebery firmly. "He committed suicide."